I0613240

Albert Gallatin Riddle

The Life of Benjamin F. Wade

Albert Gallatin Riddle

The Life of Benjamin F. Wade

ISBN/EAN: 9783337053963

Printed in Europe, USA, Canada, Australia, Japan

Cover: Foto ©Raphael Reischuk / pixelio.de

More available books at **www.hansebooks.com**

THE LIFE

OF

BENJAMIN F. WADE

BY

A. G. RIDDLE

Author of 'The Life, Character and Public Services of James A. Garfield',
'Students and Lawyers,' Etc.

CLEVELAND, O.: WILLIAM W. WILLIAMS
1886

Copyright, 1886,
By W. W. Williams.

———

All Rights Reserved.

TO
MRS. CAROLINE ROSEKRANS WADE,
THIS SKETCH OF A
VALUABLE, EXALTED AND NOBLE LIFE,
TO WHICH SHE CONTRIBUTED SO MUCH, IS INSCRIBED,
WITH THE PROFOUNDEST RESPECT.

THE AUTHOR.

CONTENTS.

TO THE READER.

It may be stated that this sketch of an eminent Western Senator was written in detached papers for the Magazine of Western History. That periodical is largely devoted to the beginnings, the hitherto unwritten sources of history. In something of the spirit of that work, the earlier of my chapters were composed—taking note of obscure things, having but a general influence on the fortunes of Mr. Wade, but showing a flavor of, if not the spirit of the times, of his American ancestors, and of the first half of his own life. These papers, unchanged, with headings, make the chapters of the volume here presented to the public. Care has been taken to attribute no opinion or sentiment to Mr. Wade not his. He is nowhere made responsible for the notions of the writer.

In my mental vision he stands apart from his fellows, a heroic, manly, rugged, unique form, of a type never too numerous, and now so rare as to seem solitary; a man provoking admiration, commanding respect, gaining entire confidence without consciously seeking either.

The writer is not without hope that his pages will realize something of this conception to a reader who may make a study of the influences which gave shape to the colossal forms of our later history.

A. G. R.

WASHINGTON, July, 1886.

CHAPTER I.

By nature, emulous and loving praise, man is the
one braggart of the universe. The Hebrews even
clothed their Jehovah with this quality as a controlling attribute. To be modest is more rare in
man than woman, and is a mark of distinction in
him. If he does not boast of his achievements,
we laud them for him ; and when a distinguished
man dies, scores of common men pull themselves
into notice by the hair of his fallen head We
boast of our achievements in civilization, and are
fond of measuring the distance between ourselves
and the primitive man, yet we retain many of the
characteristics of the veriest savages. We build
fires to attest our joy, and literally make huge noises
to celebrate our achievements. We murder and
slay as savages always have, and build up a pile of

senseless stones to immortalize our greatest man.
To-day we complete the rock monument of Washington; we celebrate the event with salvos of artil-
lery, and congratulate ourselves upon a great deed
accomplished. We have secured the stone-immor-
tality of George Washington, and have done our
duty. We are never to escape the age of
stone.

As a rule, men are remembered as long as they
deserve to be. A man's life is his only fitting
monument. What irony so bitter as the question:
" Whose monument is this ? " The man has disappeared, and here is a stone-exclamation point
against inevitable forgetfulness. The world is too
busy to preserve dead leaves even as specimens ;
let them rot where they fall, if haply the earth
may be fertilized by their timely decay.

I fear my present work will hardly be distin-
guishable from a very ordinary stone-heap near the
grave of the distinguished dead, whose memory
will survive, whatever we may do or say, with that
of the great men of the remarkable time in which
he lived and worked. How great those men were,
what the real magnitude of the events of their time,
we may never know. We were too near them, too
much a part of them, whatever may be our powers
of observation, to correctly estimate their value and
importance in the world's history or that of our
own country. Hundreds of pens are now busy
inditing what the writers call history. When the
real historian comes, fifty or one hundred years

hence, what a dusting and crumpling of waste paper there will be !

My labors will be of a man of the most singular and, in some ways, unfortunate modesty. In no way a builder of dead monuments, he was seemingly a careful, persistent destroyer of all the ordinary means from which his own personal history could be composed, or a memoir of his time and associates; an abhorer of pageantry of every kind for all occasions. Men, living or dead, were to be left as their lives and actions left them. One of the propelling forces of the War of the Rebellion—a keen observer, seeing the best and worst of men, taking their best as no more than their country's due—he was no lauder, no praiser, always speaking words of inspiration; and, one of the few just in their estimates of men, he shrank from all pomp, all parade of woe, all funereal show of grief, when they fell by the wayside.

The steadiest and most inflexible as the most radical of the supporters of the national cause, doing fullest justice to Mr. Lincoln, he shrank from the sable pageantry over his remains. In that he had no part; was not present as a spectator. The "catafalque," with its blackness of drapery and sableness of plumes, with all the weary and public wail of woe, were to him meaningless, ludicrous, vainest mockery. For himself he probably never instituted a comparison between himself and another; never spent a moment in estimating the quality and rank of his own actions

in the minds of men.   It was his fortune to be as
little the object of criticism, through a long conspicuous career, as any man in our history.   To
live and do heartily, with all his might, the things
which came to his hands to do, never shirking,
however onerous ; never evading, however unpleasant ; seeking and meeting the hardest and
worst, which yet some man must do ; living truth
in his life, doing truth in his acts, speaking truth
in his words ; seeming not to care for words of
blame or praise ; tender, strong, of the heroic in
mould of soul and heart, he lived, did his work,
died, and was loved, trusted, feared and respected
as few of his time were, and will be remembered.
The least secretive of men, the openest of approach,
the easiest to know, and one of the widest known ;
it is not easy, save in these broad, strong lines to
sketch him, or tell the story of his real life, so that
the younger generation, the men who did not
know him, will yet appreciate him for what he
intrinsically was.   He was a sayer of things to be
repeated, a doer of things to be told of.   No one
followed him around to note and preserve these ;
no one has gleaned them up for a book.   They
are already matters of tradition.   No man of his
time wrote and left so few memorials of himself.
He left none ; no sign or mark.   Seemingly without the slightest literary instinct, the few papers
he made were for a special purpose ; that answered,
they were destroyed.   He seems systematically
to have destroyed papers.   He kept no journal,

made no diary, notes or memoranda. At the end
of a session or campaign, letters and papers of all
descriptions, not in the form of printed books,
were burned. Though a born warrior, no man so
hated strife and every species of personal warfare.
He never had any. If differences arose, he settled them at once in the most direct and decisive
way ; ended them so that nothing remained—
neither bitterness nor scandal. This disposition
to make a total final end of things was at the bottom of his destruction of papers. If saved, some-
body would want to pry into them, re-open old
wounds, renew old strifes. Cut off all sources of
evidence, and the thing would have to die. With
him private history—the history of common men,
the men with whom he daily associated—was of
no account. It was a history of strifes and bickerings, of failures, at the best. Let it perish. It
was not necessary to the public history, the national annals, and he governed himself accordingly.
So he seldom or never spoke of himself to others,
save sparingly to the most intimate. Though a
man of thought, he was a man of action, of deeds,
not of words and letters ; and such, in the main,
were his associates. A few instances of literary
men who approached him for a purpose may have
occurred. Their reception was not encouraging,
and few save newspaper correspondents made him
the subject of literary labors. Though he did not
at all share in the elder Senator Cameron's attributed estimate of literary men, he did not seek,

nor was he sought by them.   Busy, content to do
his work, doing more and doing better than was
given to good workers, and when done, leaving it
for the use and help it might be without an accompanying word of explanation of his motive, he
permitted others to take the credit of it if they
would.   So he made his active, robust way, push-
ing intermeddlers out of it, dealing with the momentous issues of his time unhesitatingly, boldly,
wisely, at the centre of life and strength, careless
of nothing save what was said of him, or the part
he played in the great events of the great epoch.
When his share of the work was done, when the
underlying causes which changed somewhat the
configuration of the continent perished, without
thought or care of how history might deal with
him and his share in affairs, anxious only that
what was gained should not be lost, he died.

Such a man was not the product of accident.
Such men never can be.   Causes through generations must conspire to such results, the science of
which is still to be searched out and formulated.
We trace his parentage back through the four or
five generations of Englishmen in America, of
whom the history of the planting-time of New
England makes honorable mention.   A long-lived,
tough, sinewy strain of men and women of varied
endowments contributed their modified qualities
to his make-up and furnishing-forth ; men and
women themselves to be changed, wrought, perfected, by the severest of Puritan schools, in the rig-

orous climate and ungenerous soil of Massachusetts, in its struggle for place and existence among
new and old peoples.

Ancient Medford, five or six miles to the northwest of more ancient Boston, at the head of navi-
gation of the small Mystic river, which came to
be famous for ship-building, was the Massachusetts
seat of the Wades.   Thither came Jonathan Wade
from county of Norfolk (country of the Norse
folk), England, in 1632.   He seems for a time to
have been at Ipswich, where he was a freeman in
1634.   He receives much and honorable mention
in the history of Medford.   At what time he
transferred himself to the latter place does not
appear, probably some years later; for we find
him buying four hundred acres of land on the
south side of the river, near Medford bridge, October 2, 1656, of one Matthew Avery of Ipswich.
He is spoken of as Major Wade, a man of worship, who paid the largest tax of any man in Medford.   He gave the town a landing about 1680,
one of several which Medford had.   It is said the
house he built and dwelt in there, though a
wooden structure, was in a sound, habitable condition in 1855.   Nothing is said of his wife or
children save one.   He died—one authority says
in 1683, another, in 1689.   He was the father of
Major Nathaniel Wade, the date of whose birth is
not given.   The history mentions this Nathaniel.
Dealing with churches, it gives this curious origin
of pews in "meeting-houses" in New England.

To call the place of worship, made of sticks and
stones, a church savored too much of papacy,
episcopacy, prelacy, for the severe Puritan, who,
as is historic, made these structures like his religion, as ugly and uncomfortable as might be.
He did not believe in helps to virtue and religion.
Both were rendered as forbidding as possible.   No
artificial means of heating their dreary meeting-
houses was permitted ; but when the proximity
to fires, which have since generally died out,
where their ministers kept them, is remembered,
the rigors of even a New England winter went for
little.   By vote of the town on his petition, it was
ordered—" May 25, 1696, Major Nathaniel Wade
shall have liberty to build a pew in the meeting-
house, when he shall see reason to do so."   Of
course he was to weigh well the deed.   This extraordinary concession marks the estimation in
which he was held at Medford.   He has another
and much stronger claim upon our consideration.
His wife was the daughter of Governor Bradstreet
and Anne Dudley Bradstreet, the famous New
England poetess, in her time called " The Tenth
Muse," and a daughter of Governor Thomas Dudley.   These are persons entitled to a moment's
attention on their own account. and especially as
their descendant is to be the subject of our literary
labors.

Dudley was a great name in older English history.   It was no less conspicuous in newer English annals.   It was the name of several royal and

other officers in Massachusetts. Of these, Thomas
Dudley was born in Northampton, England, in
1576. In 1630 he was sent to Massachusetts as
deputy governor, chosen governor in 1634, '40
and '45, died at Roxbury in 1652, a man of the
sternest Puritan integrity. He had a son Joseph,
who was successively chief-justice of Massachusetts
and New York, governor of the Isle of Wight,
and finally governor of Massachusetts from 1702
to 1715. So Joseph's son, Paul, was chief-justice
of Massachusetts.

Anne Dudley, daughter of Governor Thomas
and sister of Governor Joseph, was born in 1612.
She seems to have been carefully reared, as became a gentlewoman. Her father was attached
to the service of the Earl of Lincoln, and she
spent much of her short girlhood at his castle
of Sempringham, and was married at sixteen.
Simon Bradstreet, her husband, was nine years
older, and was also reared in the the austere
religious family of the earl. The young people
were for years members of the family, and their
marriage was a love match. That occurred in
1628, and two years later they were of the wealthy
and well-born party who entered upon the coloni-
zation of Massachusetts and reached the province
in 1630. Bradstreet was of a good Suffolk family.
The coming away of these wealthy, carefully
reared people from the luxury of Old England to
the savagery and penury of the New, was a sore
trial, and to none more so than to the tender

child-wife, who had a scholarly taste for learning
and a poet's relish for refinement, pleasant surroundings and culture.   She must have recoiled,
as we know she did, from the rude, wild forms of
life in the rocky, sterile wilderness of New England.   Notwithstanding she saw the hand of God
in it, all her life was a subdued wail of a homesick
heart.

The first edition of her poems, which were extensive, was published in London in 1650, and a
third edition in 1658.   They were brought out in
our time at Charlestown, in a fine edition, in 1867,

Of her children she sang :

> "I had eight birds hatch'd in the nest ;
> Four cocks there were, and hens the rest ;
> I nursed them up with pious care,
> For cost nor labor did I spare,
> Till at last they felt the wing,
> Mounted the trees and learned to sing."

She was a fine prose writer, and not without
poetic instincts.   Her genius was too weak to escape the vicious poetic forms and spirit of her
time.   Her work was cast in the quaint and dreary
mould of that age, and was neither worse nor better than its good average.   Her dialogues between
Old England and New, between the four elements,
a long allegory, would be melancholy reading
now.   "Contemplation," a later production, is
now esteemed her best poem.

Simon Bradstreet was governor when the charter was annulled, in 1686 ; was again elected when
that worthy, Governor Andros, was deposed and

imprisoned, in 1689, and held the place till the arrival of rough and sturdy Sir William Phipps, in 1692, who brought out the new charter. He was a prudent, plain, strong-minded man, and, if he thought Massachusetts was unable to resist Charles II, whom he was sent to congratulate on his accession, he was untouched with the Salem witchcraft craze. Anne died September 16, 1672; her husband survived till 1697.

Mercy Bradstreet, daughter of Anne, and Major Nathaniel Wade were married October 31, 1672, and had liberty later to set up a family pew in the meeting-house. That he saw reason to, is matter of inference.

To these, with other children, was born Bradstreet Wade, in 1681, at Medford—the parents dying, the father in 1707, the mother eight years later. Bradstreet Wade became the husband of Lydia Newhall, October 17, 1706, and died December 9, 1738. His son Samuel saw the light April 21, 1715, married Martha Upham, daughter of James Upham and Dorothy Wigglesworth, December 2, 1741. These were the parents of James Wade, the father of our Benjamin Franklin Wade. James Wade's grandmother, Dorothy Wigglesworth, was the daughter of the Reverend Michael Wigglesworth, a remarkable man, and also a poet of no mean power. His principal work, the 'Day of Doom,' saves his name from oblivion. He was born in England in 1631, was carried to Charlestown, Massachusetts, when seven years

old, graduated at Harvard 1651, and was settled
over the church at Malden, Massachusetts, 1656.
His famous poem was first published in 1662, and
was for a century and a half the most popular literary production of New England, going through
many editions in various popular forms, the latest
in 1867.   It is the most lurid and direful array of
terrors and horrors ever made to jostle and jingle
in jerky rhyme, and became at once the burning
fountain for images and figures of speech of the
turgid Puritan pulpit eloquence of New England,
as it is now the museum of the burnt out and fossilized remains of that volcanic age of theology.
Committed to memory, recited, quoted on all occasions, it had much to do in forming the common
mind and character of the people.   Slight specimens will show its qualities, imaginative and literary.

Thus the day dawns :

> For at midnight breaks forth a light
>   Which turns the night to day,
> And speedily an hideous cry
>   Doth all the world dismay.

Many pages of this measure and form, and the
final trump sounds and there is a general scramble
of course.   As a good many had reasons for not
caring to appear for trial, a swarm of fast-winged
bailiffs are sent to prod them into court, when the
sheep are divided off and business opens rather
briskly.   The saints are first attended to, and dis-
patched to their thrones, nothing loth to take part

in judging the sinners. Business first; pleasure follows. Sinners are disposed of in classes for expedition. Finally reprobate infants are reached:

> Then to the bar they all draw near
>   Who died in infancy,
> And never had of good or bad
>   Effected personally ;
>
> But from the womb unto the tomb
>   Were straightway carried,
> Or, at the least, e'er they trangressed,
>   Who thus begun to plead :

Poor, deserted things! Left to their own resources, it must be confessed they made a stout case of it. They could not see, any more than can we, why they should burn eternally on Adam's account, especially, as the old gentleman himself sat near by on a very comfortable throne. However, according to Wigglesworth, God found little difficulty in brushing away their baby arguments, which he is made to do in this luminous way :

> You, sinners are ; and such a share
>   As sinners may expect ;
> Such you shall have ; for I do save
>   None but mine own elect.

This must have been satisfactory. However, he concludes on the whole :

> Yet to compare your sin with their,
>   Who lived a longer time,
> I do confess yours is much less,
>   Though every sin's a crime.
>
> A crime it is ; therefore in bliss
>   You many not hope to dwell,
> But unto you I shall allow
>   The easiest room in hell.

This was letting the poor things off easy considering the enormity of their offenses, and doubtless exceptionally tender-hearted devils were
assigned as nurses. Finally the whole host are
disposed of, and God is made to call the Redeemer
and Saviour to dispose of those he tried to redeem
and save. I may give but four of the many lines
in which the final judgment is pronounced:

> But get away without delay,
>   Christ pities not your cry ;
> Depart to hell ; there may you dwell
>   And roar eternally.

Of their fortunes after being thus disposed of,
the poet gives us this glowing picture:

> They live to lie in misery
>   And bear eternal woe ;
> And live they must while God is just
>   That he may plague them so.

Of course, having enjoyed the sight of these
comforting spectacles, the saints in fitting strains,
are dismissed to bliss generally. Cotton Mather
said the ' Day of Doom ' would be read in New
England till its pictures were realized by the event.*
Michael had a son Samuel, who seems to have
been capable of poetry in a milder form—real
poetry—but who contented himself with the office
and duties of a country parson. The author of the
' Day of Doom ' was equal to different work. His
daughter Dorothy, as we have seen, was the
grandmother of our B. F. Wade.

---

* Whoever would know more of the two greatest New England poets
of colonial times should read what is said of them in Professor Tyler's
admirable ' History of American Literature,' not yet concluded.

James Wade was born at Medford, still the seat
of the Wades, July 8, 1750, and would lack four
days of being twenty-six on the declaration of
independence. His birth was at the beginning
of a noisy, stirring period. He was four years old
when Washington fought the first battle that
opened the wide, long desolating war, one result
of which was the transfer of Canada to England
and establish British dominion in America. It
was a day of adventure. Medford was an old
town, was within reach of the salt wafts of the
ocean. Though born in 1750, and living till 1826
—when the writer of these sketches was ten years
old—with a son still living, no one has told us the
manner of boy or man he was. Hardy, robust,
sinewy, right-headed, he must have been, and
well educated, for such as passed for education
outside of Harvard. He grew up in the intensely
patriotic atmosphere of stormy Boston, during the
pre-revolutionary years. Heard the Adamses,
Otis and Warren, in old Faneuil—not then so
old ; was there through the times of the stamps,
the destruction of the tea, the Boston massacre—
always to be a massacre, though a jury of Middle-
sex county acquitted the officers and soldiers who
committed it. He daily saw the red-coated soldiers about the streets of Boston, and hated them
for what they stood for ; was to see more of them,
as they were to see him, elsewhere and full soon.
The lithe young Englishman of American birth
and nervous organization was early a member of

a train-band, an adept in the manual of arms.
Think of a youth thus nurtured and growing up.
Of course, he was at the first facing of the hostile
elements, not in the least premature, where the
flash of the British muskets was met by the answering flash of the armed patriots, flash for flash, at
Concord ; and so on to Lexington, and at
the decisive Bunker Hill's epoch-making battle, decisive that war was to be and so an end,
which was also a beginning greater than the end
it followed.   He could hardly fail of a predilection
for the sea, and we next see him on board a
privateer and a prisoner, after various adventures.
Privateering was then a universally recognized
means of public war, though dealt with by the
royal cruisers as but one remove from piracy.
Our maternal foe was not eminent for clem-
ency to rebels taken in arms, and distinguished
against those taken on private armed ships,
though sailing under letters of marque all squarely.
James Wade was carried to Halifax, where,
languishing for an unknown period, he was transferred to a prison ship of the "Jersey prison ship"
class, place of nameless horrors.   Here he and his
fellows conspired against their jailers, overcame,
captured them and their "old prison hulk," and
made good their escape to freedom and more war.
Restless, adventurous, he gave his time and ener-
gies to the war when not in prison.   When that
was ended, like the country he was impoverished,
and turned to peaceful pursuits, with the habits

and modes of thought formed by his many years
as a soldier, sailor and adventurer.

His mother, was Martha Upham, as will be
remembered, daughter of James Upham. She
had a brother, Edward Upham, a graduate of
Harvard in 1734, and curiously enough, he became
a Baptist clergyman and was settled first at Newport, Rhode Island—that Baptist colony and state.
He was one of the trustees of Brown University ;
was offered the first presidency of it, which he
declined. Later he made his way back to Massachusetts and established himself at West Springfield,* on the west side of the Connecticut river.
That region in western Massachusetts was then
new, remote and rude. Just when he settled there
is not apparent.

The narrow, winding, lovely valley of the Connecticut was always very fertile, while on each
side of it the country rises into a hilly, almost
mountainous region, rocky, with a starved, sandy
soil, soon exhausted.

Rev. Edward Upham's youngest daughter was
a winsome maiden, though no longer young, born
at Newport in 1752, when her cousin James, with
the romance of his career, made his way to visit
his uncle, amid the breezy hills of West Springfield. Just where they first met—probably long
before—or under what circumstances, no one has
told us. They were cousins, which made court-

* The early colonists had the English way of repeating names of
places with the prefix north, south, east, west.

ship easy.   No one has told us a word of that.
Easy or hard, they were married January 15, 1781,
and made their home in "Feeding Hills" parish,
a few miles southerly of West Springfield.   The
name Feeding Hills may still be found on the
larger maps of Massachusetts, as a small town.
A thin, sandy-soiled, rocky, hilly country, abounding in trout streams, its principal products were
fine scenery, huckleberries and wintergreens.   It
was a region early devoted to wild pasturage for
kine-herds of the more favored valley and other
adjacent places, and hence the name.

At the marriage of these thus descended English cousins, James Wade was thirty-one years
old, and we may assume that Mary, the daughter
of a Baptist clergyman of West Springfield, was
rich only in person, intellect, piety, womanly
qualities and graces, educated for the subordinate
position then assigned generally to woman, even
in the family.   There is ample testimony to her
unusual excellence as a woman of very considerable
mental endowment, judgment, fine sense, steady
courage and wifely devotion.   As a mother she
ranked with the noblest.   She had need for the
exercise of all her faculties in the place to which
she ·was assigned in life, where, as everywhere,
when she performs her duty, woman's place is
the least favored.

At what time the young pair set up their
homestead, amid the outlying Feeding Hills, we
are not told, nor of the kind of habitation they

occupied. We know it was humble, and that the implements of the young housewife were simple and primitive. No one has told us of the home-faring of this family. Human life is essentially the same under all conditions, admitting its continuance. Individuals adjust themselves to their various surroundings and unconsciously work out a portion of the as yet unsolved problem. Straitened as were their circumstances, we know their life was robust and healthful. To toil early and late, steadily, persistently, for bread, meat and raiment, wrung from an ungenial soil, with little perceptible gain or advance, save in years, and increasing mouths to feed, bodies to clothe and shelter, was the changeless though ever-growing task of James till old age came upon him in the barren, rocky hills.

To bear, nurse and rear children ; to economize, contrive and eke out from scantiest stores and meet the ever increasing demand with smallest increase of supply; to be first up ere dawn and the last to retire, caring for the infants during the night ; to work and toil early, lose her girlish comeliness ; to love and fear God, with the awful fear of the Puritan ; to rear her children in that fear ; to trust and doubt and hope for them, watch their unfolding minds, their dispositions, hearts and morals, till years enfeebled her—was the life of Mary.* Forty years of this life amid

---

* Current biography makes scanty mention of the mother, often omits all notice of wife and marriage. Whoever thus writes has

the grim, rocky hills, scrub pines and cedars, and
the family sought a new home in the newer New
England of the northern Ohio woods of the Reserve, from 1781 to 1821.

To these parents were born eleven children, all
in the Feeding Hills home. Of these the four
eldest were girls. Their names and dates of birth
were as follows :

Martha Upham Wade, born August 24, 1782.
She became the wife of Corlleain Brigden, and
died at Andover, Ohio.

Nancy Wade, born July 2, 1784, and died in
infancy.

Nancy Wade, second, born February 26, 1786,
became the wife of John Picket, and died also in
Andover.

Mary Wade, born September 2, 1787, married
William Bettis, and died in Andover.

James Wade, born June 5, 1789. For his first
wife he had Sally Mulford, for his second Elizabeth Hughes. He died in 1868. .

Charles Wade, born April 22, 1791, died in
infancy.

Samuel Sidney Wade, born May 11, 1793,
married Emily Cadwell, died at Andover.

Theodore Leonard Wade, born March 13, 1797,
three times married. His second wife was Au-

---

failed to make a study of the most important factors of a man's life.
Next in importance to birth is his marriage, and the wife shares with
the mother the labor and responsibility of shaping his fortunes and
destinies.

gusta Bettis, a cousin. A daughter by this wife became Mrs. Schuyler Colfax. His third was also a cousin. He died in Andover.

Charles H. Wade, born December 8, 1798. He married Julietta Spear, who bore him three children. He is the sole survivor of the family living in Andover.*

Benjamin Franklin Wade, born October 27, 1800.

Edward Wade, born November 22, 1802, twice married. First to Sarah Louise Atkins. His second was Mary P. Hall. He died in 1866.

Eleven children, four girls and seven boys, with twenty years difference between the oldest and the youngest! Curiously enough, no name of any of the distinguished ancestors appears among the boys, save Edward. Not a Dudley, Bradstreet or Upham. Martha Upham and Nancy of the female line. Nor is there a Jonathan or Nathaniel. A tough, long-lived family and race! All married and affectionate, remaining together in the bosom of the Feeding Hills, and making their new homes together in Ohio, all save the eldest bearing his father's name. By popular legend Edward, a seventh son in unbroken succession, was born to happy fortune. His last years were the saddest that can fall to man. He died of softening of the brain.

The year 1800 is a handy year to date from, as is that of the birth year of Frank's father, the half

---

* April, 1885.

century year before.   Edward, the youngest, was
a scarcely less remarkable man than Frank, in
some ways fully his equal.   The mysteries of
transmission and reproduction are still elusive.
That must be a fine strain of men and women,
and that must have been a remarkable family,
where the tenth and eleventh were of the quality
of Frank† and Edward Wade.   There are none
now to tell us the manner of child Frank was, this
greatest of the descendants of the Dudleys, the
Bradstreets, the Wades, Wigglesworths and Up-
hams.   He would well repay a study if the material existed.   Great men always arise in unlooked
for homesteads.   There is nothing to mark them.
No man probably could now, of all the living boys,
name one of the one hundred remarkable men of
this country forty years hence.   It is only when
one has achieved distinction that an effort is made
to reproduce his early years, and construct a fitting
child- and boyhood for him.   We can fancy him a
brave, active, adventurous child and boy, eager,
ready, studious, thoughtful, coming late into the
already overpeopled house, he and his little baby
brother Edward—little Ned, as he would be
called—taken in hands by the elder sisters, bloom-

---

†Through all his early life in Northern Ohio, and still among the
members of his family, the subject of this memoir was known as Frank
Wade, and such he will be here called, as his younger brother was Ned
Wade.   "Ben" and "Old Ben" came into use at Washington, and
though they grew into use in Ohio, were always less popular.   To the
writer, who knew him intimately all his own adult life, "Ben Wade"
was something different and less than "Frank Wade," the ideal of all
the younger men in the wide reach of his acquaintance.

ing into young women comeliness, early taught to
make his boy hands and active feet useful, scamp-
ering among the wild Agawam hills, emulous to
be with and imitate the older brothers, to whom
James, who was called Jim, of course, was an ideal
hero. This is not all fancy, for it was in the or-
derly course of things in a New England family.
The father is more phantom-like to us. The
mother stands firmly or moves materially the unconscious head and centre of her now completed
flock, teaching each and all the New England Catechism, the Shorter Catechism of the Westminster
assemblage of divines of 1646, in which the meta-
physical achievements of the Calvinistic theology
of that day are reduced to dogmatic forms and set
forth in categoric questions and answers, covering
the whole fruitful field of the nature and essence,
the will and government of God, the origin and
nature of man, the advent of the Son, the nature
and consequence of sin, the atonement, and the
ultimate destiny of men. It was a wide field
copiously treated, and among the first lessons supplied to the plastic childish mind. It was not in
nature that Mary Upham neglected to have the
docile Frank and Ned imbibe this rather dry and
innutritious bread of the life to come. So, of
course, they committed to memory, possibly, the
whole of the great-grandfatherly 'Day of Doom'*
and were properly saturated with the rather lurid

---

*This was true of Frank. He used occasionally to repeat doleful
passages from it.

religious atmosphere of that time, already beginning to break, fade and yield to a purer air and a
whiter light.   That both took long, constant and
deep lessons of biblical reading we know, as both
were remarkably conversant with the Scriptures,
especially the elder canon, which they kept up
through life.   The younger was especially famous
for his many and happy quotations in his speeches
at the bar, and on political occasions.   No matter,
Mary was a tender mother, and reared her children
under a full sense of the awful responsibility resting upon her for having brought into the world
beings born to such fearful destinies.   The boys
were docile; they took the prescribed portion,
learned it, and escaped to the breezy hills, to the
trout streams; were permitted to go to the river—
the little, shallow, noisy Agawam—and on some
distant and very rare occasions were taken by Jim
and Charley to the river of rivers, the Connecticut, a larger, longer river, in the fancy of the New
England boy, than the Mississippi or even the
Jordan, with which he was more familiar.

We know that the New England Sabbath was
more rigidly kept than was the Jewish, with fewer
privileges.   By theological mathematics it was
demonstrated that it began at sundown of Satur-
day night, and ended with the departure of sun-
light of the sacred Sabbath.   The slavery of this
Puritan institution was something awful, and it
was planted in patches in the free Ohio woods.
Of course the whole family were confined a large

portion of the holy day in the meeting-house of the Feeding Hills parish, and kept alive to the long sermons that reached *sixteenthly* and *seventeenthly*, as well as the interminable prayers.†

The later mental growth of New England, under the stimulating and shattering effects of the then late war, was escaping the religious fetters as well, and taking on new forms of expression. In this the younger generation of Wades fully shared; and although in his early manhood Edward, under the influence of his affianced, sharing more fully the religious nature of their mother, became and remained a member of her church, the less impressible Frank lived and died outside of religious communion of all forms.

The daughter of one of the best educated men of his time, Mother Mary was zealous for the mental culture, especially, of her boys. In the time and region where her fortune cast her, their education was to be largely the fruit of her work. It is now difficult, even for those whose memories reach farthest back, to appreciate the utter poverty of the period of Frank's child- and boyhood, in the means of education. Literally, like the younger Weller, it was for him "a pursuit of knowledge under difficulties." In striking contrast with the prodigality of our times in newspapers, periodicals, magazines, books of every

---

†Dr. Ely, in the South meeting-house of Munson, east of Springfield, consumed forty minutes for his main prayer. The writer fortunately was an infant when present, but his inherited experience of these seasons was vivid.

form and variety, literature created for boys in his
day had no existence. The mental air was cold
and thin. Few had books, and they were mainly
books of scholastic theology, of the quality of
'Edwards on the Will,' Baxter's 'The Saints'
Everlasting Rest,' his notes of the New Testa-
ment, for which that upright Judge Jeffries placed
him in the pillory; Watt's dreary hymns, 'Watt's
on the Mind,' long a college class-book ; 'Butler's
Analogy,' which was also; 'Milton's Poems,' regarded as the product of divine inspiration direct ;
and Bunyan's 'Pilgrim's Progress,' by the same
high authority. Other light literature there was
none. Of educational books, first and foremost
was 'The New England Primer,' * containing the
Shorter Catechism and abounding in couplets of
a moral and elevating character.

Noah Webster had already begun his reforma-
tory raids on the common language. He published his 'Grammatical Institute of the English
Language' a year or two after the marriage of
James and Mary. It consisted of three parts.
The first afterward became his famous spelling-
book, the second his work on grammar, and the
third was a widely used reading book—'The III
Part'—with rules of elocution, which many may
still remember. It may be doubted whether

---

* The first prize ever competed for in school by the writer was a
'New England Primer' in blue covers. He lost it by missing a single
word in a long spelling lesson to a boy who missed every other word
in it. That was the last of two long columns, and placed him at the
head.

Mary, whose notions were of Harvard, would favor the innovator of Yale, but undoubtedly the Wade boys were fed with this Websterian pabulum.

There were 'Dilworth's Speller,' 'Arithmetic' and 'Guide to the English Language,' all in existence since 1761. There was also Pike's—Nicholas Pike's—'Arithmetic,' long the standard in New England schools, published at Newburysport in 1788—a club for stupid heads, the delight of tough, fibrous brains. Lindley Murray was a Pennsylvania lawyer, merchant and author. His grammar, first published in 1795, soon became and long remained the standard in England as well as America. This was followed in 1799 by his 'English Reader.' What elder or middle-aged man who did not use it? Later came the 'American Preceptor'—a fresh, good book.

The method of teaching of that time was mainly to leave the pupil entirely to himself. The works mentioned contained small or no explanation of their own rules, and few illustrations. They were to be memorized and reveal themselves when they would. Sometimes a ray of light was cast into the darkened mind, and the student was expected to follow out to the source of light, a clue—something to pull himself up by. The work was his, the gain all his. The older edition of 'Adams' Arithmetic' a book with large pages, had a concisely stated problem, one or more on each page, with blank space on which the solution, when

reached, was to be written by the pupil. A boy
carried a bit of paper and a pen to school. His
teacher wrote an arithmetical problem upon it—
"set him a sum"—and with or without a word of
instruction, possibly a bare hint of what it was,
the child was left to wrestle with it as he might.

Teaching as an art, an applied science, was unknown in the common schools. The old statutes
of Massachusetts, and the earlier of Ohio, required
that an apprentice should be sent to school and
taught so much arithmetic as included the four
fundamental rules, and carry him to what was
called "The rule of Three direct"—simple proportion.

One thing was inevitable under this arid step-
mother process. The stupid, dull-minded boys
grew up dull, stupid men, with undeveloped rudimentary faculties, and remained such through
life. Their minds were the dark resting places of
the old, once popular superstitions and beliefs,
while the quick, strong, eager, sinewy minds of
Mary Upham Wade's boys were stimulated and
strengthened to their very best. The difference
between the naturally endowed would at once be
increased and widened, and the better gifted
would become as they were, an intellectual aristocracy. Nothing in our world is so essentially
democratic as a real *common* education. Now
men say there are no really great men, while the
fact is the common—the average—is so much elevated that the difference is much less between it

and the highest, so that the great men have seemed to disappear.

From what we know of Benjamin Franklin and Edward in their early manhood, whom we must be permitted to associate, we glance backward and reproduce Frank and Ned, the youngest and therefore favorite boys of Mary and James Wade, running freely among the Feeding Hills. Frank, the older, more adventurous, more silent ; Ned, tender, bright, joyous, the more hopeful, going with, seconding, standing by Frank in all the wild adventures of their boy life—in their studies, Frank the more enquiring and certain, Ned the more eager and docile, with his black, silky, curling, girl's hair twisting and falling over his dark brow, with flashing black eyes, full of fun and mischief; while Frank's burned with a steadier and more thoughtful, a mysterious and melancholy light, as if given to see things withheld from common men ; he the leader and mentor of the younger. His encounter, long tussle with and final conquest of ' Nicholas Pike,' in their growing years and minds, is historic. Few young men then or ever went through—clear through—' Pike's Arithmetic.' This he accomplished, and conducted the younger and more aspiring boy along the same rugged way. So we are told that the elder had an algebra, that later generalization of arithmetic unknown to the ancients, whose problems it solves with the aid of symbols. We do not know whose work he had. He was nearly of the same age with Davies. It may

have been something from Descartes or the older
mathematicians.   His was a mind that would have
delighted in the higher range of mathematics.   It
is easy to suppose that in the matter which came
to his mother may have been a copy of ' Euclid's
Elements,' in the old quarto form, with wide mar-
gins, the word triangle always being expressed by
little deltas.

We know that Frank worked at home on the
farm all the years from the time his child hands
were useful till the family removed to Ohio, going
to school two or three months each winter—his
only aid from educational institutions.   Self-taught,
with his mother's and elder brother's aid, when
above the reach of the New England schoolmaster,
he worked on alone.   The mental discipline of
this process is very effective, the self-taught man
always running the risk of being misled by not
knowing who is the latest and best authority.   He
makes a book his own—blood, bone, muscle and
sinew.

James Wade was becoming aged.   How many
great and grave things occurred during the years of
his sojourn in his native state !   Springfield was
quite the centre of the Shay's rebellion of 1785–6 ;
a soldier, he must have had some hand in one side
of that.   Then came the long wrangle over the
growing troubles with the mother country, leading
to the second long and bloody war, necessary, perhaps, to perfect our emancipation from unconscious
colonial vassalage, and in which we fought our way

to a place of respectability among the great nations of modern times.

The Wades removed to Ohio in 1821. Of that removal, as of the general outlook of the younger members of the family, we shall have something to say hereafter, when we hope to take up and pursue the individual fortunes of Frank Wade more directly in his maturing manhood on the Western Reserve, where the ground is firmer under our feet, though the incidents of his life are still scanty and elusive.

CHAPTER II.

THE final causes which shape the fortunes of
individual men and the destinies of states are often
the same. They are usually remote and obscure,
their influence wholly unsuspected until declared
by results. When they inspire men to the exercise of courage, self-denial, enterprise, industry,
and call into play the higher moral elements, lead
men to a risk of all upon conviction, faith ; such
causes lead to the planting of great states,
great nations, great peoples. That nation is
greatest that produces the greatest and most
manly men, as these must constitute the essentially greatest nation. Such a result may not
consciously be contemplated by the individuals
instrumental in their production. Pursuing each
his personal good by exalted means, they work
out this as a logical conclusion. They struggle
on the lines of the largest good.

Something has been said of the planting and training of the Puritan element in rugged New England. A word must be permitted of the planting of a new state west of the Alleghanies, between the lake and river, and the transplanting the modified Puritan to its stimulating soil and atmosphere, for further development.

In 1788 General Rufus Putnam organized the Massachusetts company, and secured the grant of a million acres of land on the Ohio, including the mouth of the Muskingum, a river flowing through a most favored region. There the company planted ancient Marietta and organized the county of Washington.

About the same time John Cleves Symmes, a distinguished citizen of New Jersey, secured concessions of large tracts below, extending to the Miamis, valuable and rich lands, establishing himself at North Bend, intending there to lay the foundation of a western metropolis.

A little later came men from young Kentucky and secured the site of Cincinnati, which, for the time, they called Losantiville, though it fell largely under the dominant men of the east.

The third Stuart king of England, in 1662, made a grant of American lands, sixty-two miles wide, extending from Narragansett bay westward to the ocean, which finally inured to thrifty Connecticut. Her title was none of the best, but she so managed that after her sister states had relinquished their rival claims to the infant republic,

she was permitted to reserve from her grant to the
United States, as her property, this breadth of
territory extending west one hundred and twenty
miles from the western line of Pennsylvania. This
is the origin, territorial extent and geographical
position of the famous Connecticut Western Reserve—New Connecticut, as the natives of that
state affectionately called it. The south line of
the grant—the forty-first degree north—was its
southern boundary. Her northern was washed
by the envious lake, ever encroaching on the
domain, the southern trend of whose coast line,
running west, cut the ambitious little state out of
quite half her acres. In her sweep across northern
Pennsylvania she had planted, organized, and for
a time governed her county of Westmoreland,
whose representatives sat in her legislature, and
she had a long and bloody feud with Pennsylvania, to whom she was finally obliged later to
yield it. And though she had so much *more land*
still *west*, she was constrained to yield its sover-
eignty to the United States, and it became for
political purposes part of the Northwest Territory,
and so of the state of Ohio. She soon sold the
soil to the Connecticut Land company, composed
of Massachusetts and Connecticut capitalists, who
surveyed, divided their acquisition and dissolved,
each at once seeking purchasers, which caused the
first and greatest movement westward from New
England. All this, save migration, occurred in
the last years of the last century.

These wide acquisitions on the borders of the state that was to be, show the appreciative judgment, as well as the enterprise, of the men of New England, of the importance of this new and farther west, a west that was to flee yet westward till the occident itself should vanish.   This northernmost acquisition was soon to become the home and training ground of our youth of the Feeding Hills' parish, whose best claim to notice is—it gave him birth and early nurture.

Loosely speaking, the Reserve was distant six hundred miles, the whole extent of westward-stretching New York and farther-extending Pennsylvania, both westwardly, covered by an interminable forest, traversed by numerous and generally unbridged streams, and intersected by one considerable range of mountains to be crossed or gone around.   At the beginning of the century the whole of the new domain was in the possession of the Indians, though their titles had been extinguished by the process of battle and treaty.

Immigration, left wholly to individual enterprise, by unconscious selection, secures in the main very good, often the best men for that purpose.   None but the hardy, resolute and enterprising would undertake and endure the hazard and hardship.   The most of Ohio was thus peopled, not only from New England, but from Virginia, Maryland, Kentucky and Tennessee. As might have been foreseen from her geographi-

cal position and extent, she would rapidly grow
to power and importance in the republic.

The leaders of New England and northeastern
immigration to the southern border were men of
wealth, high position and wide influence. They
sought soldiers, adventurers, border men, hunters,
men of broken fortunes, and, surrounded as they
were by emigrants from the border southern
states, the distinctively New England and northern traits and characteristics were soon lost ; and
while they modified the manners and customs of
the new communities, were in turn modified by
their new associates and environs. Migration to
the Connecticut lands was entirely spontaneous,
without the aid of the states, or of the land company, without the patronage of leaders or propri-
etors, quite without individual concert. That
region bordering the lake was from the first preferred, though in the beginning not more accessible. It may be that the unapprehended influence
of that seeming law which requires the greater lines
of transit over the western continent to be along
the parallels of latitude, controlled this first considerable movement of the eastern people. However that was, while New England early lost its
distinctive influence in southern Ohio, it concen-
trated and augmented it on the northern border,
which was so much condensed Puritan New England. It still remains essentially New England.
The immigrants thither were young, middle-aged
husbandmen and their young wives and children,

from the centres of the oldest English civilization
on the continent, with nothing warlike but the
fading traditions of the revolution and older Indian
wars, nor hunters, knowing nothing of woodcraft,
or pioneer makeshifts.   Peace-loving, law-abiding,
from instinct and habit—frugal, long-headed, intellectual, hard workers, inventive, strongly imbued with the religion of their ancestors, intensely
Protestant, believing in the God of the Bible, the
saving efficacy of common schools in this life, and
bent on bettering their earthly condition by slow,
hard work.   Beyond that, never thinking of any
part they were to play in forming a new great
state.   Purely democratic in life and habit of
thought, their organized townships would be little
democracies.   Of one of these the young Wades
are to become citizens, help form and be formed
by it, in the larger freedom of the thinly settled
woods, most favorable to the development of individual traits and tendencies, growing as the
trees grow, and, like them, largely under the
limits of natural law alone.

The county of Ashtabula (Indian name of a
creek) is the northeastern county of Ohio, bordering Lake Erie and bounded east by Pennsylvania.
It was organized in 1811, containing twenty-eight
townships, of the five-mile square pattern of the
Reserve, to which the exceptions, save those
caused by the lake coast-line, are few.

The township of Andover is one of the eastern
range, lying along the Pennsylvania line, and the

fifth going south from the lake, from which it is
something over twenty miles distant. Its settlement began in 1805 or 1806. It was organized as
a body politic in 1819. This implied at least ten
resident voters in its territory. The organization
was after the Massachusetts pattern, with three
trustees—the government proper, one or more
justices of the peace and constables—old English ;
supervisors of highways, overseers of the poor,
viewers of fences, the erection of common school
districts by metes and bounds, of which the
residents were *quasi* corporators. All native or
naturalized citizens, with the qualification of residence, were freemen, and settled their township
affairs at an annual meeting of all the voters, held
then, and now, on the first Monday of April.

In the history of Andover* I find it recorded :
'' In 1820 the three brothers Wade—Samuel Sidney, Theodore Leonard, and Charles H.—came
into the township. They were unmarried." The
record says further of these young Wades, that in
1821 "Theodore taught a three months' school
in Madison (then in Geauga county, some distance west) and received therefor six barrels of
whiskey ;" and that "Charles taught the same
winter in Monroe (down toward the lake) and
received five barrels." It may be stated that at
that day the only disposition to be made of the
surplus wheat and corn was to turn it into whiskey.
Its capacity of being turned elsewhere rendered it

* Williams' 'History of Ashtabula County,' p. 216.

one of the few merchantable products of that
remote region, which then had no outlet, except
across the woods southeastwardly to remote Pittsburgh and the headwaters of the Ohio river. The
history also says that the new Wade homestead
was established on lots 38 and 48. What were
distinguished as lots were quarter sections, a half
mile square, containing one hundred and sixty
acres of land each. This may answer for the
beginning of current history as usually written.
It will be remembered that James Wade, Jr., the
eldest of the sons, early pushed off to the neighborhood of Albany, west of Springfield and not
very remote, where he taught school, studied
medicine, married, and came finally to be a physician and surgeon of much local celebrity.

It is quite certain that the first to reach Ohio
were Charles H., his sister, Nancy Picket, and her
husband, John. They left Springfield late in
1819, and there is a legend that they walked much
of the way, lingered in Pennsylvania and reached
Andover in 1820, where they settled. The next
was Samuel Sidney. Samuel Sidney Wade, second
son, left Feeding Hills and made his way to his
brothers, in eastern New York, where he remained
for a time teaching school. He reached Andover
about the time or a little later than did his brother
and sister. He was accompanied by Theodore L.
They joined the others. The exact date, whether
in 1819 or 1820, of this reunion is of little consequence to us. The three young men, brothers,

these young and vigorous Wades, fell to the first
and only work of pioneers—axmen—chopping
down trees, building log cabins, tracing out trails
and lines, and "blazing trees" (hewing off the
bark) to mark the way, and picking up the rudiments of woodcraft, this and school-teaching in
the winter.   Here in the woods, Samuel Sidney,
the wit of the family—who ranked high for shrewd
and pithy sayings, esteemed quite the best con-
versationalist—found sweet Emily Cadwell, then
two years with her father's family, Roger Cadwell,
from Farmington, Connecticut, and wooed her in
such fashion that they were married in September,
1821.*   He it was who "took up" the land in
the east part of this Andover of the west, and
built there a new homestead, of which the young
bride became the mistress.

It must have been in the fall of 1821 that the
Wade brothers fitted out a team and sent John
Picket to Massachusetts for the residue of the
family—James and Mary Upham, Frank and
Ned, who reached the cabin in the woods at the
near approach of winter, now sixty-five years
ago.

How rudimentary everything was—a little
framed school house at the centre, built the year
before ; an old-fashioned, small-stoned grist-mill,
picked from native boulders ; a little, new, slow-

---

* They became the parents of Judge E. C. Wade of Jefferson, Ohio,
and she was a sister of the later born Hon. Darius Cadwell of Cleveland.

going saw-mill, on a forest stream that dried up
when the woods were cut away ; trails and winding, scarcely trodden roads and forest paths,
through the endless woods, with here and there a
small opening, a rude log cabin, a little, stumpy,
blackened clearing, and for the rest, woods—trees
and woods.   There was a court house and a hamlet
at Jefferson, a larger village near the mouth of the
Ashtabula creek.   Buffalo still showed signs of the
late war, and then the solitary shore of the lonely
lake, a waste of desert water.   There was a little
village on the Grande river west, and a rude, straggling town of six hundred inhabitants at the
mouth of the Cuyahoga.   The lake had a single
steamer launched that season, called *Walk-in-the-
Water*, after the old Wyandot chief, who deserted
Proctor the day before the battle of the Thames ;
that and four or five small craft, without a harbor
or barely an accessible creek, on the whole southern lake coast.   The great state of the near future
was a wide, dim outline, hiding in the shadows of
its scarcely broken forests, still echoing with the
cries and din of savage warfare—its half million of
pioneers.   Columbus, a straggling, muddy village
on the Scioto, had been but five years the capital
when Frank Wade, this lithe young descendant of
the Puritans, strode into the woods of her northeastern border, as unconscious of what this coming
portended to him as of the future greatness of the
infant state three years his junior.   He was then
twenty-one years of age, full American height,

broad, heavy shouldered, slender in the loin, well limbed, straight and supple, manly featured, to whom Jupiter had already sent a beard; dark eyed, and bearing his head well up with unconscious dignity, wholly unassuming, frank, courageous, virile manliness early characterized his bearing, with a mind well developed, quick, observing, alive to all that was about him, he came, as did the other youths of the East, to war with the forests, reduce the earth to the purposes of the husbandman and become a tiller of its fresh, vigorous soil ; less aspiring than his younger brother, this was known to be his purpose. His first study was the wonderful forest, not the lush gigantic tangled growth of the sub-tropical, humid regions of the south, but the open, clean, tall, large, splendid product of the strong soils in that northern temperate belt, stretching from the Hudson westward to the treeless plains, composed of nearly every variety of *deciduous* trees, with but a slight sprinkle here and there of *conifers*. This was particularly the character of the forest lying along the southern border of the lake, extending indefinitely southward and westward.

The younger Wades had already become accustomed to the woods. They, nor no men, had ever seen a finer growth of splendid forest than shaded the wide sloping plains and hillsides of the Western Reserve.

It is curious, the effect of a sojourn in the forest upon civilized men. All revert more or

less toward primitive conditions—toward savagery. It is essential to existence there, where
everything is taken first hand from the woods, the
waters and the soil itself. Some became hunters
in a day, some instinctively grasp the lore of woodcraft, while the majority remain obstinate citizens,
to whom the forest is a prison whose walls they
flee or labor to destroy.

Frank early became, and always remained, an
expert rifle shot. I never heard that he was a
hunter or greatly a woodsman ; he was an observer,
a student, and alive to impressions. From wondering at the individual trees, wondering at the
trees in grand masses, he passed to studying their
peculiarities and economic values. He came to
know something of the forest, the woods as a whole;
came to appreciate it as the realm, the world of
nature, who wrote a common character upon all
her children that found standing room and homes
in its thickets and glades. *Wild*, men call it,
from insect and bird to the elk and Indian. Wild,
gamey, the hunters and pioneers said of the flavor
of its meats and fruits. Men living long in it
themselves become more or less possessed of its
subtle, elusive, yet pervasive spirit.

The latest arrived took up their abode with the
newly married Samuel and Emily, and so the
family were reunited. The Pickets were near, the
Brigdens and Bettises soon came, and save the
long absent James, jr., the Wades were all together again. Three of the five young men taught

school that winter.   Those at home kept the fire
agoing, "chopped down browse " maple, elm,
beech and basswood for the cow and oxen.   As
the spring approached five axes were helved and
ground, and five stalwart young choppers assailed
the forest.   A cornfield must be planted in May.
From eight to ten days a single fairly good axman
required to fell and cut into proper lengths the
standing trees of an acre of land and pile up the
small limbs and brush for the first burning.
What a falling of trees and resounding of axes
as these five youths *Waded* into the woods.   Then
came sugar making, and the pigeons, the suckers
and mullet, the pike and other lake fish up the
undammed creeks.   In mid April the newly cut
and piled brush in the chopping, under the sun,
winds and rains, would burn, and the "fallow"—the
chopping—was fired.   The winds arose, and there
was a great conflagration—which darkened the sky
—and the fragrance of burning leaves was on the
air.   Then, with a specially trained yoke of oxen—
Bright and Brown, the same with shoes and working in breeching, which drew the wagon from the
Feeding Hills the autumn before ; the young men,
armed with "ironwood" handspikes, strong,
hardy and lithe, piled up and burnt the already
blackened tree trunks, and the denuded,
smirched, virgin earth was given to her husbandman.   The vigor of her response to the young
New Englanders, was a wonder to them.   Whatever they entrusted to her she returned an hundred

fold, their plantings of one day putting forth their
blades almost on the next. What lush growths
of rank and fragrant herbage on the wide slopes of
the woods and along the pleasant watercourses,
the early season brought ; even the uplands were
clothed in deep verdure as a savanna. What
myriads of new and strange flowers, what a world
of song birds, and then the wild small fruits as the
summer deepened. There were the plum bottoms,
raspberries, crabapples, in endless profusion, and
the fragrance of wild thyme and oxbalm. Through
the summer, there was more chopping and clearing
for wheat. Then the rich, ripe autumn and the
splendor of the gorgeous forest, with the profusion
of nuts. Winter came with more school teaching,
and so as the seasons came and went. They were
much alike. The fields grew, the woods receded ;
rich grasses clothed the earth, fruit trees and
shrubs took the places of the wilder plantings of
nature, which she in turn fostered with the same
care.

What a household was that—these five young
Wades—the eldest with his bride-wife; James already venerable, telling his stories of the old war,
his memory failing; Mary, grown a little stout,
with her square, intellectual brow, bright eyes,
white hair, her softened, sweet face and winnowed
wisdom, still the head and centre ; the young wife
ruling by the divine right of blessed womanhood,
surrounded by these youths taught by Mother
Mary to reverence and cherish womanhood. Some-

thing of this old-time, rare circle has been told
me.

These five vigorous, healthy, intellectual, witty
and fairly cultivated young men, emulous, hungry
for mental food, eager, searching for everything
within reach, reading every book that any of their
ten hands could be laid upon, and discussing it as
they read, and so of everything. The Cleveland
Herald was established in 1819, the Painesville *Telegraph* in 1821. One or both of these they secured
with something from the east. A joyous, gay-tem-
pered, light-hearted, laughing, joking, rollicking
band of brothers as ever migrated into the western
woods ; kindly doing everything that came to their
hands ; helping and being helped, as was the then
golden rule of the pioneers ; widely known, widely
respected and loved. What a power such a band
is ; how helpful to each other.

Two years—two cherished years of this life, hard,
and in many ways stinted, in a cold, thin atmosphere of toil and self-denial, yet robust, sinewy;
free, pure, active, unselfish, healthful, Frank
Wade's first of pupilage and acclimation in the life
and fitting for his future duties—two years, and he
turned from that book of the lessons, a little with
the uncertainty of one who has not yet seen his
way to the thing he wants, or is in doubt as to the
thing itself. He would not be an Ohio farmer.
For many, many waiting years the young communities were without markets or outlets. The
lake was useless. The Erie canal was yet incom-

plete, and notwithstanding the thrift and enterprise
of the people, the settlements languished, stood
still, the years were moveless; values of all products disappeared;* money was not; the silver
coins were cut to fractions, and the utmost economy was necessary to secure enough to pay the
moderate yearly taxes and buy salt and leather.
Black salts commanded cash at Pittsburgh. Whiskey has been mentioned. The wide and rich
forest pasturage made the raising of cattle easy.
These could be driven eastward to a market. Early
this was an extensive business on the Reserve.
Enterprising men made it a calling. It was full
of risk, laborious, required skill and enterprise.
The larger merchant made it a means of purchase
and sale. He supplied his customers on long credits and received cattle in payment, sometimes
paying a small part in cash. Philadelphia was the
great eastern market where the droves were sold
and the proceeds invested in goods. New York
was no market. Boston was oftener resorted to
for commercial purposes. The purchases were
herded and driven "over the mountains" through
Pennsylvania, taking five or six weeks to make the
transit. Later, sheep and swine were in like
manner disposed of.

In the autumn of 1823, Frank Wade hired him-

*My father's noble pair of oxen were sold for forty dollars, part cash.
A fine mare for thirty dollars. He sold wheat for thirty-five and forty
cents per bushel, receiving "store pay." He paid ten dollars for a
barrel of salt and thirty-five cents a yard for poor domestic cotton. A
man often worked a day for a yard of cotton cloth.

self to a drover, and aided him in driving a herd
"over the mountains" to Philadelphia. He
probably walked a large part of the distance,
and received eight, ten or twelve dollars—his
personal expenses paid. The name of his em-
ployer is lost, and so escaped the one chance of
immortality. From Philadelphia he made his way
to Albany and joined his brother, Doctor James.
He spent two years in the neighborhood—two
years teaching school, and as is said, he also under-
took the study of medicine under his brother's tu-
ition. He could never have more than toyed with
the text-books, his reading making no show in his
after mental equipment, as it would had he ever
seriously undertaken it. It is certain that during
this time he resorted to the line of the great canal
in the course of construction, and worked for a
time with pick and shovel and barrow with the
common laborers, for means to carry himself forward, receiving, probably, not exceeding forty-five
or fifty cents per day. Had any one then told the
brave, independent youth that he was destined to
hear this incident of his life related in the senate
of the United States, and himself spoken of as one
of the most talented members of that body, by the
foremost statesman of his time, he would have regarded it as a prophecy too silly for even derision.*

---

*Speaking of the great work and of the foreigners who performed it,
William H. Seward said in the senate : "Whence came the labor that
performed that work? I know but one American citizen who worked
with spade and wheelbarrow upon those works. Doubtless there are

Little as we know of these two years, we know they were not lost. Nothing ever is in the lives of such men. They may not have been the most helpful—they were not without their use. He may have been slow in growth and development; I am inclined to think he was, and his mind got the utmost help from all discipline.

The great waterway was commenced in 1817, was completed in the autumn of 1825, and the regal Clinton made his progress in a famous barge from Buffalo to tide water, through it, at the close of that season. Unquestionably young Wade returned home upon it by way of the lake. Of all the west the Reserve was the first to be vivified by the new life it slowly kindled in all the north.

Frank returned to find his youngest brother, Edward—the most aspiring of all the brothers, a law student in the office of Messrs. Whittlesey & Newton, at Canfield, now Mahoning county, toward the south line of the Reserve, then the great private law school of northern Ohio. This ingenious youth, though full of fun and fancies, nevertheless had a turn for mathematics, and had composed and written a new arithmetic, which occupied his thought and spare time for a year or two. When completed, and he was studying the means of publication, a brother-in-law's house, where it was deposited, was burnt, and it was consumed. It was said

---

many others, but I know but one, and he, I am glad to say, is a member on this floor—Mr. Wade of Ohio—and one of the most talented senators.

he went about dejectedly for a day or two, and then announced his determination to become a lawyer, and that soon after, with his scant wardrobe and six dollars in his pocket, he made his way to Canfield, was received, and at once entered upon his novitiate to the law. This must have been in 1824 —year memorable in American annals for the first great contest between the second Adams and General Jackson for the Presidency, in which were sown the seeds of mischiefs innumerable.

In that day the profession of the law was, if anything, more exclusive and exalted than any other calling in America. Its members were limited, and they jealously guarded all the avenues of entrance to its ranks and priveleges, then wholly committed to their keeping. They received as students and educated the carefully selected few, whom they finally admitted to this favored circle. Always dressed with care, dignified and distant in manners, associating socially with none but the conceded select, when lines and classes were still well marked, as a body, a profession, the members always remembered and exacted their collective and inividual dues. It was long regarded as arrogant in the average young man to aspire to the honors of the bar. Wealth and education could not always find the way to it. The ministry and medicine were comparatively free. To be received into a law office as a full student, at once marked a young man and set him apart. It required courage and enterprise on his part to face this aristocratic set, meet their exactions and steadily contemplate the awful presence of the court itself. The idea of assaulting and winning his way into this favored profession was Ned Wade's own. Who vouched for him, if voucher he had, is now unknown. He was aspiring, had faith and capacity for work, and when Frank returned from Albany he was a well established and favorite student.

Elisha Whittlesey was then fairly among the three or four great lawyers in his section of the state, and had just entered upon his long, distinguished and very valuable career in the national house of representatives. Eben Newton, younger, was in the opening of a long and exceptionally brilliant course at the bar, in the Ohio senate and congress. The firm ranked with the best in the west, and educated as many able lawyers as ever graduated from any law office in Ohio. The senior was a gentleman of the old school, had served with distinction in the late war, was the centre of an exceptionally exclusive circle, the olden Canfield, where was much of wealth and pretension. There resided the Whittleseys, Wadsworths, Churches, the Canfields and others. Ned had a modest youth's confidence in himself, had boundless faith in his brother Frank. He quite appreciated his strong, sinewy mind, his capacity and will for work. Just what line of argument he pursued we know not. Upon his return he besought him so earnestly to enter upon the study of the law, that through his efforts Frank, ere

winter, was an accepted student in the office of
Whittlesey & Newton.*   He was then twenty-five
years old, with a mind fairly unfolded, a good age
to enter upon the acquirement of the rudiments
of the law, by no means an exact science, and even
at this day of inquiry and criticism, little of its
philosophy has been written.   While it demands
long and arduous mental labor to master its numerous and often artificial rules, and the grounds
and reasons upon which they depended, it still
has a considerable element of apprenticeship,
which those who undertake the law, toward even
early middle life, rarely acquire and become adepts
in.   Though slenderly equipped by scholarship,
Mr. Wade in many respects was admirably fitted,
not only to acquire, master, the theories of English common law, but he had the courage, will
power, the capacity for long, continuous, persistent work, mental and physical, without which the
higher positions of the profession never were attained, and with which no man ever yet failed at
the bar.   The curious layman who glances around
the book crusted walls of a good working law
library, wonders if a man must know all they contain.   Not at all.   He is a good lawyer who knows
where to find what law he wants at a given time.
The student is not asked to master more than ten
or twelve volumes, purely elementary, the accepted formulas of the law, arranged under heads,
as expounded and enforced by the courts at West-

---

*Edward Wade was my authority for this statement.

minster, Washington, New York, Boston, Baltimore—the courts of the last resort, among the
various English speaking nations and states.

The well selected library of that time would
seem meager and poor to the richer surrounded
lawyer of our day. Blackstone's still incompar-
able work, first given to the public in 1765, of
course these leading lawyers had ; and the first of
Joseph Chettys, which still maintain their place.
Chancellor Kent's first volume was not published
till 1826, nor was there any important American
work. For the rest, there were Coke and Fearne
and Fonblanque, Plowden and Powel ; Bacon—
not him of St. Albans and Verulam ; Bacon's
abridgement, in ten huge, dull volumes ; Comyn's
digest ; a stately row of Hargrave's state trials,
old folios, and Espinasse, and hardest of books of
legal problems ; Buller's *nisi prius*, where complex
cases were condensed into five lines, and a half
score to the page. For the law of crimes there
were Hale and East and Hawkins. Above all
and over all, and " blessed forever," there stood a
huge folio—' Jacob's Law Dictionary'—good old
Father Jacob, who required a good deal of recon-
dite learning to consult and understand, but who,
in a last push, in that strange old land of mediæ-
val scholasticism and hidden meanings, of bad
law Latin and worse law French, where solid
black letter cast a mystic gloom over the page,
never did fail the bewildered, wearied student.

It would be interesting to note the early steps

of the plucky, sinewy mind of Frank, with its
inherited tendencies, in this new field. How he
scoffed and fought everything ! What battles
royal he had with the already indoctrinated
Edward, till by degrees the spirit and life, the
reason and light—the last sometimes a little
lurid and sometimes a little ghostly, yet always
steady—came to be apprehended and appreciated as the weird, quaint spirit of the realm
came to possess him. Its sturdy efforts to
reach a practical right, sometimes failing through
its own subtleties, sometimes losing its true
spirit in its own dead and empty names, yet
always reviving and coming forth strong and vigorous for the rights of the individual man, and
effectively interposing to shield and protect him
from the oppression of the crown, which, while
the law presumed it could do no wrong, betrayed a
vicious tendency to do no right. No vigorous,
ingenuous mind can explore the law and apprehend the historic significance of its English career,
without cherishing a profound veneration for *habeas
corpus* and trial by jury. Rapidly the strong, primitive mind of the young man—a mind that boldly
questioned all things, which took nothing second-
hand, which, when deepest imbued with the color
of the law, still retained its native apprehension
of the white light, in which a healthful intellect
sees all things—became truly studious of the common law—that distilled product of so many generations of the strongest and most practical of the

minds of men, compelled to deal with, adjust and settle the innumerable differences of men, arising in their endless commerce with human property, its acquisition, transference and transmission, each generation accepting the results of its predecessors, working them over, broadening, deepening, correcting, limiting, modifying and improving the whole, as new and better lights arose, new wants arose, and farther general human progress attained—that infinitely greater mass of law, not originating in acts of parliament, of congress and state legislatures ; older and wiser, the atmosphere in which they are created, underlying, overarching, surrounding all statutes, the background against which they are drawn, by the rules of which the meaning of all enacted law is ascertained, adjudged and enforced.   An admirable mental training say the doubting, jealous laymen, for a lawyer, but its tendency is to narrow the intellect and render it less competent to deal with broad subjects and large interests.   Let these remember that the broadest minded statesmen of America, from Hamilton to Webster and Clay, from these to Lincoln, Seward and Garfield, were all thoroughly learned and trained common lawyers.

The statutes of Ohio required two years of diligent, preparatory study ere examination for admission to the bar.

The life of a real law student is narrow, absorbing, intense, exclusive and most uneventful.   He has appreciated its importance to himself and cor-

rectly apprehended the demands of his future profession.   Shy, silent and retiring, the allurements
of society, the charm of outdoor life, the roar and
clamor of the great outer world, cease to distract
him.   Let no young man who does not seriously
intend the law as his life work, waste his time in
dwaddling over books in orthodox sheep, and
kindred vices, for vices to him they will be.   He
will not dip deep enough to ensure useful mental discipline.   He will secure just law enough to mislead
himself and those who trust in him.   He will never
know how little he does know, small as it is certain
to be.

The young Wades made the law theirs—made
themselves over to it—imbibed its spirit and acquired the capacity to become real lawyers.   There
is now scarcely a legend of their student days.
There used to be many traditions of the brothers
about the older Canfield, particularly of Frank,
who impressed all men.   I have tried in vain to
find how he impressed women.   Shy of women,
diffident of power to please, he seems to have
never sought the society of ladies.   I am sorry for
that.   His decided ways, pithy sayings, original
views of men and things, his well marked individ-
uality, left a flavor of his presence that took many
years and three generations to dissipate.   Two
years, then he was to face the not apprehended
examination, beyond which, gray and misty, was
the great world of the unknown.   Yet ere the
trial for admission, James, the father, and Mary,

the mother, were laid to rest in the shadow of the western forest.

James Wade, the elder, was seventy-one at the time of the westward migration. His vigor was in the decline. He was boyishly eager to start for its west. No land since that first paradise of the occident has ever been made more alluring by stories of returned explorers than that favored region. Mary Upham, a little stouter, never very tall, retained her full mental vigor and was still strong of limb. She knew she was going forever from home into a literal wilderness. Quietly and silently she bade adieu to the small, well-kept mounds over baby Nancy and baby Charles, lingered about the spring and in one or two pleasant nooks in the garden; went out to the orchard, took a final look off from a near summit, with her own hand closed the outside door, and took her place by her impatient husband's side, as so many women had done and would do. Bravely, when they started, she refused to turn her eyes backward. They had looked their last on what she loved of that earth, and steadily and cheerfully she set them westward. Nancy and Sidney and Theodore and Charles were there. James was weary before they reached James junior's, where they lingered. The full significance of the enterprise to him began to reveal itself when they again moved on the returnless journey. Very well he endured to Buffalo. Further lay the Cattaragus swamps and woods. Where were the boys going,

and into what ? Beyond, on the wave-beaten beach
of the solitary lake, were days to him of reverie
and half dream. The endless waste of water, the
boundless border of trees. He grew weary of the
monotony of the woods—all woods. Such trees
he had never seen. He soon lost the power to
admire and wonder at them. They wearied and
then wore him. The endless level plain became
unendurable. It was quite all the brave, tender
Mary could do to keep him up. All the way and
from the first he deluded himself. Ohio-Andover
was a place dreadfully level, but there were cleared
fields, pleasant, grassy meadows, white houses,
and lazy, fat cattle, a place where he could see
through and out of the woods. Yet the further
they went the more endless seemed the everlasting forest. Finally the wagon stopped beside a
rude cabin, with the tall, great trees thick about
it. There, tripped out to him comely, sweet-faced
wife Emily, and here were Sidney and Theodore
and Charles—what were they all doing here in the
woods ? Then it came to the old man that this
was the final end, this was Ohio-Andover, home.
He went into the woods too late ; children never
comprehend how cruel they are to attempt to
transplant an old man. It is hardest on him ;
a woman is more transferable. He never took
root in the new, strange soil.

The strong, fresh, abounding life, so inspiring
and invigorating to the young, the middle-aged,
never thrilled his shrunken veins. He was recon-

ciled, passive, even cheerful, a little querulous, and went pottering about, resumed the stories of his early advetures whenever anyone would listen, then grew forgetful and told the same thing over and over to the same person, as a thing he never had heard before. He would sit watching the circling shadows of the trees as the sun cast them over the low cabin. As time wore on and the woods receded, came the natural wish to return to the Feeding Hills. He dreamed of it, planned the journey, the time it would take, the money it would cost, the places where they would put up for the night. He finally thought he and Mary would start and go alone—would walk it—and she indulged the idea. As she made no preparations for the journey, he concluded to go alone, and put together a few things and set times to go, and finally it was a source of disquiet to faithful Mary fearing he would start away alone, on a pilgrimage to the old home, and she watched and was on guard.

Mary's self, so bright, cheerful, patient and hitherto so strong and hopeful for the rest, took the new, strange life pleasantly. The winter of 1825–'26 was severe. It was too much for her. It became apparent to all save James that unless the warm weather came early and genially, she would see none but the early flowers in bloom, would never hear her favorite, the hermit thrush, at twilight in the near wood again. She died April 10, 1826.

James had now no wish to go back to Massachusetts. He was only eager to follow Mary.
She had not long to wait for him, and he set out
on the same way, the eternally old road, May 9,
following.   In age, death does not long divide the
really married.

CHAPTER III.

Frank Wade, with his brother, was admitted
to the bar late in the summer of 1827, at a term
of the supreme court, held at Jefferson, the seat
of Ashtabula county. That then, as now, was
the highest court in the state, and could alone
admit applicants to the bar. It was originally an
"ambulatory court," always "on the circuit." It
had to hold one term in each of the ever-increasing
number of counties. Two of the three judges
constituted a quorum. They exercised the right
of reserving cases for a full bench—*court in banco*—
the origin of the court as it now exists. The
earlier of Hammond's 'Ohio Reports' (first of
the state) contain cases decided on the circuit and
in *banco*. The judges were paid a thousand dollars a year, were allowed nothing for traveling
expenses, and were expected to visit every county-

seat each twelvemonth, and did when accessible. A part of the noithwest at times could not be reached.* A history of the early jurisprudence of the state would be in order and interesting. Maugre the meagre salaries, Ohio was fortunate in its supreme judges—Pease, Tod, Huntington, Hitchcock, Sherman, Grimkie, Wood, Lane, and others. They established its jurisprudence on very enduring foundations. Few of their cases have been shaken. The court had appellate and jurisdiction in error from the common pleas—the only other court of record. It also had a jury, and might and did try cases of murder directly. The later attempts to relieve suitors by increasing the number of courts is a weak device. It but makes endless the already wearying way of the law.

Admission to the bar was then not a mere matter of form. The examinations were thorough and searching—often conducted by the judges themselves. No standing conundrums were proposed, as "the rule in Shelly's case."† It is said that Frank Wade had never been in a court of record, had never seen a supreme judge, until called to the ordeal of his examination, which we know the Wades successfully passed. There is

---

*Judge Peter Hitchcock used to drive a sorrel horse in a wooden springed, light wagon, painted yellow, annually over the state for many years.

† It is one of the curiosities of the older law that while this famous rule is preserved as one of judgment, the case itself is lost, was never reported.

no profession so uncertain as the law. Of all who
study it, twenty per cent. is a fair estimate of
those who succeed. Lawyers are grown rather
than made. They are never born. No gifts can
make a lawyer. It is largely the youth's own
work. Will and staying power—years, many of
them, are necessary—natural aptitude, talent,
genius, are great helps; industry, patience and
time will do more. In no other calling can men
so little forecast results, and I may say in no other
are the final results of the mere lawyer more un-
satisfactory. He may sit and contemplate the
leathern backs of his two or three thousand law
books, and for the rest, innumerable pigeon holes,
filled with yellow papers, tokens of work and
woes innumerable.*

Frank Wade was now an attorney and coun-
selor at law, and solicitor in chancery. He has
taken the oath of office, his name recorded on the
then small roll of men, some of whom are to be
honorably distinguished, and he has the clerk's
certificate of the fact bearing the broad seal of the
supreme court of the state of Ohio. It was very
unusual then for a farmer's boy to attempt to
break away, escape to a profession, most of all
the law. He is always subjected to criticism
more or less sharp. "He feels above farmer's
work, he wants to wear broadcloth every day."
"He's a lazy chap." "He'll never come to any-

* These are the reflections of the weary *old lawyer* at the close, not
the anticipations of the *young barrister* at the beginning

thing," and more of that sort. The law was supposed to open to the fortunately fated, an easy road to riches, honor, leisure. The average mind has no conception of the labor of those to whom labor comes, of the wearying soul anguish of those to whom it does not. In Ashtabula at that time, there had been but one or two instances of young men who had studied law. Young Joshua R. Giddings had been admitted in 1821. He was looked upon as a rarely exceptional young man. It was not likely these Wade boys—two of them —would prove to be of the same order. Of the two, less was expected of the more silent, thoughtful elder. So wise is the world. Frank heard that he was talked about when he went off with the drover, and more when he went with Ned to Canfield. All that was past. He was safely at the bar. He felt he had the pith in him. It must now work to the surface and show itself to the world.

The usually perplexing problem with the young lawyer is where to plant himself. He often supposes that somewhere is a place—an opening— yearning for him. He sometimes spends months in looking for it. I never knew one of these young men to find it. They find all the places taken, all the openings filled. In the nature of things, they always are. I like better the answer of the young man who, in reply to the question of a lawyer in a western town, "Are you looking for an opening?" said: "No. I am looking for a place *to*

make one." For the Wades there was small choice.
They were west. No one thought of going east,
and few south. At about the geographical centre
of broad Ashtabula was the township of Jefferson.
The region was monotonously level. The earth
at the centre had managed to lift itself by an im-
perceptible swell, a foot or two, and here in 1811
the commissioners of the county established the
county-seat. No one now can form an accurate
idea of the muddy, sodden little town, largely of
log buildings, when the young Wades went there
for examination. The woods were very near,
walling it in all round. They still covered the
whole country, with stumpy and muddy roads
through them leading to it; the wide swampy
lands were traversed on log-ways of sections of
trees twelve or eighteen inches through, laid side
by side, sometimes for miles in extent. Here
the court of common pleas, consisting of a president-judge—a lawyer elected as were the supreme
judges, by the legislature—and three associates,
laymen, sat three times a year. It had universal
jurisdiction, civil, criminal and probate; also
licensed public houses, then called taverns, as was
the better old English way. It also had appellate
jurisdiction, and in error, in all cases arising
before justices of the peace, who collectively dispose of infinitely a larger number of cases, and
settle the rights to a larger sum total, than do
the courts of record. Like all new communities,
the pioneers of the Western Reserve were litigious.

The causes of their suits and the sums involved
would throw a curious light on their character and
time. To go to a lawsuit between others, above
all go to court at Jefferson, Warren or Chardon,
was a great thing. To be called as a juror gave a
man importance. He not only heard the lawyers,
they talked *to him.* He was a part of the tribu-
nal ; ever afterward a man of note in his neighborhood. The young advocate, whether in the
log house of the magistrate or the larger forum of
the common pleas, was sure of a large and very
appreciative audience, than which nothing gives
so much interest and consequence to a trial and
the man conducting it. Trial by jury is incidentally valuable, as it so largely adds interest and importance to the ordinary administration of law.
Contrast the usual *nisi prius* courts, with the
supreme court of the United States in session.
Note the attentive throngs, the presence of re-
porters in the one; the emptiness and sleepy
silence of the other. Day by day, in the capitol,
the third coördinate department of the government discharges its high and sacred functions
without a solitary spectator. At the best a casual
visitor flits in, with, perhaps, a lady. A minute
satisfies their curiosity, and they glide away. The
gravest cases are heard and decided in the presence of counsel and the officers and pages of the
court only. The philosophy of the history of
a free people may be largely drawn from its legis-

lation, its character and bent, its genius from its litigation—its crimes even.

For aids in practice the young Wades had Tidd and Chitty. The Ohio legislature and the courts had secured for them about the best system of procedure the common law was capable of— simple, practical, safe. The gains by the later code were of doubtful value. Its good was nearly all due to the modified English practice. Its bad was its own, abundant, and due to the tendency of the later years for mere detail, which mars alike constitutions and statutes—a weak love for an- alysis, which has rendered trials interminable and multiplied sub-issues until the few verdicts ob- tained cannot be sustained. These are faults of the bar, as courts and lawyers. If the young bar- risters looked for adjudged cases, they must still go mainly to England. Hammond's first volume was published in 1823. There were about twenty- five volumes of the United States supreme court reports, a few United States circuit court volumes, and from twenty to thirty of each of the oldest states.* No old lawyer had them all. These young men had none of them. The Ohio statutes at that time were found in the twenty-ninth volume, "The Sheepskin Code" of the lawyers.

Of the more notable lawyers they found at the

---

* Happy time! Ere the weak wash of the forty odd volumes of state reports each year, the despair of the lawyer, adding immensely to his work, and nothing to his learning. He wants to know what the law is. He need not care what the courts of Beersheba say about it.

bar of Ashtabula Samuel Wheeler, Mr. Giddings and two or three others. O. H. Fitch, Horace Wilder, S. S. Osborn and O. H. Knapp were admitted at about the same time, as was Seabury Ford, the future governor of the state, in adjoining Geauga. William L. Perkins and James H. Paine were at Painesville of that county, as was S. W. Phelps. Rufus P. Spalding must have come to the bar about the same time, and Sherlock J. Andrews and John W. Willey were at Cleveland. Warren had its bar; so had Ravenna. The practice of "riding the circuit" like a Methodist preacher never largely obtained on the Reserve as in the middle and southern parts of the state.

No one has ever told us of Frank Wade's first case, which usually stands in the lawyer's memory as the hunter's first deer, the lover's first kiss, and costs him as many tremors and as much fever. Of course it was before a magistrate. It may have been a small trespass, or a case growing out of the universal course of business, of giving notes of hand payable in specific articles, as "neat stock," "grain," "store pay," or, more general still, "in produce." These were a fruitful source of litigation, small and large, reaching to my time.*

---

* Among my first considerable cases in the Ohio supreme court was one on a writing to pay for a farm in wool. The case of Hostatt was another, in a small way, before a justice of the peace. He had a due-bill for two dollars and a half, payable in produce. The maker tendered wheat. Of course Hostatt failed, a tender being kept good. He wanted whiskey. "W'eat! w'eat! w'at kin I do with w'eat?" he demanded. "W'iskey now, I knows right w'ere I kin *turn* that."

It is possible his first case was before his brother-in-law, Cadwell, to settle a controversy about some "saw-logs." That, or Cadwell was a party. Frank had no case and was beaten.*

Another source of litigation arose from the method of land sales on the Reserve. Few paid for lands at purchase. They took contracts of sale from the owner or agent, called in the language of the time an "article." The buyer "articled" the land. They should have been recorded. They seldom were. Of course the land office knew of the sale, strangers never. Often the purchaser either never took possession or abandoned it if he did. Years ran on without his being heard from, the owner knows nothing of him. The articles become forfeit for non-payment, without notice to the buyer. Many "lots" or fractions so held were "bought out from under him"— the holder still in possession, as it was called. There were grave questions of "betterments," as the improvements were called. Most of the owners were non-residents. The legislature came to the aid of holders. The cases were numerous, sometimes difficult, important and interesting.†

* S. S. Osborne, a student and partner of Giddings, had the other side. Himself became prominent at the bar, and later a leading member of the Ohio senate. He was my informant. He said at that time Frank could hardly speak at all; but, though modest, was the most courageous man that ever faced a court.

† N. D. Webb of Warren was a noted lawyer in this class of cases. Nearly all the leading lawyers had many of them. It may be remarked that lawyers' fees were then ridiculously small, usually paid in kind

Mr. Wade, like most young lawyers, did a good deal of waiting for clients. That is the ordeal. He had to see himself passed for other men his inferiors, because they were his seniors. The cool, phlegmatic New Englanders have always been slow to trust young men. "I was always too young," said a witty man in his decline, speaking of them, "until it was discovered that I was too old!" It is still the rule with them. Such was his standing, however, that in 1831 he formed a partnership with J. R. Giddings, which introduced him to a much wider practice, and more important cases. The position of junior, for a young or ordinary man, to one of the standing of Mr. Giddings, is full of peril. He is apt to be overshadowed, dwarfed. He keeps the books, looks up the law, runs of errands, serves notices, helplessly dependent upon the senior, whose clients never become his. He never secures any of his own. He merely answers questions as to *him*— his engagements. In court he is helpless alone. Always leaning on his partner, he can never go alone. Frank Wade never filled this role. He was of good age, had confidence, courage and will power. He had taken root and made healthful growth. He was now to occupy a larger, wider field for himself as for the firm.

It is said that few young men ever showed less

and stipulated—the amount in advance. I once received twelve bushels of wheat for trying a case before a J. P. and a jury. Wheat was fifty cents per bushel.

aptitude for public speaking than did he. The
testimony to this is unanimous. Probably no
modern people possess more native aptitude for
effective speech than the born Americans of the
the present time. No people, ancient or modern,
not excepting the old Greeks, more readily
become fluent speakers. As an art, oratory is
everywhere lost. One wonders when he thinks
what a controlling part speech exercises in all
human affairs, private as well as public, that so
little attention is paid to training men, and women
as well, in the use of words orally.

Wade seemed an exception to his countrymen,
who do now, in schools, give very ineffective attention to elocution. They did then, some, but
he knew nothing of the higher schools. His efforts for a long time were dead failures—so fla-
grantly so that he was laughed at, ridiculed, for
the sorry showing he made. The shame and mortification it cost him, the effort of will, persistence
and endurance of actual labor and agony, to finally
win success as a speaker, were never known to
others, not even to Ned, who had some of the
same difficulties to overcome. He had never attempted a declamation, or to recite, save from the
'Day of Doom,' of the great-grandfather. The
moment he rose to his feet, ideas fled, memory
was annihilated, language was dead; a more sen-
sitive, less self-sustained man would have never
tried but once—making such failures. Many instances of abandonment of the profession for this

cause are well known. The American young lawyer must become an advocate—that was the rule. Frank Wade was to be an advocate—not a mere halting, hemming stammerer, but an advocate, an orator, strong, bold, effective ; and such he became. Not merely an average, a fair speaker, but he pushed, battled, toiled, to the first rank, and among the very foremost of that. Even in his worst day he refused to write and commit a speech. It is rare that a lawyer can find the time for that. He scorned it. He would become a ready, effective, fluent speaker—and he did as stated.

The faculty of rising in court, stating the case, conducting the examination of numerous witnesses, arguing questions of the admissibility of evidence, during a protracted, sharply contested trial ; and on the close of the evidence, without intervening time, then proceed to the presentation of the case, law and evidence, clearly, strongly, logically, with pertinence, wit, eloquence, perhaps pathos, always astonishes the lay spectators, as it well may. Such efforts rank with the best work of the human intellect, and the men capable of it, habitually, must have much mental excellence of a high order. An advocate who at will did such work, Mr. Wade, after years of failure, became ; and he enjoyed the fruits of it while he lived. Perhaps this was really his greatest success.

The first necessity of successful advocacy is entire belief in the justice of a cause. It is the first duty of an advocate to convince himself he is right, however he may fare with the court and jury. It is a poor advocate who cannot do this ; a careless one, or a very bad case, where he does not do it.

It is a reproach to the bar—many good and very pious men are called upon to shake their heads over it—this constant spectacle of honest men, earnestly contending on the opposite sides of the same case, one of whom must be in the wrong, and must know he is. They with charitable effort cannot understand it. Indeed ! Divines, the most learned and pious, differ as to the meaning of passages of writ called holy, given as both sides aver by divine inspiration. They used to burn one another for this difference. As for lawyers, it should be remembered that of civil cases not one in ten involves directly a question of moral right and wrong. . They usually are to determine which of two parties is to suffer a loss, occasioned by the act of a third. One man liable to a loss goes to a lawyer and gives him his version of the provable facts, who, making fair allowance, honestly finds the law with him and commences a suit. The party sued tells his version to another lawyer, who making the same allowance, finds he has a good defense and denies the cause of action. From that day to the trial each party looks for witnesses to sustain his statement of fact and the laws for authorities in support of their versions of the law. When we remember that a man can argue himself into or out of anything,

we may be assured that each lawyer sits down
to the trial with the conscientious belief that
he is right. The trouble is not in the law nor
in the lawyers, but in the facts. Neither party
knew them all. The best and most honest efforts
of both sides in proof still leave them in some
doubt. This fairly illustrates the true position of
the really good lawyer, who would not intentionally deceive himself, and who would no more tell
a lie to the court or jury than would any true man
in an ordinary transaction. If he did, the lawyer
on the other side would instantly expose him.
The fact that the contests of lawyers are face
to face in the open courts, in presence of interested and curious spectators, keeps men at their
best, true, honest and chivalrous. Even criminals
must be defended with learning and zeal. The
state appoints the judge, the prosecutor ; the jurors
are its citizens, a part of the state. So are the
sheriff and his officers, the press and public are
against the accused, have cornered him. They
bring him from the jail and place him in the dock.
In the name of decency, has not the state sufficiently the advantage ? A lawyer can perform no
more sacred duty when called to his side than to
give him his best and most effective services. I
utterly repudiate Lord Brougham's rule—as do
American lawyers generally. A lawyer's first
duty, over and above his client, is to the law. He
must make fair and honorable use of such means
only as to him appear clean and real. This ex-

cludes perjury, and simulated evidence ; with these
let him not forget God, and do his best. He will
then only secure a fair trial, such as the law and
all good men award to the worst criminals. These
were the rules of Frank Wade's professional life.

Unquestionably he seldom tried a case without
believing he was right, ought to succeed, and so
did his best. That best was usually among the
very good—the best of his time and opportunities.
His excellence as a lawyer consisted in the clearness with which he apprehended the real matter
in dispute, where and upon what it rested, upon
what it turned, and what in the white light of law
would govern and control it. These means were
to be found and applied. Law with him was a
science, not a trade. Its reason—philosophy—he
mastered, could deliver them into the easy apprehension of the court in strong, well-selected language, best adapted for forensic presentation. As
an advocate he had the rarest of powers—that of
clear seeing and clear statement—statement which
outruns argument; precludes it; statement which
argument sometimes obscures. All great truths
should be left to their own simple assertion. The
advocate should place them in clear view and leave
them. A good advocate must be a good lawyer.
While he was an admirable lawyer, he dealt equally
well—perhaps better—with facts. He never made
that common mistake of overestimating the mental
capacity of a jury. He never fired over their heads.
He knew their inability for long-continued, hard,

intellectual labor.   He never overloaded them.
In the language of his mother and sisters, learned
in the Feeding Hills before he was ten years old,
simple and chaste, he laid before them the real
matter for them, delivered it safely into their
custody.   He first cleared the field of all mere
rubbish, then made two or three strong, conclusive
points, the fewest that would dispose of the case,
in the most direct, possible way.   His conclusions
were irrefutable—his premises admitted.   It was
only when his foundations could be assailed that
he was successfully replied to.   All his figures, his
illustrations, were drawn from their own lives—
forcible, laughable at times.   Not a soft, bland
speaker, he never attempted to persuade, lead or
mislead.   No sham, no affectation, no flattery, no
semblance of demagogueism, no cant, no hypocrisy,
but plain, honest, intense sincerity, working for
conviction.

He had a good, well knit, well proportioned
figure ; erect, flexile, well turned ; a noble head,
grandly borne ; a face well featured, striking ; a
fine mouth, black, melancholy eyes that had a way
of burning with a deep, smothered fire ; voice
good.   He usually began to speak standing very
erect, his right hand in his breast within the vest.
When something striking, emphatic—a point—
was reached, he rose on his toes, threw out his
hand, sometimes both, with force and grace, rising
and sinking on his toes in a peculiar, and in a very
effective way.   Behind all his clearness were force,

strength, logic intense, never overwrought earn-
estness, and more than all, better than all, stood a
pure-hearted, clean-living truthful man, every fibre
a man.   All these made him one of the most dangerous as one of the most successful advocates of
his day.   I had heard him spoken of as a strong,
coarse, unpleasant speaker.   Early in the forties I
heard him argue a demurer at Warren. I thought
him a handsome, graceful, as well as a strong,
bold speaker. My early impression always remained.   He and his brother were the best, or
two of the best, special pleaders in the state, as
practically they handled the rules of evidence the
most effectively.   Hence, they were the most
successful lawyers, the most dangerous opponents
of those now old contests of the Northern Ohio
bar.

While the elder brother was of rather rude—
unpolished—manners, his manner to his opponents was kindly, his treatment generous, unless
provoked by unfairness, chicane or some species
of pettyfogging, when his wit and sarcasm were
something awful.   His own practice and conduct
never gave occasion for complaint.   Witnesses,
even on cross-examination, were always treated
with considerate kindness, unless he suspected a
deviation from or concealment of the truth.   To
the court always respectful; and such was his
faculty of impressing courts that they differed
from him reluctantly.   His was the will-force that

sometimes carried juries and courts because he would carry them.

An instance of the kindness of his nature, akin to weakness, illustrates the manner of man he was. He once discovered a man filling his bag from his corn crib, and he quietly withdrew to save the man the mortification of discovery. He mentioned the incident; he never told the man's name.

His wit partook of the character of his intellect, incisive, and if men sometimes winced under it, we know that the man who could be thus tender of the feelings of a thief, could not intentionally wound. Like other men accustomed to wielding trenchant weapons, he was possibly unaware of the effect of his blows and thrusts.

The firm of Giddings & Wade became the leading law association of their immediate neighborhood, when under the changed character of the business habits of denser population and the consequent diversity of employment; by the opening of channels of communication, the growth of lake marine, the causes and character of litigation changed and multiplied. It was not until comparatively recently that the admiralty laws of congress were extended to the great lakes. Their want in the meantime was supplied by legislation of the state, which permitted suits for supplies, wages, claims for damages, for all causes of action against a craft by name, in any county along the lake coast, in whose waters service of process could be made, no matter where or by whom owned.

Geauga had a port. Ashtabula had two. There was power in the courts to change the venue of marine cases, as of others. Shipping increased. Lake Erie was stormy. There were many cases for collisions, especially between steamers and sailers, as between steam vessels or sailers. Many of these became famous cases. They paid well. In the autumn of 1835, Mr. Wade was elected prosecuting attorney of Ashtabula county, which office he held for its term of two years. The rules of evidence are the same in criminal and in civil cases. A good law pleader will not fail in his indictments. Mr. Wade became the model of his successors. The so-called criminal laws are purely for the suppression of crime by penalties, punishments, investigated and applied by the courts. In Ohio, as in all the younger states, there are no so-called common law offenses, although in the administration of the statutes, the common law, its cases and rules are in constant requisition. The law-makers alway use its terms, and are guided by its lights, so that it becomes the great exponent of their labors. The criminal law lies in a nut shell. Any good commercial lawyer will master its specialties in a short time. Criminal trials have attractions for many young lawyers, and sparingly indulged in may be of service. The defense usually consists in showing the inconclusive nature of the case made by the state. They give scope for the apt advocate, and have something of the fascination and danger of the gam-

ing house. The most heinous crimes of the Reserve were then horse-stealing and passing
counterfeit money.

Wade was a vigorous, safe and popular prosecutor ; relentless where he was satisfied of a cul-
prit's guilt. He put no others on trial. The
kindness of his nature ever prompted him to see
that convicts were as leniently dealt with as the
public good permitted.

During all these years, as all the preceding years
of his life, the still young, rising, risen, well-grown
and ever growing young lawyer was the most popular young man of his time, and widely extended,
ever-widening circle. A democrat in life, with
the frankest manners—the few he possessed—cordial, unpretending, warm-hearted, quick, strong,
fearless, decisive, magnetic to men, the most virile
of men, he was a born leader. Men admired,
were drawn to, and followed him. Never exact-
ing, never haughty, never imperious, obtrusive or
overbearing ; simple, truthful, considerate, tender,
a doer for others all his life, in no way a self-seeker
ever, the atmosphere of him alway true, manly, a
hater of a lie, the scorner of sham, the ridiculer
of effeminacy. Young men were drawn to him,
became his students, adopted his manner—it often
set badly on them. They combed their hair back
over their heads. Where he was merely frank and
abrupt, they became coarse and rough ; where he
indulged in the stronger English, they became
profane. In a few years the bar of northern Ohio

was invaded by these rude, swearing caricatures of
the strong, magnetic man.

His influence, save in the matter of manners,
was wholly good, directly in the line of honor,
integrity, manliness, truth, clean living, industry,
and thorough mastery of the law for the student,
enterprise in all pursuits. The austerity, the
lurid theology of the Puritans, drove his free,
masculine mind, his tender nature, to open revolt.
The reverence of his self-poised soul remained;
was ever strong. He stepped from the prison-
house of bigotry into the whiter outside light and
perfect freedom of thought. The frankness of his
nature gave utterance to his impressions, views,
opinions. Jefferson, Ashtabula, the Western Reserve, were orthodox. The revolt had begun in
New England. The healthy intellect and soul of
young Wade had taken the new spirit into the
Ohio woods. It found its own utterance. Not
offensively; he was not a propagandist of these
ideas. His regard for the feelings of others, his
memory of his mother, forbade that. These, his
skeptical notions, were the one drawback to his
immense personal popularity. These, too, infected his personal followers. Indeed, so many
marks, so much of the obvious Wade, were borne
about by them, that those of us who were beyond
the outer ring of his growing circle could generally tell one of them in five minutes, if he did not
sooner proclaim himself. This was the estimate
of him by men. I have enquired by letters in

vain for the estimate of him by women. Thus
far, the form of no woman has flitted across
the field of vision. He had much to win the respect, admiration and confidence of women. I
presume that he did not seek their society. So
manly a man must have been anxious for their
good opinion. Men widely differ in this regard.
I have known many strong men to whom the grace
of women was not necessary. Wade may have
been one of them. I may secure more light.

At the October election of 1837 Mr. Wade was
elected to the Ohio senate. In 1839 he was placed
in nomination again for the senate and defeated.
The causes were peculiar. In 1841 he was reëlected. He resigned, but was elected again the
ensuing autumn. I shall have ample occasion
later to deal with the politician and statesman,
after the judge.

The firm of Giddings & Wade was dissolved in
the spring of 1837, by the retirement of Mr. Giddings, and the new firm of Wade & Ranney was
formed. Mr. Ranney had been a student of the
late firm, was to develop, perhaps, one of the
best, if not the first, legal minds of the state, and
take rank with the great American lawyers and
jurists.

The year 1837 saw the first of the great, widespread commercial disasters of the country, and
presented a new test, a new ordeal, a new problem for the American people. Its causes, though
then well understood, were less obvious than, with

wider induction and larger experience, they appear
to us now. One of them was the war of Andrew
Jackson on the old United States bank, the removal of the public monies from its vaults to the
seven pet state banks; the over issue by them;
stimulated by him; the general consequent infla-
tion of bank issues; the monstrous growth of
credits; the wild and universal epidemic speculation, mainly in real estate; the multiplication of
new cities, mostly on paper. The collapse came
of course. It is mentioned here because the late
firm of Giddings & Wade had been among the
speculators, especially in the city and water lots
of the Maumee—platted for cities from its mouth
to Fort Wayne. The firm, the individual members and many friends, became bankrupt. Wade
made large, timely sales, but they were caught.
For him, as for his younger brother, there was but
one way of escape—liquidation, payment. All
the large earnings for years were henceforth devoted to this, a sacred purpose, until the last
dollar was honorably extinguished. Mr. Wade
had to become thrifty and careful of expenditure.
The country at large took refuge in a general
bankrupt law. Two have been enacted, amended,
carefully administered and repealed within our
time, indicating that the sense of the American
people, enlightened or otherwise, is adverse to a
bankrupt law as an institution of commerce. However that may be, neither member of the old firm,

nor did the younger Wade, think of shelter in the provisions of the older act.

The next year, 1841, witnessed the second of the most important events of the life of B. F. Wade. It would be quite in accord with the usages of personal history to state a marriage in parenthesis or a foot note. These papers are constructed in my own way. This thing is of too much importance to be mentioned at the end of a desultory chapter.

CHAPTER IV.

FRANK WADE became a very busy, hard-work-
ing man before 1835. In the latter part of 1834
a young man became a student of Giddings &
Wade, attracted by the fame of the senior of the
firm, from whom I learned more of Mr. Wade
personally at that interesting time of his life than
from all others. During his novitiate a great
change appeared in the dress and something in
the manner of the lawyer. From one of the most
careless and indifferent in the matter of attire, he
became one of the most careful and fastidious.
The gentleman referred to had rare taste in matters of dress, and was much in Mr. Wade's confidence in the things of coats, cravats and shirt
frills, then much worn, and to whom the lawyer
presented a complete outfit, the work of a New
York tailor, before he left the office. Various

were the speculations as to the cause of this change in the tastes and dress of the advocate. If there was anything special it never transpired. It was the impression of my informant that some to him unknown maiden was the inspiration of it. So far as known he distinguished no lady by approaching her, nor did he seek the society of women. He passed his thirty-seventh birthday, if not untouched at least in safety. Thirty-eight, thirty-nine, forty, and yet unmarried. Not thus solitary was his life to remain.

There is a universal delusion that love romances are the special events attendant on actual youthfulness of years. Youthfulness may be necessary to their beautiful existence. It is the youthfulness of heart and spirit often perennial. Old poets have sung sweetest of love—old men have written some of the most charming of romances. There is in most normally structured and grown men and women the elements and tendencies which lead to their most intimate association. Nature knows what she is about, and secures her own purpose. Until that is accomplished in the individual, and usually till the birth of children, the spirit and flavor of poetry and romance linger in the heart and atmosphere of most men and women. Whoever doubts this let him seek the confidence of some middle-aged bachelor or spinster. Even in the oldest of these unmated he will find low down in the heart a little drop of condensed sweet—a preserved nectary, though the flower perished, its petals withered in the long, unblessed past. "All the world loves a lover." The proverb had its life in this law of the human race. Art compels his appearance in song and story, epic and novel. The elements of romance and tenderness were as strong and as yet unsunned in the deep nature of the lawyer at forty as of the young man of twenty-five.

Caroline M. Rosekrans was born at Lansing-burg, New York, July 30, 1805. Her father, Depin Rosekrans, was a merchant of that place, where he died while she was in her second year. Her mother, a daughter of Nehemiah Hubbard, then a retired merchant and banker of Middle-town, Connecticut, her native place, returned to that city, where later she contracted a second marriage with Enoch Parsons, esq., a son of revolutionary General Parsons, also one of the first territorial judges of Ohio. Of this marriage a son, Henry E. Parsons, esq., was the issue. The new family continued to live in Middletown until the younger Parsons removed to Ashtabula, Ohio, in 1832, where he still resides. His mother and Caroline became residents there in 1837.

A child of affluence and of cultured parents, Caroline was educated with as much care and attention as were at the beginning of the century bestowed upon the minds of the fortunately surrounded young American woman. Nature was kind to the young girl in the bestowal of a well-formed, pleasing person, a blonde, attractive face,

vigorous constitution, and a mind of unusual
strength and capacity. The education she received was one to leave the person to develop and
mature much as nature intended, healthfully and
in just proportions—a fit residence for a mind
which for its grasp and intelligence was more like
the vigorous reach and play of an educated, well-
read young man, than of the thin-soled-shoe, wasp-
waisted, pale, simpering girl of that day. Sex is
not a garment that a woman can throw off at will
—that she can lose or be parted from. She may
say and do the things that a man does and says.
In her hands and mouth they are womanly. Sex
is the inseparable character and quality of her
heart, soul, intellect, of her acts and speech, as of
her physical form, and cannot be separated from
either. Caroline Rosekrans grew to be one of
the most womanly of women, as at her maturity one of the most attractive. She doubtless had her fancies, her preferences and repug-
nances, as all healthful girls do. Not a prude,
not affecting to dislike or avoid men. Doubtless
she sympathized with their intellectual labors,
their free, robust life. She early became a great
reader, and such she always continued to be.
Not a reader of novels—of them but sparingly.
A reader of histories, of biographies, of politics,
newspapers—well-informed. So she reached her
full womanhood, and lived on—growing, developing
mentally, morally; ripening in person, extending
her acquaintances; living cheerfully an active, vig-

orous, womanly life, neither pining or sighing for any possible future, cheerfully awaiting it, what- ever it might be.

Ashtabula, at the time of the arrival of Mrs. Parsons and Miss Rosekrans, was one of the most active and important places on the lake. Nearly every one of the great lake-going steamers called at its wharf—sometimes half a dozen in a day. The lake at that time for five or six months of the year was the sole highway for the immense transit of passengers and property. Ashtabula had much of wealth, and there were the marked beginnings of class distinction, which have not yet been evolved out of the race of men.

The newly arrived were a real accession to the place. Mr. Parsons had capital, character and business capacity. The young lady had marked character, womanly accomplishments, and a rarely cultivated mind. She had no position to attain. She quietly took what was hers of right and by use.

In the absence of certain information, it is easy to fancy how the first meeting of Miss Rosekrans and Frank Wade came about. It was in the kindling of the fires of the never to be forgotten though now grossly misrepresented campaign of 1840, which was in the first months of that mem- orable year. Wade was quite the first to sound the trumpet call to arms in his region, and was one of the most effective and popular speakers of the state, already widely known. There was to be a meeting at Ashtabula, at which he was to speak upon the new and old issues of the shaping campaign, hereafter to be dealt with. Caroline had heard of him. The Astabula ladies spoke of him—an interesting puzzle to them. No one was much acquainted with him, they said. He was very popular with men, but seemed to care nothing for ladies' society. Never did. Not only a bachelor, he was "an old bachelor." Had he never courted a girl—had any heart history? No one had ever heard of such a thing. No, he did not like women, though there was much in him to interest them. It is not at all likely that the healthful fancy of Caroline Rosekrans was in the least attracted by what she heard of him. She had doubtless wondered what such a man could see in the average pink-faced girl to attract him. By intelligence, temperament and association, she was a Whig. She was much interested in the popular rising against the party in power. She went with her brother to the meeting to hear Mr. Wade's speech. She never had heard a political speech. As usual in that region, at that day, it was presided over by a New England "moderator," who called on a clergyman to open it with prayer. Caroline had no trouble in distinguishing Mr. Wade, and while this was going on she noticed his face, and at the first did not very well like it. Though well-featured, it was a little pinched at the temple, but the head was good, the figure as he arose manly, the attitude striking. He at once

launched himself on his theme, the arraignment of
Mr. Van Buren's administration and the Democratic party. Strong, bold, sustained, manly.
After he closed, Mr. Parsons, who had met him,
lingered with his sister at the exit for a word of
congratulation. He presented the successful orator, still aglow, to his sister. Mr. Wade had several times caught her handsome, intelligent interested face during his hour and a half of a speech
—a stranger he noted, as also that it pleased him.
For once he was glad to be presented to a lady.
They had a few pleasant words, and he carried off,
for him, an unusual impression of the personal
charm of a woman's presence. Something infinitely sweet, attractive, delicious in this fully matured, virginal, womanly woman. They were
near each other long enough for Mr. Parsons to
ask him to call. He remained in town over night,
as much of the ensuing day, and did call ere he
returned to Jefferson.

Something of this we know to be true. The
acquaintance begun, ran on during the summer,
autumn and winter. Wade was frank, direct and
manly in his wooing. The lady was greatly
pleased with his attentions and let him see she
was, as a woman might. "During the courtship
he came often to see her. They were congenial
spirits," is the statement of one who knew all
about it.* That was an important, an interesting,
a memorable year to Mr. Wade. What with his

* Letter of Henry E. Parsons, esq.

prosecution of Mr. Van Buren and the Democracy, his attention to the courts of law, his suit to Miss Rosekrans, in which he was no laggard as we have seen, it was a busy year as well. They were married, May 19, 1841, and took up their residence in Jefferson, where the bride of that far-off day still resides.

All marriages worthy the name, though possibly less to a man than to a woman, are of the gravest moment to him. No man can open his heart, his life, and admit another life into it, become a part of it, become in turn a part of another life, without great and important consequences to himself and others. This marriage was exceptionally fortunate, happy—a love marriage, not so rare as is supposed. We hear mostly of the unfortunate ones. By this marriage were born two sons—Lieutenant-Colonel James F. Wade, in 1843, and Captain Henry P. Wade, in 1845.†

A financial disaster—a panic widespread and general—always precipitates a vast volume of credits to the bottom as dead debt, to be got rid of, cancelled or buried ere business can revive, or any degree of prosperity restored. Generally the revival brings forward new names, a new, younger set of men, new commercial houses. The disasters of 1837 were not repaired save by a lapse

---

†Both were appointed to the regular service, as soon as of military age. The elder is with his regiment. The youngest resigned at the end of the war and is now a farmer in Jefferson.

of many years, involving the overthrow of the
Jackson *Locofoco*—or as it came to call itself the
Democratic party, in 1840.‡   The Whig tariff and
other measures of the successful party had much
to do with the restoration of confidence, the crea-.
tion and employment of new capital.

Lawyers and courts were busy for years with the
fossil remains of the former world.   Judgments
innumerable, followed by creditors' bills, to un-
cover properties and reach equities.   There was a
large crop of cases.   Contrary to popular impression, the legal harvest in money was small.   The
profession fares best when business is healthy.
The new firm had its full share of this unsatisfac-
tory business, procured its full share of never to be
satisfied judgments.   Clerks and sheriffs are paid
before lawyers.   They, too, performed immense
labors never to be compensated.

With the new men, the new era, came new
methods of business—the old commercial rules of
the older communities not created, but recognized by statutes and enforced by courts.   "Truck
and dicker" made way for cash.   Later, the Whig
legislature enacted Alfred Kelley's bank bill ; this
and later a new tax law, and Ohio, her canals

‡At a famous meeting in Tammany hall to determine a grave and
bitter local quarrel, it came to be known that upon a given contingency the lights would be turned off, and each man of the other side
carried with him a box of *locofoco* matches.   The lights were turned off
and thereupon were lit a thousand of the sulphurous pine sticks.
Hence the name of *Locofoco* applied to the prevailing faction speedily
transferred to the party at large by its opponents.

completed, took her place henceforth with the
states whose industries and trades were organized
in accord with the established usages of the modern world, to remain until reorganized without re-
vulsion under the quiet revolution, to be wrought
in the near future by railroads and the telegraph.
New cases, new questions arose for the bar and
courts. They are the last to be reached in
changes by new processes. Questions and con-
troversies arise, pass the stage of discussion by
the parties, their correspondents and brokers,
then the lawyers are called in and they take them
to the courts. During nearly the whole of the
late war, the supreme court of the United States
sat serenely adjudging the old cases involving old
well established rules, in contemplation of law,
oblivious of the new and awful issues discussed and
decided in the red forum of battle. They were
there settled ere the momentous constitutional
and legal issues springing from war reached it, for
which there were no rules, no precedents.

With the revival of business in Ohio, the profession and practice of law passed a new phase.
The firm of Wade & Ranney had quite the lead
in Ashtabula. The rapid rise of Mr. Ranney at
the bar and the constant calls to Trumbull, were
such as to warrant, require, the opening of an
office at its shiretown—Warren—now a flourish-
ing city, and there Mr. Ranney took up his residence, which soon brought the partners to the
lead in that wealthy and important county also.

From this time forward there were few important
cases in the two counties that one or the other or
both were not engaged in.   Mr. Wade had occasional calls to Geauga, Ravenna and Cleveland.
It is not to be supposed that Wade & Ranney
had things their own way, even in their own counties.   Horace Wilder, Ned Wade and Sherman
were in Ashtabula; Tod Hoffman & Hutchins,
the Sutliffs, John Crowell at Warren; Van R.
Humphrey, Otis & Tilden at Ravenna; R. P.
Spalding and L. V. Bierce at Akron; Reuben
Hitchcock, E. T. Wilder, Perkins & Osborn,
and Benjamin Bissel at Painesville, quite their
equals, with a host of younger men coming on at
the bar, without mentioning Cleveland.   It has
always seemed to me that the period between the
formation of the firm of Wade & Ranney and the
election of Wade to the bench, was one of a very
high degree of excellence, of strength and learning of the bar of these Reserve counties.   Cleveland then had H. B. Payne, Andrews before
named, Bolton & Kelley, Backus and others, and
certainly the north was in this respect the equal
of any part of Ohio.   The practice of law under
the guidance of the bar, with occasional judicious
legislation, also at their hands, so far as procedure
was concerned, was very well perfected, was really
a useful, expeditious method of adjusting the differences of men.   The courts were able and in-
dustrious, and nowhere was there the great drift
of dead wood damming up the administration of

the law, and damning the courts and bar for inequality to their duties. A class of men who have the entire control of the third department of the government, national and state, are certainly responsible for its working power and efficiency. That it is now absurdly behind the other two is mainly their fault. Let them be held to account.

It must have been at about the commencement of this period that the encounter between Frank Wade and Millard Fillmore occurred. A steamer owned at Buffalo was libelled—we should call it now—under the Ohio statute, in Ashtabula county, for running down a sailing vessel. Fillmore was then at his best, learned, able, handsome, elegant, eloquent. He came to Jefferson with the owners and witnesses to find out the reason of the detention. There he met the younger, full-grown, alert, strong, comparatively rough Frank Wade, to whom he was no more than any other man. Frank had never been heard of at Buffalo, then the largest city of the lakes. He had the advantage of the home forum. The case must have been tried before Humphrey, an able judge of much presence and dignity. The case was important, was closely contested, and conducted with great and probably fairly matched ability. The Buffalonians began by underrating the leading counsel for the plaintiff. The trial attracted much attention, and the Ohioans felt a special pride in the splendid manner in which their champion met, and as they claimed, overthrew the eastern knight supposed to be peerless. Victory declared in his favor, and it was claimed the strangers retired to their city much discomfited. †

It is the habit of the multitude to lose sight of the real issue on trial, and fix their gaze on the leading counsel and regard it as a contest between them personally, in which the best man wins. There is less difference between fairly good lawyers than laymen generally suppose. Something there certainly is in temperament and aptitude, dependent upon endowment. One man, strong and able, a master of his case, arises seemingly at a distance from the jury; he never overcomes it. He is strong, logical, convincing. They may be constrained to find for him, but he aroused their combativeness, arrayed them against him. Another gets up within the charmed circle of their sympathies, addresses them as one of themselves. They go willingly with him. They may be compelled to return an adverse verdict. They will do it reluctantly. One man cannot examine a witness so as to get from him all he knows, even when he is anxious to tell it. Another gets it all, and more too, even when the witness wishes to conceal it. Still one lawyer can do about as much as another, and one good lawyer is better than five equally good. There is seldom room for more than two. It is a mistake to increase the

---

† The late Hon. O. P. Brown, a student in Wade's office, was my informant.

number. In the courts, safety does not dwell in a
multitude of counsel.

And so the years ran on. The state grew in
population and wealth, the two lawyers in business,
fame and influence, the younger going on to his
proper place at the head of the bar in his section,
giving their time, talents and best labor to advise
and advance the material interests of men greatly
their inferiors. This was their business, their
profession, having few or no material interests of
their own. Wise, sagacious to counsel others,
negligent and inefficient in the management of
their own property affairs. So the years bore
them on, until the change came which necessarily
severed their association and the senior from the
bar. As said, the state of Ohio was niggardly in
the matter of compensation in its public service.
The salary of the president-judges of the common
pleas courts reached a minimum of seven hundred
and fifty dollars in the early years of the reign of
Wade & Ranney, the time of an anti-lawyer spasm.
Here and there a fairly good lawyer, who wished
to retire and was ambitious to sit on a bench,
accepted office under it. There are always a set
of legal deadbeats, who hang about the courts
talking of other men's cases, and trying the triers
allowable of neither men or the gods, who eagerly
sought places on the bench. The act reducing
salaries brought it within their hungry reach.
The experiment was bad every way, and the
good sense, or the better sense of the legislature

removed the poor demagogical law, and placed the judiciary on a better footing.

/ In February, 1847, the legislature of Ohio elected Mr. Wade president-judge of' the third judicial circuit, then composed of the five important counties of Ashtabula, Trumbull, Mahoning, Portage and Summit. That was the second year of the fateful war with the unfortunate Mexicans, and the battle of Buena Vista was fought during the same February. The seed once sown was quickening in the greater field of his final labors. He was still unconsciously preparing, maturing for the work. Patience for a little space. The time will be short. Four years will he judge his people in righteousness, and when summoned will then be surprised as now by this call to the judgment seat.

The counties of his circuit were among the most populous, wealthy and prosperous of the state. Though still largely agricultural, they were traversed by canals, infant cities were springing up, mines were opened, and various extensive manufactories were coming to importance. The new justice at once entered upon his new duties. He was greatly needed. There was a large arrear of business on the calendars. In the five counties collectively, there would be fifteen terms of his court during each year. The initial days of the terms were fixed by statute. Under his administration, the last day in a given county was the first of the succeeding in the next shire.

B. F. WADE.

No man ever reached the bench better equipped for its best and highest duties than did Mr. Wade. He was of good age, young enough to adapt himself readily to the place, a mind thoroughly trained—had acquired the *legal instinct*—great capacity for work, an even, healthy, good temper, a man of secure popularity with the people, admired, loved, profoundly respected by the bar, he took his place not only by right of unsought election, but the divine right of fitness. Imbued with the robust spirit of the common law, his native love of right and justice still prevailed, and his knowledge of the law enabled him generally to secure that, so strongly entrenched that his judgments were rarely disturbed.

I was never in his court. I was for the four years of his presiding in the adjoining circuit. Heard of him constantly. There now lie before me two well-written accounts of his career on the bench by lawyers who practiced before him, both of whom since sat on the bench;* and I am surrounded by ample information from various sources. If it is all friendly, and from appreciative admirers, it is to be said that, robust, virile as his nature was, trenchant as were the blows he dealt, caustic as was his wit, he never made enemies, was never the object of detraction. The real man stood so palpably before all men's eyes that whoever spoke of him praised him, and often in terms that seemed laudatory to strangers.

---

* Hon. Darius Cadwell and Hon. R. F. Paine.

I once heard an educated man—a lawyer and a judge—a man of fine ability, while occupying the place of presiding judge on the bench in Cleveland, and who since sat on the bench of the highest court of another state, say: "I never sat in the trial of a case in which I cared two cents which side gained it." This was a mode of showing his utter indifference. I heard it with amazement. He fortified himself by quoting a similar declaration of a really much admired judge, well-known to us both.

Mr. Wade, as I think, was not that sort of a judge. He saw at once the right of a case. No man saw the moral right, when involved, quicker. He was, of all things, loyal to the law, and this, in the absence of a controlling moral question, was to prevail. It is generally found, when a case is cleared of foreign matter, that the rule of common right, when involved, and the rule of the common law coincide. With his mastery of the law, mastery of men, he usually so shaped a trial that ultimately the right prevailed. The American judge declines to deal with the case itself in his instructions to the jury. Wade's ingenuity enabled him, by the aid of a supposed case, to bring the real issue broadly within their apprehension, in the clear light of its right and wrong.

It was useless to attempt to blind him with mere technicalities. He usually found a recognized legal way to the right. Securely independent, no considerations of party or favor to per-

sons influenced him ; nor was he ever suspected
of being so influenced. We have heard of doc-
tors who never lost a patient, lawyers who never
lost a case, and of judges never reversed. To say
that a judge of a *nisi prius* court, in the multitude
of cases, the hurry and pressure of business, never
committed an error, would be a preposterous
statement. Of Judge Wade this is quite true.
He generally gave reasons so satisfactory for his
conclusions that, as a rule, his decisions were acquiesced in. No judge ever put himself more
unreservedly on the record than did he. Of the
few cases taken to the supreme court from him,
very few were reversed. As a rule, he was there
held to be right. A notable exception may be
mentioned. A case arose before him of considerable difficulty. He gave it full consideration and
decided it. It was taken to the supreme court
and there reversed. On mandate it came up before him. He disregarded the mandate and followed his own first decision, and such was his
judgment. "But, your honor, the supreme
court reversed your former judgment!" exclaimed
the now re-beaten counsel. "Yes, so I have
heard. I will give them a chance to get right,"
was the quiet reply. It was again taken to the
supreme court and re-presented there, and this
time with Judge Wade's reported opinion. On
reconsideration this was found to be the better
rule. The court, instead of attaching him for
contempt, reversed itself and affirmed his last

judgment. This must be the one unique instance of adherence to first impressions by a subordinate court in the judicial history of an English speaking people, and honorable to both courts.*

There used to be much " retaxing of cost bills " by the court, bills of the cost in cases as made up by the clerk, under the sometimes obscure statutes, often of no little difficulty. Such a case before him may be mentioned, as more illustrative of his character as a man than of his learning, perhaps, as a judge. The case was quite fully presented and taken under consideration. On his return at the ensuing term it was called up, talked over, and with a promise to "dispose of it" at the next, the third term, he took refuge in the causes awaiting him in the next county. That the third term lapsed, he was closing up the final session, settling exceptions and journal entries (the Yankee lawyers of the Reserve of that day were very particular about these), was about to order adjournment *sine die*, when the nervous counsel ventured to remind him of the mooted matter of costs. "Mr. clerk, what is the amount in dispute?" he asked. " Nine dollars and —— cents," was the reply. "I'll pay the —— thing,†" he observed as to himself, throwing a ten-dollar bill down to the clerk with " Enter the costs sat-

---

* Judge Cadwill.

† If the curious reader should fill the above blank with an English *damned*, he might do the otherwise model judge and history no injustice.

isfied.   Mr. sheriff, adjourn the court without
day." It was disposed of.

Judge Wade's industry was great; his faculty
for the dispatch of business remarkable. The bar
was worked to its fullest capacity by him ; the
over-heavy calendars were brought within working
compass, and the shortening years ran on.

On the fifteenth of March, 1851, while presiding on the bench at Akron (county of Summit), a
telegram was handed him, announcing his election
to the senate of the United States for a full constitutional term.   He read it, handed it down to a
gentleman of the bar near him, and went on with
the pending trial, as if no unusual thing had
occurred.   In one way it was the usual.   The
position, in many respects the most honorable
and desirable in the Republic, came unsought,
unexpected.   The unexpected ruled his life in the
matter of the public service.   He was aware that
his name had been mentioned at the state capital
during the winter in connection with the pending
senatorial election.   The selection of himself,
finally, to fill the august place, was a complete
surprise.

His all too short service on the bench was now
concluded.   Had he not been called to a higher
field, we should greatly regret it ; had he in any
way failed in this new field, we should deeply
deplore it.   He had the making of a great judge.
In his obedience to this last call, the administration of domestic justice suffered a loss never fully

repaired. While the state lost the Republic, the cause of broad national justice, the large cause of freedom and the rights of men, were large gainers. On the twenty-seventh of March following his election, a bar meeting was called at Akron to take leave of Mr. Wade as judge. Many able men of the three political parties were present, and several from points remote. The assemblage was large, and with entire unanimity adopted the following as their sentiments on the occasion :

Resolved, That, as members of the bar, we cannot but regret the departure of the Hon. B. F. Wade from his position as president judge of the Third judicial circuit, a position he has maintained with dignity, courtesy, impartiality and ability in the highest degree creditable to himself and the common public, suitors, and improvement of the bar.

Resolved, That we congratulate him upon his election to the highest legislative council of the nation, and take pleasure in expressing our confidence that he will discharge the functions of his new office with the same extended intelligence, high integrity and sound judgment that distinguished him upon the bench.

From the *Mahoning Index* of February 22, 1850, a Democratic organ, edited by a prominent Democratic leader, I quote the opinion of a hostile political partisan contained in a single paragraph. Speaking of Wade while presiding in the Mahoning county court of common pleas, he said :

Our court of common pleas has been in session since the twelfth, Hon. B. F. Wade, one of the best, if not the best, judge for the people and justice in the state, presiding ; a man of superior legal attainment, and one that the bar and the community may well be proud of.

These, papers are but preliminary to the large

work before us.   It will now be necessary to turn
back to Mr. Wade's election to the state senate,
make brief mention of service there and before
the people as a popular political teacher and
speaker, and also make a rapid survey of the rise
and status of the slave power at the time of his
first assault upon it to his election to the national
senate, from which time his personal history will
be drawn against its gigantic struggle as a shifting
background, necessary to be studied with some
care to an accurate apprehension of his services
and character as a senator and a patriot.

CHAPTER V.

ACCORDING to American ideas every man, and
woman as well, is born a politician. If the
right of self-government is inherent, the right to
the means of that government, though artificial, is
a natural right; and as in association we cannot
govern ourselves without governing others, government among Americans imposes mutual and
reciprocal rights and duties. Under a universal
abstention from the discharge of this duty, for even
a short period, the visible government would perish.
Any neglect of this duty by the better class, which
seemingly is becoming onerous to many of it, is
attended by grave mischiefs to the public, though
the government goes on and will, however derelict
they may become. There is nothing men so

cheerfully undertake as the government of their fellows, curious as that may seem to the thoughtful. We saw Mr. Wade elected to the senate of the United States, but advised the reader there was much matter to take account of before we could accompany him to the capital. Something of his earlier political career, also a rapid sketch of the rise and progress of the great slavery contest, down to the time he entered upon his new duties. These labors are mainly for the younger readers, who will not take it amiss if I deliver into their easy apprehension an outline of what led to one of the great epochs of human history. Many who witnessed the earlier and less important incidents of it may care to have their memories revived, perhaps corrected.

If a relation, an institution common to all nations and tribes of men, is to be classed as a natural relation or institution, then is slavery of that class. It is a law of man's nature that he can only associate with men and brutes by finding a plane where they can associate in common, where, while he influences, governs them, they also influence him. If he elevates them they reduce him, and the more there is in common between them, the greater is their influence on him. A horse exercises great influence on many men, a slave on many more, hence the institution of slavery is the most hurtful of all influences upon a people. The higher forms of selfishness, which lead men to pursue their own highest good, would induce a people to abolish slavery, eradicate all forms of vice, and permit the fewest possible of a lower class. These considerations are too broad and absolute for more than mention. They range with the higher morals.

"Slavery," says a late English writer,* "was in England never abolished by law, hence Lord Mansfield's decision in the Somerset case (1772) was without legal foundation." This is a misstatement. Slavery in England, at that time, was without legal foundation, and hence Somerset's master could not hold him there. At common law men could not be held as slaves by custom, no matter how universal, or long continued. Hence slaves escaping beyond the reach of the statute which made them such, to free territory, were free. So we ordained constitutions and laws for their return to slavery.

The law of the Somerset case did not reach the English colonies. Some of these were taken from Spain, notably Jamaica, where slavery existed. In others, as in the continental colonies, slavery was planted by England herself. Sir John Hawkins, as is said, made the first venture in this commerce in 1562, bringing a well assorted cargo of negroes and prayer books. Curiously enough negro slavery was introduced into Spanish America by the good Spanish priest, the sympathetic Las Casas, to save the more tender natives from servitude, under which they sunk. The Portuguese were the first traders in negroes to America, in

---

* Dictionary of English History-Slavery.

which all the western Maritime nations had a share.
England finally by treaty obtained a monopoly of
this commerce by the peace of Utrecht, secured
by "the *Assiento.*" Ten years after the Somerset
decision, Clarkson, Zachary Macaulay, father of
Thomas Babington, and Wilberforce, moved
against the slave trade. Pitt's aid was secured in
1792. Effective steps were not taken till 1805 and
1806. The heaviest blow was dealt in 1807. In
1811 to deal in slaves was made felony and piracy,
punished capitally in 1824.

The English colonies politically, legally, morally
and religiously, were a unit in the matter of negro
slavery. Its oponents few, and had no hearing.
Massachusetts enslaved Indians. Down to 1776,
it is estimated that 300,000 native Africans had
been imported into the Anglo-American colonies.
The census of 1790, showed the number of slaves
to be 698,000. In 1800 the slaves had increased
to within a small fraction of 900,000. There were
1,100,000 in 1810; 1,538,000 in 1820; in 1830,
2,000,000; in 1840, 2,400,000. They had increased to 3,200,000 in 1850; in 1860, to 3,952,000,
their last enumeration. After the Revolution
some of the southern states abolished the foreign
slave trade, while it was maintained at the north.
Vermont was the first to abolish slavery, which
she did in 1777. Pennsylvania by gradual eman-
pation in 1780, of her slaves 64 remained in 1840.
A judgment of the supreme court ended the institution in Massachusetts, in 1780. Rhode Island

had five slaves in 1840, Connecticut had 17 at that date. New York, which had 20,000 in 1799, the date of her emancipation act, freed the last on the fourth of July, 1827. New Jersey also pursued the gradual process and had 236 in 1850.

The Revolutionary patriots declared all men born free, and tacitly held negroes not men, and so not within its meaning and spirit. It was of this quite universal sentiment of the Revolutionary period, that Chief-Justice Taney, in the Dred Scott case, truly said: "At that time it was generally held that negroes had no rights that white men were bound to respect.*

The national constitution recognized slaves under the euphuism of "persons held to service in a state under the laws thereof," and pledged the states to their return if they fled from it, as so many did.†

For the purpose of representation in the national house of representatives, five persons thus held were counted as three, and congress was prohibited from legislating against the African slave

---

* Nothing better shows the spirit of the slavery contest, when that unfortunate case was decided and since, than the fact that this sentiment, excusable, perhaps, in 1776, but atrocious in 1857, attributed by one of the ablest and purest of American judges to the men of the preceding century, were popularly accepted, charged upon him, as *his sentiments, his judgment* of the black man's true status, on the day of its declaration. The old man died with this imputation strong upon his name and memory, and good men died believing it true.

† It was estimated that at least thirty thousand thus held reached and found shelter in Canada alone, where no fugitive law or rendition treaty could exist.

trade for twenty years. July of the year of the production of this national instrument (signed September 17) saw the promulgation of "the ordinance of '87" (1787) which dedicated the great unknown northwest to freedom. ‡

So stood this thing of slavery when the young states and younger nation, under its charter, entered upon their interesting career, unconsciously to be wrought upon by the ever active unseen laws of evolution, which mould politics, government, morals, and religion, as all organic and ignoranic matter.

At that time slavery was no way sectional. Thoughtful men in common everywhere vaguely regarded it as evil, temporary to be sure, and at some time in some way to be made rid of. We have seen the northern states dispose of it for themselves, also that some of the southern had put an end to the African slave trade, and we know that Mr. Jefferson and many leading southern men favored not only the ordinance of '87, but emancipation in their own states. The utter incompatibility of slavery with the institutions of a free people, resting on the declared equality of men by birth, so shocking to our logical sense now, was not then apparent. Men were too pressingly engaged with the devouring necessities confronting them on every hand, to study and speculate of the less obvious and seemingly remote

‡ The authority of which was called in question in the Dred Scott case, the power to pass it by congress.

dangers, then not deemed possible. There was a continent to subdue ; many robust, strong, free peoples to be made homogeneous, educated, governed ; Indians to be dealt with ; foreign nations to be treated with, fought with ; cities to be built, rivers to be navigated, ways to be opened, commerce to be created—a thousand pressing things to be done. Slavery was a seeming means, a help, and not a bale. So things went their blind unconscious ways, as they always do. Slavery became sectional. Slaveholders were homogeneous. It became their bond of union. Long before the north was aware of its dominating power, even at the south it had consolidated that and became dictator. The great parties at the north were compelled to bid against each other for its aid. The way for it there was already prepared. The sentiment of the north was proslavery—always had been. Its conscience slept, had never been developed toward this thing. When that came to life, to seeing, and assailed slavery, on its hitherto most indefensible side, it had become too profitable to part with, too powerful to be easily overthrown. It was the foundation and controlling element of southern civilization and industry. It needed but one thing more to become seemingly invulnerable—to be accepted as right in itself, approved of God, sustained by the Bible, accepted of his prophets and the patriarchs. The greatest work of slavery propagandists was in fashioning the southern conscience

and church to this view.   Enmeshed as it was in
the constitution, constituting their property, their
life, hope, memory and aspiration, this task was
feasible, and in a few years effectively done.
Rapidly and certainly with the accomplishment
of this process, the north was also necessarily consolidated.   Its morals, its conscience, its political
necessities, united it.   Slavery, itself a state of
chronic war, is by necessity aggressive, bold and
unscrupulous.   Its enemy necessarily the north.
It can live only by plunder and outrage.   As long
as the north aided or acquiesced in its aggressions
upon other people, semi-peace ruled the sections;
when it felt compelled to plunder the north, war
was inevitable, and the more so as each party
would conscientiously believe it was right.

Some of the more prominent incidents scenes
and acts of the opening of the great drama, are
to be mentioned.

In good faith to their national undertaking, the
northern states passed laws for the rendition of
escaping slaves.   Slavery has been declared by
able southern courts, a state of chronic war by the
masters upon their slaves—a not modern doctrine
—and thus the northern people became the active
allies of the masters in their war upon their bondmen.   These state laws were not satisfactory to
the south, however, and in less than four years
after the adoption of the constitution, and seventeen after the great Declaration, congress passed
the first fugitive slave law—the first national depar-

ture from its preamble and bill of rights. This was followed sooner or later in many of the northern states by laws repressive of the rights of free blacks, glaringly by the state of Ohio, the first blossom of the ordinance of '87.

Ere the passage of the fugitive law, the Quakers of North Carolina emancipated their slaves, which the state speedily reduced again to servitude. Slaves escaped in large numbers from Georgia masters to the *Creeks*, within the state borders. When the Creeks were threatened with war on their account, they fled to Florida, becoming *Maroons* (as the Spaniards of the West India islands called their runaway slaves, who maintained themselves in the mountains), where uniting with runaway Indians (Seminoles), they sustained years of war to avoid recapture, first in 1818 and in the times of Jackson and Van Buren. In 1800 congress reëstablished the slave code in the national capital. In 1803 the settlers of Indiana asked for a suspension of the ordinance of '78, to enable them to hold slaves. That year we purchased Louisiana, to become a slave empire, its far-reaching influences, a great factor in the destruction of slavery itself. In 1805 a proposition that the children of slaves born in the District of Columbia after that date, should be free, was rejected by congress.

In 1806 we broke off commercial relations with San Domingo, where black slaves were in arms for freedom, having just closed a war with Barbary to free white slaves. In 1810–11 Georgia sent an army to Florida, a Spanish province, to capture the *Maroons*, who, combining with the Seminoles, drove them out. Georgia seized the afterward infamous Amelia Island, which from that time became the headquarters of African slave traders and other more honest pirates. Meantime we had abolished the foreign slave trade, and largely in the interest of the home producers of slaves, as it proved, a curious application of the doctrine of protection of home industry.

Slavery becoming economically profitable, men began to find it less immoral. The trade in slaves at the capital became so flagrant that John Randolph pronounced a phillipic against it on the floor of the house, in 1816. The year 1818 saw the first Seminole war, in which old Fort Nichols, where the fugitives found shelter, was blown up with hot shot fired into its magazine, and a few of the survivors were delivered to our Indian allies for their amusement, after known methods, a costly entertainment as negroes went. After two severe battles General Jackson retired with doubtful honors and small profit. Georgia then clamored for the acquisition of Florida itself.

The first contest over the admission of a state occurred in 1811, on the application of Louisiana. The opposition was violent and bitter on the part of some of the New England men, not so much on account of its characteristic slavery as that it was a form of foreign territory—had been a foreign possession.*

This contest excited little popular interest. Missouri applied six years later. Her case came up in December, 1818, and lasted for two years. The first great trial of the bands of the Union. Sudden and almost inexplicable was the deep, far-reaching excitement it caused, ending in the famous compromise of 1820, and followed by a calm, a profound apathy, as mysterious. This rise, long continued, furious war, and its sudden subsidence, are still a problem of our political history. In this, slavery itself was the sole cause. The first battle was on Mr. Talmage's (from New York) amendment, prohibiting the further introduction of slaves, and securing the freedom of all slave children after a named date; it passed both houses. At the next session Maine and Missouri both sought admission. They thus became united, remote as they were geographically, in the interests and genius of their peoples; in the all-embracing arms of slavery. The contest was renewed with more than the first heat. Mr. Clay, though speaker of the house, became the pro-slavery leader of the floor. The house would not admit the two together; and Maine was uncon-

---

* Josiah Quincy of Massachusetts, a remarkably able man, took the ground that the admission of a foreign possession and people was a virtual dissolution of the Union and threatened to give this effect to it if persisted in. So the first threat of dissolution came from Massachusetts. The same objection was urged with much force against Texas later.

ditionally received in March, 1820. An enabling
act containing the famous dedication of all the
Louisiana purchase north of thirty-six degrees
thirty minutes, was passed for Missouri. Angry
and resentful, her people complied, but inserted
also a provision against free negroes. When this
constitution came up in congress battle royal en-
sued, with more than the former heat and venom.
Twice the house rejected the constitution with this
obnoxious provision. During the struggle the
Maine senators, Holms and Chandler, voted steadily with the south. Finally a second compromise
was secured, by which the Missouri legislature
were forever prohibited from giving effect to the
obnoxious provision. She was admitted, and this
startling and ominous episode, as it was regarded,
and the spirits it conjured, passed into speedy forgetfulness. Stephen A. Douglas was then but
seven years old. His voice was to recall these
spirits, the Kansas border war—the prelusive
skirmishing of the real war, which was in the fullness of time to follow—coming out of the great
compromise.

The next step was the purchase of Florida, in
1821, and, notwithstanding the provisions of the
treaty with Spain for their protection, an interminable war was begun to reduce the *Maroons*, their
wives and children to slavery. In 1826 came the
second great discussion of slavery in congress, on
a proposition to send commissioners to the new
southern republics, who had abolished slavery.

The south feared for the institutions in Cuba and Porto Rico, and the remote consequences to themselves. The next year saw the debate on the long pending controversy with England, for the slaves deported by her in the war of 1812. The question was finally referred to the Emperor of Russia, who good-naturedly awarded that England should pay the United States one million two hundred thousand dollars.*

We have glanced at the institution under English dominion. Long before any agitation for emancipation in this country, Elizabeth Heyrick, a Quaker lady, published an important work in England entitled, 'Immediate and not Gradual Abolition,'† which finally produced a profound impression there, and led to a change of views and action on the part of English abolitionists. Such advance had then been made that upon the assembling of the reform parliament of 1832, the government announced its determination to bring in a bill for the emancipation of the slaves. The abolitionists demanded immediate emancipation. In 1833 a bill was passed abolishing slavery and providing for an apprenticeship of the slaves.

---

* After paying all the claimants for the thus stolen slaves, there remained about one hundred and forty-one thousand dollars. Toward the end of the Jacksonian reign this was quietly paid to Georgia masters, to compensate for the children the slave mothers would have borne them had not the faithless things run off with the Indians! How that was divided, or by what rule, I never knew.

† Immediate abolition has recently been deemed as the discovery of the late William L. Garrison, who is said also to have discovered Whittier, the poet. 'His Life,' by his sons, Vol. I.

This was disregarded by the masters in Jamaica, followed by a bloody insurrection in that land of slave insurrections, in which thousands were slain, when parliament abolished the apprenticeship and slavery disappeared August 25, 1838, in all the British dominions.

Things in this connection happened in the United States the year following, which recalls our attention to our seemingly forgotten immediate personage who now takes, if a brief, an important part, his first, in the incipient contest on this continent. With a pro-slavery sentiment pervasive through the north, slavery bold, arrogant, aggressive, had, as we see, then made large gains, rapid advance toward unquestioned supremacy in the so-called free republic. The open opposers of slavery were slow to appear, won few, and at the first unheeded, north and south. Several books had been published against it. Anti-slavery societies had long existed. Between 1820 and 1830 several anti-slavery papers were published, notably by Benjamin Lundy in Ohio, and Baltimore, Maryland. In this last William Lloyd Garrison served his apprenticeship in his press room as in prison, and then went to Boston where he planted the *Liberator*. Hammond, in the Cincinnati *Gazette*, produced a series of strong articles against slavery. Theodore Weld had caused a secession of students from the Lane seminary, on anti-slavery grounds, and had lectured through the north, then a very young man of remarkable powers. James G. Birney had arisen in Kentucky and gone north, a man of rare gifts and marked character. The American anti-slavery society had been organized and disrupted for difference of opinion as to whether, in a matter largely political, political action should be had. In 1831 John Quincy Adams took his seat in congress and was soon in open war against slavery, on the narrow and seemingly remote issue of the right of petition, logical only because the illy advised slaveholders elected that issue. Mr. Adams was at the beginning no abolitionist, might never have become one had not the war made by them on the right of petition compelled him to be one, born warrior that he was. He alway opposed the abolition of slavery in the District of Columbia until it should disappear in Maryland and Virginia. That same year occurred Nat. Turner's bloody insurrection in South Hampton, Virginia, followed by many pro-slavery riots at the north. Indeed, to begin with, the entire north had to be first conquered from slavery to freedom. The conquest, in fact, never was completed while slavery anywhere existed, and it left many mourners there, over what, to them, seemed its untimely demise.

We have noted the early action of the Ohio legislature in favor of slavery. This was followed by various acts which together came to be called the black laws.*

---

*The first act was in 1804. This required every black or mulatto, before

These together, the shame and reproach of the young state, were not satisfactory to Kentucky and Virginia, the south. There was the memory of South Hampton, the recent bloody insurrections of Jamaica and Demarara. England had abolished slavery in all her dominions, and notwithstanding actual murder, bloody riots, and burnings at the north, an anti-slavery sentiment was increasing there. The slave trade had actually been presented by a grand jury of the District of Columbia. Ohio was now in the hands of the Democrats, and she at least should be asked for additional safeguards and pledges. She was asked for them, and the most humiliating incident of her history is to here find brief mention. She readily rendered

---

he could reside in the state, to file with the clerk of the county of his intended abode a certificate of a court of record of the state whence he came, that he was free. This act also authorized claimants of runaway slaves to make summary proof before any judge or justice of the peace that a named person was an escaping slave, when a warrant was to issue to the sheriff of the county, who was to sieze and deliver him up to the claimant, to be returned. *First Chase's Statutes 363.* Two years later this was supplemented by an act requiring all colored persons, before they could be permitted to remain in the state, to give a bond with two good sureties, conditional for their good behavior, and that they should be maintained, with stringent provisions against harboring fugitives. There was a section making blacks and mulattoes incompetent as witnesses in any case, civil or criminal, where a white person was a party. *Chase* Id. 555. To the credit of the supreme court of Ohio, it should be stated that it held all persons with more white than black blood, white for all purposes, 4 O. R. 353, 11 Id. 372, 12 Id. 237, *Wright* 578. All blacks were excluded from the public schools by act of 1831, 3 *Chase* Id. p. 1872 ; they were precluded from lawfully becoming paupers by act of the same year, Id. p. 1832.

what was asked of her. Mr. Wade was of the
young Whig party. †

In the fall of 1837, as stated, he was elected to
the Ohio senate by the Whigs, nominated without
his knowledge or consent. He was then, as will
be remembered, thirty-seven years old. The state
was temporarily largely Democratic, both houses
of the "General Assembly" overwhelmingly so.
Though one of the youngest members, he was at
once placed on the judiciary committee, then the
most important committee of the senate. At that
time divorces were obtained by legislative action.
A report of Mr. Wade's on this subject put an
end to this practice. This was the day of roads,
canals, really inter-state improvements by state
action—transitional period from old to new methods—and the financial collapse of that year (of
which the reader has been reminded) led the
people to look to the structure of public works as
a source of relief. They clamored to have the
state at once enter upon a wild scheme in that
fatal field of municipal enterprise. The sagacious

† While the patriots of the Revolution called themselves Whigs—
the name of their English friends (derived from Scotland, first in
derision by their enemies, who in turn were called Torys, a term of
reproach derived from Irish outlaws), the name Whig was adopted by
the young National Republicans of New York in 1834, who then supported young William L. Seward (who was a year younger than
Wade) for governor of New York, but was then defeated by Marcy.
The name was at once adopted by all opponents of the Jackson-Van
Buren *Loco Foco* party (except the anti-Mason), then beginning to call
themselves Democrats. Three-fourths of the voters of the Western
Reserve were Whigs.

senator from Ashtabula opposed it with great vigor, as did several of his colleagues in both houses from his section. At that day the Western Reserve was as broadly marked from the rest of the state as was the north from the south at any period of our history. The measure prevailed. Mr. Wade suffered for his opposition, and the state suffered deeply because of the failure of his efforts.

Quite his first action was to secure the passage of a resolution against the annexation of the new republic of Texas, which passed the Ohio Democratic senate unanimously.*

During the second session of Mr. Wade's term, in the winter of 1838–9, came the Kentucky commissioners, created by her legislature, and commissioned by her governor.† They came to secure the passage of a more vigorous and stringent fugitive slave law, although it had been shown that it was with the utmost difficulty that

---

*We are to hear much of this. Texas was first occupied by an American colony under a grant to Austin of Connecticut, in 1823. The colony was attached to Coahula and governed with gross injustice, exclusively by Mexican methods. The first outbreak was against the state, and fully justified. The battle of San Jacinto was fought April 21, 1836. The United States acknowledged the existence of the Republic, as an independent state, in March 1837. The project of its annexation to the United States became at once a _burning question._ It dictated policies, nominated and defeated Presidents, and was with the agitations consequent of the purchase of Louisiana, the immediate active cause of a destruction of the institution it was to perpetuate.

†Mr Moorhead (afterward a Whig senator) and Price a Democrat.

the existing laws could be executed, as they rarely were.

The utmost good feeling had until recently prevailed between the people of the two states. They had fought the Indians together, and Ohio was grateful for the aid of gallant Kentucky, when invaded by Brock, Proctor and her own Indian son, the greater Tecumseh, in 1812–13. Indeed, most of the men of that day of peril and blood not slain in battle or massacred by the foe, were yet in vigorous life. Recently, however, several slave-hunting cases had arisen in Ohio, of doubtful character—doubtful as to the real status of the alleged fugitives and the means of capture, —which had disturbed the otherwise pleasant relations of two peoples.

The Kentucky commissioners were received with open arms by the majority of the two houses. In the senate but five opposed their wishes. Mr. Wade was quite the most determined as the ablest of these. They could only debate, delay and obstruct. The courtly Moorhead and colleague waited upon the senator from Ashtabula, and in moving—quite pathetic terms—laid before him the tender and benignant character of the institution in Kentucky, where the slaves were barely servants, and treated more like children, yet would run away. Mr. Wade thought there must be some inexplicable mystery in this, when such a docile race sought every opportunity to escape from such parental love and tenderness.

He had decided objections to becoming a slave
hunter and bailiff, and asked if gentlemen like
themselves ever engaged in the business in Kentucky. Moorhead admitted they did not. Price
laughed and told his colleague that the northerner
had him at disadvantage. "No," said the indignant native of the Feeding Hills, "you send
your drivers rough and desperate to decoy, steal
and kidnap them, and were I master here, every
man of them should be placed in irons, and our
people spared the pain and terror of their presence." It was in this spirit he met the bill. He
assailed it when reported from the committee in
all forms, details and provisions. It is to be
remembered there was then no source or supply
of anti-slavery arguments. The place of the
Democratic legislative caucus was in a large upper
room of the Ton Tine coffee house, on the main
street of Columbus. An elevated Whig member
of the house, in his exhilaration on the floor one
day, irreverently called it *Tin Pan*, and so it was
ever after known. The bill was "*tin panned*," *

---

*Of *Tin Pan*, after the production of a batch of new judges, in 1839
40, the following *jeu d' esprit* had wide circulation:

> Our vulgar English verb—create
>   Means really this and no more,
> Nor less in fact—it is to make
>   Things, of what nothing was before.

> This power, as said, don't dwell with man—
>   That's mistake, it dwells in *Tin Pan* ;
> I prove it maugre all your grudges,
>   By its act of making judges.

and came up for final action in the senate at 9 A.
M. of the twenty-first of February, 1839. Those
were working-day times. It was passed in the
form it then wore—a bill of fourteen sections
alleged to have been prepared in Kentucky. It
began with an elaborate whereas, glorifying the
compromises of the constitution and asserting the
duty of Ohio in the premises as one " reaping the
largest measure of benefits conferred by the constitution, to recognize to their fullest extent the
obligation it imposes," etc.

The minor provisions authorized the pursuing
party, before any judge, justice or mayor, to swear
out a warrant for the arrest of any alleged fugitive
addressed to any sheriff or constable, whose duty
it was to arrest the party anywhere in the state
and return him before the officer issuing or some
other judge, justice or mayor most convenient.
It secured to the claimant sixty days to prepare
for the hearing—no delay to the captured, who
meantime was to be committed to the county
jail. The hearing was summary, without a jury,
and the warrant of the court authorized a removal
to the state whence escape was made. Everybody was prohibited from interfering, or consult-
ing as to means of interference with the pursuit,
and from harboring, concealing or in any way
aiding the pursued, or any fugitive, under severe
penalties. †

The session ran from the morning of the twenty-

† See act of February 26, 1836. 37 Vol. Stats. of Ohio, page 38.

first into the morning of the twenty-third.   After midnight of the last hours, Senator Powers of Akron arose and delivered a strong, bold, vigorous, manly speech against the bill.‡

It was two o'clock when Wade arose, weary but determined, to conclude the opposition to the bill. From this, as reported, I quote to show specimens of his then style of dealing with grave subjects, as well as the spirit, courage, firmness with which he confronted the greatest issue of his country of any time.   The details of the bill, as stated, had been discussed at its earlier stages.   This was a final assault from the high and broad ground of large fundamental opposition.   He began with a rapid sketch of the course of the majority, the efforts of its opponents in good faith to relieve it of some of its worst features by amendments.   "In sullen silence you voted them down. No friend of the bill deigned to raise his voice in its defense."   He then spoke of the treatment by the majority extended to its friends, obsequious to give them every opportunity, and churlishly denying every courtesy of needed opportunity, to its opponents to debate it.

‡ Gregory Powers was worthy to stand, as he did, with the best men of Ohio.   I never saw his speech.   It was widely spoken of as a noble effort of manly argument and indignant eloquence.   He was then not more than thirty-four, tall, dark, black-browed, one of the most promising men of the state.   He died early.   As was told us, the younger, he was compelled to argue a heavy case, with a severe cold upon his lungs, and died of the effects.   I am glad to add this note to the memory of Gregory Powers.

Such are the contemptible expedients resorted to by you to silence discussion upon this infamous bill of pains and penalties. It shall not avail you. I stand here at two o'clock of the night, after a continuous session since nine of yesterday morning, and though I speak to ears that are deaf, and hearts impervious to right, justice and liberty, I will be heard, although from the servile policy manifested by the majority on this floor, I have no hope of arresting this measure—a measure which shall ere long stamp its supporters with deeper infamy than did the alien and sedition laws their inventors. Like the heroes of old, the champions of the bill, before taking up the gauntlet in its defense, have prefaced their remarks with a history of their own births, habits and educations. As I suspected, they were born in the murky atmosphere of slavery, or of parents who were. Were I to follow their examples, and speak of so unimportant a subject as myself, I would say I was born in a land where the system of slavery was unknown, where the councils of the nation were swayed by the great principles of equity, where right and justice were deemed the highest expediency. My infancy was rocked in the cradle of universal liberty. My parents were of the Revolution ; their earliest lesson taught me was to respect the rights of others, and defend my own, to resist oppression to the death ; neither do nor suffer wrong ; do to others as I would they should do to me, and though my venerable instructors have long since passed away, the God-like principles they taught me can never die.

This elevated strain he pursued for some space, rapidly sketching the great genesis of free institutions of this country, and bringing into relief the startling departure from them that found expression in the measure under consideration. He made forcible reference to the ordinance of '87, which dedicated the entire northwest to freedom, —freedom for all, forbidding slavery in all forms. He spoke of the great expectations of the great wise men who declared this purpose.

Dare you disappoint them, and with them the hopes of the world? Did they intend you should become the mean apologists of slavery, throw down these barriers against its encroachments, built up with such cautious care. Make the state its great hunting ground, and this to reassert a title in human flesh, which the laws of God, of nature, your constitution, alike refuse to recognize   To affirm that these great men intended this is to pronounce upon them the foulest libel.   Yet such is your argument.   While I have a seat on this floor, am a citizen of this state—nay, until the laws of nature and nature's God are changed—I will never recognize the right of one man to hold his fellow. man a slave.   I lothe, I abhor the accursed system, nor shall my tongue belie my heart.

Proceeding then to admit that slaveholders for the time were safe behind their state barriers—" I ought not to disturb them there.   There let them remain and cherish and hug the odious system to their hearts, as long as they can brave the focus of public opinion of the nineteenth century."   He taunted Kentucky with her pusillanimous position. Yesterday haughty, arrogant, calling "hands off;" to-day imploring help to catch her runaways.   He would not thus become party to her great crime, would in no way aid in sustaining her in it. "Kentucky no longer asked you to let slavery alone, but to become active agents in its support. Mr. Speaker,* do you approve of slavery?   Let me answer for you—'No.'   Would you deal in slaves?   'No.'   Is it right to deprive a man of his liberty?   'No.'   Can you conscientiously, by your legislation, aid in doing all this?   *Yes*, Mr. Speaker, I know you will.   I know your servility."

Kentucky, he went on to say, having solicited our aid in support of slavery, would by this act be estopped from charging us with unwarranted interference if we should hereafter ask her to relieve

---

* The president of the senate—Joe Hawkins, at that time—was called the speaker, and as such signed himself.

us of the abominable burden, by the abatement of the nuisance. This idea he worked up with effect. He warned her not to make up an issue on slavery with Ohio, and especially not to put trust in this bill. "As a friend of Kentucky, as a lover of truth and fair dealing, one who despises deception, and who has some knowledge of the people of the state, I declare here, and now, in my place, your law will be of no validity, it will remain a dead letter on the statute book. With the frankness of honest and honorable men, you should have declared this to the agents of Kentucky. Sir, your legislation is mean, deceptive, unworthy the dignity of this state, and you know it to be so." He asked, demanded, if the senators would aid in the execution of the law. "Dare you make a law which no decent man will execute?" he demanded further. He drew a strong picture of a community, once free, who should become so abject and craven, that an act of the character of the one under consideration could be executed in their midst. He took higher—the highest ground, which he reverently approached—the "higher law," as it later was derisively called. "No one has yet compared your bill with the paramount laws. The subject has not been broached. Should your bill be found conflicting with their provisions, it will not only be void, but we must answer for consequences. You cannot violate these laws with impunity. If you oppress the weak and defenseless, no power can shield you from the consequences ; the evil

will recoil upon your heads, upon the heads of
your children, to the third and fourth generation.
Such is the order of nature—the will of God. The
neglect of this great truth has filled the earth with
violence and crime, from the first ages to this day.
You can not deprive a man of his liberty, however
lowly and weak, without endangering your own.
The practice of tyranny becomes habitual, weakens
the sense of justice, respect for the rights of others,
stimulates the malignant passions, engenders
pride, renders a man helpless, dependent; is
scarcely less fatal to the oppressor than to the op-
pressed. The influence of this example will remain when we are forgotten, to influence unborn
generations and jeopardize the well-being of pos-
terity."

He pursued this high theme at length, and drew
this distinction between man's enactment and the
laws of God. The first may be evaded, the latter
execute themselves—the penalty inexorable. In
the light of this code he proceeded to a careful
analysis of the principles of the bill, especially the
provisions denouncing penalties for acts of charity
to the fleeing, famished fugitive from slavery. It
had been urged that the comity of states required
this act in behalf of Kentucky. To this he replied,
comity could never require a mean, base or tyran-
nical act. In handling Kentucky's claim to our
consideration, he cited with great effect several
recent outrages of the Kentucky agents and
authorities on citizens of Ohio, among them the

once well-known case of *Eliza Johnson* and *John
B. Mahan.*

His discussion of the constitutional question, then
comparatively new and fresh, was remarkably
able, and his handling of authorities admirable.
His plea for trial by jury, to settle the status of a
claimed slave, has been rarely surpassed. He
read a notable case from New Jersey supporting
his view, and concluded that point in these words :

Does not the constitution of Ohio, equally with that of New Jersey,
guarantee trial by jury? Are you dumb? Thank God a crouching,
time-serving legislation is not the last resort, else freedom in this state
would find a grave before this session closes. But the doings of this
night must pass in open day a sterner trial, before they can be made
effectual, and you may read their doom in the case I have just cited.

"The night is far advanced," he said. "The
measure under consideration by its friends is
adjudged more congenial with darkness," and he
went on for three columns, more, to batter it and
them out of the little remaining semblance of
legislation and law-makers left to them. The
threat of dissolution by the south was then chronic.
He defied them to execute it.

His speech, like all complete work, needs to be
taken entire. No quotation can do it justice ; no
description realize its force and effect to the
reader, or any reading give its effect as delivered.
On going over with it now, one is surprised to
see how little has since been really added to this
great argument against slavery. It stands as one
of the ablest legislative speeches of the state. It
was amongst the ablest delivered against slavery.

The whole subject was then new and fresh. It was a long stride in advance of public opinion, even on the Reserve. It was widely printed and read, and became one of the sources of education, argument and influence, ere the great anti-slavery cause was well in the milk—so to say of it.

Mr. Wade, as before said, was nominated for reëlection at the October state election, 1839. His district had a Whig majority of four thousand. He was defeated by a majority of sixty, by the Democrat, Benjamin Bissell of Geauga, who was soon to press after him on the same side in the anti-slavery struggle. Whatever may be said, this result was due entirely to his course on the pro-slavery bill. As already stated, the entire north was steeped in pro-slavery sentiment, every rood of which had to be literally conquered to the cause of freedom. The work was rapidly accomplished on the Reserve, and when, two years later, Mr. Wade was again placed before the people for the senate, no one thought of seriously opposing him.

I may, in anticipation, mention that this speech of Mr. Wade, and that of Mr. Powers, under the aroused sense of right, acting on the state pride of the Ohio people, made the Kentucky act utterly odious. No case ever arose under it. No man of the south had the hardihood to seek its enforcement on a soil in which it perished at once. As Wade said, in the dimly lighted old senate chamber, full of bad air, foul breaths, and mephitic vapor, it was a snare to the slaveholders, and the leaves of the Ohio statute book became its winding sheet, where it was laid dead from its birth. The state improvement act was also short-lived. The two were not lovely in such lives as were theirs, and they were not widely separated in their timely deaths—way-marks of the momentary weakness and folly of a great young people on their way to the van of the republic, where their lead was to be wise and their deportment modest.

CHAPTER VI.

HAVING passed the great cataclysm caused by
slavery, being able now by the broad light of perfected events to examine and estimate the influence
and significance of the first signs of the rise and
steady progress of the anti-slavery cause until its
revolution of politics, and the industry and civilization of one hemisphere of this Republic, historically we deem no intervening events of the least
importance. We have seen the awakening of the
forces that are to overturn existing institutions and
change the configuration of the Republic, and are
impatient of everything that seeks to withdraw us
from their process, and the process of events im-
pelled by them. True, from 1840 to 1861 are
twenty-one long—or short—years as we estimate

them. Short to those who deplore the change—
long to those who prayed, hoped, fought for its
consummation. In these years the struggles, the
politics, the rise and rule of parties, the elections
and policies of Presidents are of no possible importance, save as they influence the great thing that
was to be. In the grand onward march of the
ages—the centuries—this is very true. When we
turn our eyes backward to earliest historic events,
the perspective of time is entirely lost. Its se-
quence cannot be apprehended. The great old
ages seem to march abreast and confront us in a
mass. The centuries loom on us in groups—as if
contemporary. We forget that all of them, all
time, have marched, filtered through the narrow
succession of days in grains of sand, from the first to
the present, that we never have seen two days come
at the same time. Each has delivered to its successor all it had that survived it. In our gaze
backward whole centuries have sunk from our vision, leaving things wide apart standing side by side.
We may not pause to grow sad over the utter in-
significance of all human labor and achievements,
which such retrospect and reflection might cause.
There may be nothing *really* great or small in the
history of individuals or nations. All may be essentially of the same size. No matter—the events
of each day are of importance to it, to the busy
men who toil and perspire under its sun, and we
cannot afford to permit these twenty-one years of
our life and time to disappear from even this slight

memoir.   Great men, on the upper and thinner
growing crust, beneath which the great forces were
storing their might, were laboring on questions of
issues and policies which have survived the cataclysm, and in some form entered into the great
campaign of 1884, as into the greater campaign of
1840, which must have a passing word—several
words, I fear.

It was the mission of the Federalist to construct,
invent, create, adopt the constitution, elect, or-
ganize and set the new government on in a healthful, vigorous, successful career.   Had he but the
capacity, with his prestige, to adopt new ideas and
work them into governmental processes, he would
have remained at the helm.   None but a man of
progress can govern a progressive people.   The
Democrat of to-day has shown this capacity, and
is now ruler.   If he gives the Republic a better
government, on substantially the Republican basis,
than did its inventors, he will remain there for a
time.   The Federalist was unequal to the new
demands, and disappeared, as did the later Whig,
and for the same reason.   Mr. Jefferson's task was
to correct the tendencies of Federalists, place the
barque more directly with the Republican current,
and give fuller effect to Democratic influences,
though to claim him as the founder of the present
Democratic party is absurd.   That was more the
work of Andrew Jackson.   No two prominent
Americans were ever more dissimilar than Jefferson and Jackson.   Their only resemblance was—

they were both demagogues. For the rest they contrast.

Mr. Madison fought the war, and though on the whole we were worsted in it, we made vast gains by it.

Andrew Jackson destroyed the national bank. Whether that was a good or a bad thing is still debatable. Whichever it was, the task was wholly his. So he introduced the feature of personal government—was the government pretty much. He originated the causes which in action overwhelmed his successor.

To Mr. Van Buren is due the credit of separating the government wholly from the banks. Mr. Jackson removed the national deposits from the national bank, and dividing he placed the public monies with the state banks. Mr. Van Buren invented the independent treasury—"sub-treasury" it was called—still the method of holding and disbursing the revenues. It was one of the potent causes of his overthrow, which, added to those he inherited, were too strong for him. The bank influence was largely with the administration while it employed the state banks. It was quite unanimously against him when he placed the public money in the vaults of his own treasurer.

Mr. Seward was defeated by Mr. Marcy in 1834. Mr. Seward defeated Mr. Marcy in 1838, prophetic of Mr. Van Buren's fortune two years later. A Whig national convention assembled at Harrisburg, December 4, 1839, to nominate for the Presidential

election the ensuing year. General Harrison had
made a splendid run, "mostly on his own hook,"
in 1836. Largely it was the wish, as well as the
expectation, that Mr. Clay should be named.
Many Whigs had been followers of General Jackson, and in no event would vote for him. They
called themselves *Conservatives*—the first appearance of that now odious term in our political nomen-
clature, of whom Senator Tallmage was the head.
Mugwumps these would be now called. Twenty-
two states were present by delgates at Harrisburg.
Three names were placed before them, Mr. Clay,
General Harrison and General Scott, all three
natives of Virginia. On the first ballot 103 votes
were cast for Mr. Clay, 94 for Harrison, and 57
for Scott. On the last ballot, taken on the third
day of the ardent but perfectly friendly contest,
Harrison received 148, Clay 90, Scott 16. With
Harrison was placed John Tyler, also a Virginian.
Mr. Clay, in advance, gave the most cordial assurance of whole-hearted support of the nominee, be
he whom he might. He redeemed it in the most
effective manner. A Whig electoral ticket was
placed in the field in every state but South Carolina, whose legislature cast her vote.

Mr. Van Buren was nominated at Baltimore,
May 5, 1840. One branch of the Abolitionists,
under the lead of Myron Hawley, placed James
G. Birney, then of Michigan, also in nomination—
of which more hereafter.

Generally, the policy and course of the whole

Jackson party and administration were broadly i
isssue. There had been many frauds, peculations
and defalcations. There was the Seminole war,
and the proposed Cuba bloodhounds as foreign
mercenaries. The declared issues, formally taken,
were upon the veto power, which had been exercised more times by the self-willed Jackson than
by all his predecessors.* Mr. Van Buren, though
his supporters were in the minority in the twenty-
fifth congress, had not employed it at all. Then
there was the great issue of the currency, which
involved banking and the sub-treasury, a protec-
tive tariff, internal improvements and the public
lands. Slavery—even under the head of Texas
—found no place, nor could the Liberty (or third)
party force an issue with either of the great parties,
save under the right of petition, an issue wrought
out by Mr. Adams. This in some sections was
effectively used, especially on the Reserve, by
Mr. Wade and Mr. Giddings, then in the house,
against the Democrats, who were the offending
party in this matter, so that incidentally the institution directly suffered.

A notable theme was the famous New Jersey
"Broad Seal" election case, of the twenty-fifth
congress. The house consisted of one hundred
and eighteen administration men to one hundred
and nineteen opposition of all sorts. After a long
contest R. M. T. Hunter, an Independent Democrat, was elected speaker. Of the six New Jersey

---

* Written before the present use of the veto.

claimants of seats all brought the same evidence of right, under the broad seal of the state. Of these, the ex-clerk, who made up the list and called the house, on the initial day of the congress excluded five, which was the final award of the organized house. It was during the chaos occasioned by the contest that Mr. Adams early arose, made a motion which the clerk refused to entertain, and he put it himself, declared it carried—himself became chairman by common consent of the body in its transition from raw units to the firm ground of a parliamentary house, contemplated by the constitution.

Unfortunately for both parties—for the history of the time, perhaps—some illy-advised Democrat ridiculed the person, life and habits of General Harrison, a man of pure life, exalted character, an accomplished civilian, and one of the ablest commanders of raw troops of our history, though it must be conceded that his soldiers were of the finest material in the raw that ever followed an intrepid leader. He was said to be a weak-minded garrulous old man, living in a log-cabin, and solacing the straitened twilight of life with hard cider. The child then unborn rued the scurrilous libel. The men of the west who had fought under him, whose wives and daughters, in their absence defended their cabins against Indian forays, took it up with a flash. They ignited the continent with their indignant enthusiasm. Log-cabins with the coon pelt nailed to it, hard cider barrels pictured in every fashion and color on banner and flag, borne in endless processions, became the emblem of the battle, the badges of the party. All the poetic and rhyming talent of the country became inspired, and poured from every quarter a swollen, mingled tide of rhymed sarcasm, wit, humor and coarse ribald blackguardism upon Mr. Van Buren and his supporters. There were occasional gleams of wit, real humor and touches of poetry. The words, set to simple airs, were sung from Canada to Mexico, from the Atlantic to the remotest march of the westward-going immigrant. Literally, the administration was sung and stung to death.

All of these were but the bubbles, the foam of the wide, deep ocean, lashed by a real storm. That was a period of exceptionally able—of great men, never more than twice equaled, and never surpassed in our annals. All the political talent, knowledge and skill of the country were called into action and marshaled on both sides—not to sing songs, march in processions, and on one side guzzle hard cider. The whole of that liquid in the country, a fixed quantity at the most, if put in real requisition, would have been exhausted in the first month of the campaign. There was an able, exhaustive and exhausting discussion, not only of the policy, measures and conduct of the administration, but of the great principles of the government itself. It was the first great popular discussion of them—never equaled since. Whatever may have been the direct gain by the labors of the Whig orators and writers, who made the onset, and maintained an aggressive war from the first to the last, indirectly the gain in the education of the people—apt pupils as they were—was of incalculable benefit permanently.

The campaign opened on the Reserve in mid-winter, with mass meetings at nearly all the county-seats, at which popular speeches were made, denunciatory, hortatory and argumentative —the first introduced in that part of the state—or anywhere north, among men of New England origin, and then first and generally called stump speeches.*

Frank Wade, as we saw, won his spurs as a political speaker in the Ohio senate the winter before. A great state mass convention of the Whigs was holden at Columbus the twenty-second of February, 1840, at which he was one of the principal speakers. Four great Whig state mass meetings were early holden in Ohio, at which General Harrison was present. The first on the site of Camp Meigs, May 4, which continued three or four days, commemorative of the siege by Tecumseh and

* The term, as the practice, originated in Kentucky, where the outdoor orator usually spoke from the top of that part of a tree remaining in the earth where it grew, after it had been felled with axes. The term soon came to mean any and all addresses of a political character, and is now thoroughly Anglicized in England as in this country. Stormonth's dictionary (Eng.), Webster, Worcester, *et al.*—another instance of the almost sole mode of the accession of entirely new words to the language—adoption by custom from pure slang.

Proctor, of May, 1813. One was also holden at Eric, September 10, an anniversary of Perry's sea fight, of the same year, at which time and place the Democrats held a rival convention.*

Thomas Corwin was the Whig candidate for governor of Ohio, and accompanied by Thomas Ewing, visited the Reserve in May.†

Mr. Wade took rank in that great canvass with the best speakers of Ohio, and was second to but very few in the thoroughness of his information, and the rather rude vigor with which he handled the great variety of subjects dealt with, in the wide range of topic and mode of treatment, characteristic of the contest.

From the first there were signs unmistakable of the result. The Whigs could that year have elected Mr. Clay, General Scott or almost any candidate. There was never in the history of our

---

*At the Democratic stand the writer first saw and heard James Buchanan and John W. Forney. He was very favorably impressed by the first. Forney was then a very young man.

†That was the year of Corwin's famous reply to "the *late* Mr. Crary" of Michigan, as John Quincy Adams called him in the house, a few days later. I first heard him at Ravenna, of that May. In the Lincoln campaign of 1860, I was one of a party, including Columbus Delano, Benjamin F. Stanton and others, who attended Mr. Corwin several days through the interior of Ohio; saw and heard a great deal of him at the capital, later; was present at the supper party, and one of the group of Garfield and others listening to his flow of story when smitten of paralysis. I have heard very many of the good American speakers of my time; have read nearly all the best published of the English and Irish. I believe Thomas Corwin at his best, the rarest orator who ever spoke the language, and for varied excellence in every range, never surpassed by the speaker of any tongue—of any age or time.

popular politics so much and such widespread excitement, agitation and popular enthusiasm. The conditions and material for its parallel can probably never again exist in such proportions. The success of the Whigs was almost fatal to the party. At each successive Presidential election it attempted to arouse the same wide, deep, popular enthusiasm by the use of the same devices and methods which were the *effect*, the *product*, of the agitation of 1840—the forms, utterance, in which that spontaneously expressed itself. "We felt good in 1849," said a melancholy and disappointed Whig leader, upon the nomination of Taylor, during this last year, "and we want to feel good again." Alas! first love is but for once, and the very youthful.

Of the electoral votes, General Harrison received two hundred and thirty-four, Van Buren sixty.‡

‡ Mr. Van Buren had a curious personal connection with the war of 1812-13, on the northern and western frontier. He was the special judge-advocate appointed from civil life, and prosecuted the unfortunate General Hull for his failure in the first campaign, tried by court martial at Albany early in 1814. His final address, extemporized by special permission of the court, was never reported and published, at least it is not found in the official report published soon after. Hull was defended in a masterly manner by Harrison Gray Otis, as will be remembered. His summing up, reduced to writing, and read by the accused as the rule was, is a masterly performance.

A few months later, Mr. Van Buren was also appointed to prosecute General Wilkinson, tried for failure on the Niagara frontier. General Dearborn was president of both courts. When the special judge-advocate presented himself to enter upon his duties, he was met by a motion from the accused to exclude him, which on a full argument was sustained. 'Wilkinson's Memoirs,' Volume III, page 15.

The popular recoil against the successful Whigs for a time overwhelmed them. They never did recover. Even Corwin was defeated for governor in 1842, and the party was everywhere forced back. True, General Harrison died, and Mr. Tyler vetoed their national bank bills in all forms. At the extra session and later they made an honest effort to redeem all their pledges and, save in the instance of the bank enactment, passed all their measures. Had General Harrison lived, the result would have been the same. No set of men could have met and satisfied the popular expectation, which was fittingly expressed by the popular formula—" Two dollars a day and roast beef "—for the most ordinary laborer. One should fully understand the years of chronic depression and rates of wages of that time to appreciate the irony of this saying, invented by the Democrats and placed in the mouths of Whig demagogues, neither few or over-scrupulous.

In turning to resume the sketchy thread of the incipient struggle against dominant slavery, in which the great contest of 1840 is a pure episode, I am tempted to say generally that when in the progress of a people or state the time is ripe for an advance in mechanics, science, politics or art, the thing to be done often suggests itself to several who then happen to be in the van of the required movement, and there are many contests as to the real discoverer, mover, leader. Were it not for this general tendency, which may detect contemporaneously, the thing itself would not gain recognition, and so secure accomplishment. A discovery, however intrinsically valuable, which the men of the time cannot appreciate, remains as a thing practically hidden.

Savonarola, whose life and fate are the most pathetic of modern history, found his age adverse, and he and his work perished. Luther was one of the many, yet the force which bore him on spent itself ere what the Protestant world deems complete success, was accomplished—the overthrow and extinction of the Romish church. Peace! the world could not then nor now be governed without it.

To claim the arousing and marshaling of the force of the mind and conscience of the men of the north against slavery, as preëminently the work of one man, is a totally unwarranted assumption. There is a way of writing history, lately attempted, which, if accepted without protest, would for the time seem to accomplish this thing. The writers of the biography of the late W. L. Garrison rely quite extensively upon his *Liberator* for authority, and thus sustained there really was but one champion of God and freedom in the north. Should the sons of the late J. G. Birney accept the chal·lenge, work as largely and as narrowly, drawing their authority from a similar source, they would for him make a case every whit as strong. Neither work would be accepted finally as history ; both would be great contributions to it, of value beyond estimation. This last work should be at once set about. It would have this unequaled advantage —slavery was overthrown by political means. Mr. Garrison refused their use, opposed with the might of his trenchant pen and resounding voice their employment, and the men who used them.

Mr. Birney was among the first to see that the most effective single thing was the employment of political power, backed of course by all the moral forces. He was the first to employ it. He, too, was a candidate for the Presidency in 1840.

He was hewn from the mountains, rejected of politicians, to become—I am not to anticipate. He was placed in the field largely by the clear-seeing Myron Hawley, as mentioned, and received but seven thousand and fifty-nine votes, provoking jibes and sneers from the Whigs, derision and sarcasm from Garrison. They were allies against Birney.*

The Liberty party—third party—was to be one of many evidences, itself an illustration that a party in the United States cannot be made. It was and will be mainly recruited from the Whigs, and treated by it accordingly, smiting it back in its hour of might. There will be individual war by it against leading Whigs, at one with it, save its independent organization.

---

* I am glad to be able to say that General Wm. Birney is now engaged on a biography of his late father which will be of great value and interest.

Frank Wade, it was insisted, must leave his
party and join it.   Mr. Giddings was denounced,
yet he was to abandon his organization while
Wade still grasped its remains, fossilized in his
hands.   If the Whigs hated it, the Garrisonians
did the more abundantly, and so the wars within
a war would go on.   Men in the struggling grasp
of a common great enemy will still find time to
clutch each other's throats over the things of
means and leaderships.   This many-cornered war
was to gather strength and fierceness till everything was hidden and lost in the smoke and din of
the battlefield, no longer a figure of speech.

Much important matter occurring in congress
must be passed without note.   Mr. Slade of Vermont, early in the twenty-sixth congress, presented
his memorials against slavery in the District of
Columbia, which caused the southern representatives, under Mr. Wise, to withdraw in a body from
the house—the first secession.   Mr. Giddings entered this congress.   It was the one during which,
under the lead of Atherton, inspired by Calhoun,
slavery secured the adoption of the famous twenty-
first rule, which sent everything touching slavery
to the tomb of the table without a word.   Those
were the days when the ponderous Lewis of Ala-
bama left the house to inspect "coffles of slaves"
from Maryland, halted in front of the east portico
for that purpose, and the hall of representatives was
the scene of constantly recurring disorder, caused
by the brutal violence of southern members, under

provocations of Mr. Adams and Mr. Giddings.
The "*Amistad* case," so productive of abolition
sentiment, had arisen, and other things of the same
tendency. The new Whig President called a special session of the twenty-seventh congress, was
himself called, and left his party to go to pieces,
under the unexpected exigencies flowing from his
absence, and its utter inability to deal with the
new questions, thence to be an abiding presence
till slavary should disapear.   The twenty-seventh
congress saw the attempt in the house to censure
Mr. Adams, the Creole case, the censure of Mr.
Giddings for his platform of the rights of slaves on
the high seas, beyond the reach of slave laws, his
resignation and triumphant reëlection, followed by
his *Pacificus* letters.   The close of the congress was
the publication of a strong address on the aspects
of the slavery contest, from Mr. Adams, prepared
by Gates, and bearing the names of twenty Whig
representatives, including that of J. R. Giddings,
S. J. Andrews, Slade and Gates. Its immediate
purpose was to warn against the annexation of
Texas ; its influence extended much farther.   A
hasty treaty for that purpose was patched up by
Mr. Calhoun, who had succeeded Mr. Webster,
Le Gaire and Upshur in the state department,
and summarily killed by Mr. Benton in the senate.
Meantime Mr. Clay, whose contemptuous treatment
of President Tyler caused much of the trouble between that worthy and the men who elevated him,
brought forward his propositions of policy, made

his retiring speech, resigned and awaited in serene
security his call to the Presidency. He had already received Mr. Mendenhall's Quaker petition
for the emancipation of his slaves, and made that
insolent reply which, with his letter against Texas
annexation, made his *call* sure. Their united effect on his *election* was another thing. He was
placed in nomination May 1, 1844, by acclamation,
at Baltimore.

The Democratic convention assembled in the
same city on the twenty-seventh of May. Mr.
Van Buren was largely the choice of the Democratic party. Mr. Cass *would* be a candidate, and
was. The Democrats were also more largely in
favor of the annexation of Texas ; Mr. Van Buren
had written a letter against it. The convention
adopted a former rule, requiring a two-thirds vote
to nominate. On the first ballot, 146 were cast
for Mr. Van Buren. 83 for Cass and 37 scatteringly.
On the eight, Mr. Van Buren 104, Cass 144 and
J. K. Polk 44 ; Mr. Polk was unanimously nomi-
ated on the ninth with a resolution demanding
Texas and Oregon to 54 degrees and 40 minutes.
The convention dispersed.

No more conspicuous figure has ever appeared
in American political history, none so grand and
really imposing as Henry Clay. Lofty, magnanimous, far-seeing, intensely American, creative,
chivalrous, of unsulied fame, an eloquence of the
rarest excellence and power ; none ever before or
since, secured the love and devotion of so many

men, and men of diverse opinions, habits and pursuits.   No American statesman has yet connected
his name with so many and such important measures, due only to causes arising in the scope of
the ordinary political necessities of a progressive
people.   He in his youth was an Emancipationist.
He came too early to have his fine impulses lit and
fanned to flame by the later arising spirit which
inspired the great upheaval.

The admirers of an exceptionally brilliant politician of our day are fond of running parallels between him and Henry Clay.   They may be exhibited on the same canvas by contrasts ; one will
live, the other's place is, perhaps, undetermined.

The contest of 1844 was next the preceding, the
most sharply contested of the national canvasses
to that time, its consequences infinitely more important than those of that.   Incidentally, great but
unintended help was given to the anti-slavery cause
in the thorough discussion of the Texas issue.   It
would be curious to note how Whig blows against
that helped to demolish the Whig party.

No man in Ohio was more zealous and effective
than Frank Wade in the advocacy of Mr. Clay's
election.   He was the first man in public life
of his state, as will be remembered, to take
ground against Texas annexation in the Ohio senate.   He gave quite his entire time and strength
to this canvass.   None were more sorely disappointed by the result.   Never was there such

widespread heart-break occasioned by the result of a Presidential election as that of 1844.* Of the popular vote, Polk received 1,337,243 ; Clay, 1,299,068.

Another power is now to be taken account of. At this same election James G. Birney received 62,300. These defeated Mr. Clay and made our subsequent history possible.

Nothing is more profitless than speculation of what might have been, if the actual were not. Seemingly, the election of Mr. Clay would have postponed the crisis of 1861 to the next century. It came none too soon—is over. Let us be comforted.

Great events crowded each other under the influence of the Democratic success. The Texas ten million bill bought its way through congress. President Tyler approved it, and Texas was annexed. Among Mr. Polk's first acts was to dispatch General Taylor across the old Spanish Texas into Mexico, stopping only at the Rio Grande, which the Mexicans crossed, and fought the first battles of that fateful war—with discussions in congress of the Wilmot proviso, ultimate annexation, which brought in California, gold, and the exclusion of slavery from the new state. Preceding these was the adjustment of our Oregon boundary with England. Fiercely the Democrats clamored for the whole. Mr. Adams and Mr. Giddings frightened

* The author, an ardent young Whig of twenty-seven, was more depressed at the result than by the death of his hero, General Harrison.

them out of it with a threat of war with Great
Britain, in which, as Mr. Adams claimed, a general
at the head of an army could liberate all the slaves,
as a military measure, while Giddings appalled them
with pictures of slave insurrections in the presence
of the British forces. No time was spared. Mr.
Polk made haste to conclude a treaty, by which the
Democracy shrunk to the forty-ninth parallel.

At the Whig convention of 1848, General Taylor was nominated for the Presidency over Clay,
Webster and Scott—a signal for the first large
secession from the Whig party in various sections
of the north.

In Ohio a young Whig lawyer of the Giddings-
Wade school called a convention over his own name,
at Chardon, of those opposed to the Whig nomination. The result was such, that similar conventions followed in each of the Reserve counties,
and the party in Ohio ceased to be potential.

Mr. Cass was nominated by the Democratic
convention of May 22, at Baltimore. The Wilmot
proviso delegation of New York bolted. This
gave the Van Burens an opportunity to avenge
on Cass their wrongs of 1844. Under the name
of "Barn Burners," derived from the Patroon
war of their state, they united with the Free-soil
party of that year, and placed the elder Van
Buren in nomination for the presidency also.
What a campaign was that! Mr. Seward and
John Van Buren—Prince John—were both on the
Reserve. Of the popular vote General Taylor

received 1,360,163, Cass 1,220,544 and the Free-soil candidate 291,262.*

Ohio was left without a dominant majority in the legislature, and her capital given over to misrule for a time. Mr. Giddings became a Free-soil leader. His course cost him a seat in the senate. A coalition of Free-soilers and Democrats placed Salmon P. Chase in the senate, and launched him on a great national career. Opportunity always comes to such men. Perhaps Mr. Giddings' place was really in the house.†

Mr. Wade, as will be remembered, was elected judge in 1847, which withdrew him from participation in the many-angled contest of 1848, though he was known to adhere persistently, obstinately, to the Whig party, to the grief of many admiring friends, who but half knew him. It may be a problem whether those who withdrew from it could not as well have served the paramount cause by remaining in it. Certainly in the case of Mr. Wade, it left him in a position where the men who refused to vote for Mr. Giddings for the

---

* The author voted for—he does not care to name him.

† He had richly earned the promotion, if such it is. He was the unanimous nominee of the Free-soil organization, consisting of eleven. The Whigs, with the persistent stupidity which preceded the death they merited, refused to aid his election. This enabled and justified Mr. Townsend to enter into an arrangement by which the Democrats aided in the election of Mr. Chase. The position of the author has not the slightest historical importance. He voted for Mr. Giddings till the Whigs demonstrated their inequality to their opportunity, when he notified his Free-soil associates that if Mr. Chase failed on the pending ballot, he should vote for him at the next. Mr. Chase was elected on that pending ballot.

senate, gladly conferred their united suffrage on him.

He doubtless chafed under the decorous restraints of his judicial position, which held him from the political tribune—restraints which he regarded as suspended, by one great event, in the history I am so imperfectly outlining. The winter of 1849-50 was memorable in congress as that of Mr. Clay's omnibus bill—the sum of his great compromises, where as usual the concessions seemed to us all on one side. It was a session of great debates in the senate, between Mr. Clay and Colonel Benton, whose great difference was mainly whether the republic should be given up to one huge monster, with one maw and many mouths, or several equally voracious, small, with each its own maw. Mr. Benton prevailed. That, too, was the session of the fall of Mr. Webster—for fall it was.

The passage of the fugitive slave act found Judge Wade holding court at Ravenna. All men heard it with equal detestation and horror. A public meeting was called at the court house. On being approached, he expressed his entire willingness to address it. Timid friends would dissuade him. He brushed them by and delivered a powerful phillipic against it. That this was not out of place nor out of character is apparent when it is remembered that, within less than a year, his judicial career and character received the thoughtful consideration and approval of the ablest and

best men of the bar, already quoted.   Now, after
this long retrospect and these many pages, the
time is at hand when the senator will take his
place.   We will certainly attend him to Washington.

CHAPTER VII.

WASHINGTON had been the capital since 1800. At the time thus taken possession of by the government, save the little corporation of Georgetown, the Maryland side of the Potomac was an unpeopled region. It was soon occupied by folk who were drawn thither to become the tavern and boarding-house keepers, livery and hackmen, the servants and boot-blacks, market-men and small shopkeepers, of the office-holders and employés of the government, the waiters, servants and lackeys of senators and members of the house, and the visitors of the home and residence of what made the state the visible government of the great Republic—their incomes derived wholly from the personal expenditures of congressmen and govern-

ment employès.   In any estimate of the city, this
origin of its population is not wholly to be lost sight
of even now.   At the time it became the senatorial
residence of Mr. Wade, the district had a population of forty thousand.   Of this, fifteen thousand
were colored, including about three thousand
slaves, reckoning every human being supposed to
have a tincture of servile blood.   On Seventh
street, at the margin of the malaria-breathing
canal, was the slave-pen and persuasive whipping-
post, in full sight of the capital.   This found its
counterpart in the city prison, on the northeast
corner of Judiciary square.   The Maryland slave
code was in force, and a more unlovely and un-
wholesome town did not exist in the civilized world
than the city which straggled up and down the left
bank of the Potomac calling itself Washington.
The capitol was the older structure with its ancient
dome.   The foundations of the new house-wing
were laid in 1850; the senate chamber was the present supreme court room.   The then hall of the
house is now given over to the effigies, in mar-
ble or bronze, of the great men of the states,
two and two, as the present generation may
elect.   Congressional and social life at the capital
were not then what they now are.   It was then
much more to be a member of congress.   It cost
much less money and more brains.   American
colossal fortunes did not then exist.   Journalism,
railroading, telegraphy, were in their infancy.
The capital had few attractions save to politicians,

few visitors, and sojourners of the wealthy, who sought it as a social centre. A very few senators, and rarely a member of the house, had their families with them at Washington. They formed "messes," lived in boarding-houses, in the kind of *he* way that men will, severed from the ties, influences, and it may be added, restraints of home and home life. A more dreary, unattractive state, for a cultured man of social instincts and habits, nowhere was endured, than that of the average congressman of the time of Mr. Wade's advent at Washington. He suffered less by it than did many—most of the men of his time.

Members of congress then received eight dollars per day, counting all the days of the week, and a liberal mileage by any roundabout route. They provided also for perquisites, in the way of stationery and cutlery, and enjoyed the franking privilege—so long the target of Horace Greeley's assaults.

Mr. Wade fixed himself in Mrs. Hyatt's boarding house, on the south side of Pennsylvania avenue, between Sixth and Seventh streets, west of the capitol, where I found him in 1861.*

The Thirty-second congress convened December 1, 1851, when Frank Wade entered upon, became a part of, that public life of which he had before, with the mass of men, only read and heard. Of the three greatest American senators, Calhoun died

---

* East, west, north, south and their intermediates, in Washington directories, mean the given direction from the capitol.

the year before, at sixty-eight ; Webster, of the same age, born in 1782, left the senate the year Calhoun died, to become secretary of state ; Clay, in many ways the greatest of the three, born in 1777, was still in the senate.   Can any one explain the law by which great men come in groups ?

Wade's old foe of the forum in the collision trial was now President of the United States, stepping to the place by the death of Zachary Taylor. He favored the compromise measures, opposed Taylor's administration, and placed Webster at the head of his cabinet, with Corwin secretary of treasury—of all men not a financier, and to that time a pronounced anti-slavery Whig, as Fillmore had been.   In 1848 he was a possible President. Upon the passage of the fugitive slave act the President referred it perfunctorily, one must think, to his attorney-general, John Jordon Crittenden (a year younger than Webster), a born slave-holder, who found it to be entirely constitutional, and he signed it—a measure decisive of his political fate as of that of his financial minister and many others.

At the opening of the senate Mr. Chase presented the credentials of Mr. Wade, and he was sworn in.   He was then fifty-one years old, as will be remembered.   Mr. Chase was forty-three at the time.

The old senate chamber is a semi-circle.   The straight side its eastern wall, at the centre of which was the vice-presidential chair, then filled by

William R. King. The senators' seats were
arranged in four arcs of the circle. The Whig
side was the left of the President, the south of the
chamber. Mr. Wade took one of the innermost,
the second from the left. Mr. Seward, as will be
remembered, entered the senate the congress before. He was a year younger than Mr. Wade.
He introduced his colleague, Hamilton Fish, born
the same year with Chase, 1808. Charles Sumner
entered the senate the same day. He, as will be
remembered, was elected by a coalition of the
Free-soilers and Democrats, after a long and
exciting contest. He was then forty years old,
and was introduced by General Cass, and took his
seat on the Democratic side. No American of his
time had been so favorably received in England as
he was, unless we except N. P. Willis. He was
always English in his air, and his presence produced a solitude. Cass was then sixty-nine. Mr.
Wade now saw the senators together, had seen
many of them before. In glancing around the
now spacious chamber, Clay, old, worn, and feeble,
like a dying lion still kingly, sat in the outer circle,
almost behind him, with Seward at his left.
Following that circle round to the seat next the
broad corridor, leading from the front entrance,
his eye fell on the compact, squat, jug-like form
of Stephen A. Douglas, with his large head and
short legs.*

---

* "No, sir ; no, sir! He can never be President," declared positive Colonel Benton ; " his—(not the skirts of his coat, as has been

The Virginia Mason, captured by Commodore Wilkes, with Slidell, a few years later, sat conspicuous on the Democratic side—outer circle. There was also his chief, Jefferson Davis, with Henry S. Foote for colleague. Next Mason sàt Chase, beyond Chase, Hannibal Hamlin. John Bell of Tennessee was there. James A. Pearce of Maryland sat in that senate a Whig. There, too, was Rhett and " Duke " Gwin, now from California, with Ohio's John B. Weller, whom Ford beat for governor, for colleague. John P. Hale had a seat on that side also. Sam Houston, gigantic, rosy and handsome, was there, as were Hunter and honest John Davis, Sumner's colleague. Of course there was a Bayard from Delaware. Pierre Soule was there, as was Jesse D. Bright ; so was Mangum, with Berrien from Georgia. It was àn exceptionally able body, even for the American senate, and an abler man than Frank Wade would be slow to gain recognition and make position for himself in it—which no man did in one congress if we except Seward, Chasè and Sumner. A full senate numbered sixty-two. Dividing on old party issues, now disappearing, there was a decided Democratic majority.

There were but five senators certain under all conditions to oppose slavery. John P. Hale, the hero of the New Hampshire revolution of '45–6, and elected to the senate in 1847, at the age of

reported)—is too near the ground, sir !" Benton had been defeated for the senate by Henry S. Geyer.

forty-one; Seward, Chase, Sumner and Wade.
Of these, Seward and Wade were pronounced
Whigs. Hale had been a Democrat, as was
Chase, though he supported Harrison in 1840.
Sumner, by education and instinct, was a Whig.
It must have cost the Democrats an awful strain
to vote for him, as it certainly did their brethren
of Ohio to vote for Chase.†

It was supposed that congress now convened in
a period of universal calm, under serene skies, on
ground never again to be agitated. The incipient
struggle of the forces was hushed to supposed
perpetual silence. Slavery triumphant, the en-
ergies of freedom and justice were tied down with
the spinnings of the grim congressional spiders
beyond recovery.

If the senate was exceptionally able, passing
fifteen or twenty names, the house was a common-
place crowd. There were Stevens and Toombs
from Georgia, Orr of South Carolina, Humphrey
Marshall and Breckenridge of Kentucky, Giddings,
Cartter and Townsend from Ohio, Clingman from
North Carolina, Andrew Johnson from Tennessee,
Thaddeus Stevens from Pennsylvania, Preston
King from New York, Cleveland from Connecticut,
Hibbard from New Hampshire, Robert Rantoul
and Horace Mann from Massachusetts. The

---

† " Here, Lord, I give myself away,
'Tis all that I can do,"
was the pious exclamatory quotation of devoted Luther Montfort,
Democratic representative of Darke county, when he cast his ballot for
Chase. Darke would not stand it.

caucuses began by quarreling over the compromise measures, but the members elected Lynn Boyd speaker on the first ballot. Thaddeus Stevens received sixteen votes, the radical anti-slavery strength of that body.

The two houses exchanged messages and congress advised the President of its readiness to receive executive communications, and he responded with his second annual message.

Mr. Seward had supplanted Mr. Fillmore in the leadership of the New York Whigs. A virtuous, upright man, the handsomest of the Presidents, Fillmore was not without ambition; was desirous of succeeding himself. He was aware that a northern man must do more for the south than she would exact from one of her own sons, to secure her favor. It is probable, had General Taylor lived, the compromise measures would have been defeated. Mr. Fillmore began by opposing his administration. He favored and approved these measures, and his first annual message declared them a final settlement. Still the north was restive; the new slave rendition act was resisted, and this gave him a coveted opportunity to remind the south of its obligations to him. The message dealt—with calm, level ability, in the hum-drum style of state papers—with the topics of the time, and, recurring to the violations of the fugitive act, the President requoted the constitution, and went over the weary corpse-strewn way of the vain argument of constitutional obligation and duty, in the track of which his own remains were soon to rest and be reviled. He again declared these measures a "final settlement."

On the conclusion of his papers' reading, Mr. Foote of Mississippi introduced a resolution enumerating these measures, declaring that they were the final adjustment of the several matters and things involved in or lying under them severally. There never was such a restless, unsettled, unsettling settlement.

In the assignment to committees—a work of the senators—it is curious now to note the disposition made of the anti-slavery men by the Democratic majority. Mr. Seward was last on that of commerce, Mr. Chase second on revolutionary claims, Mr. Hale at the end of private land claims, Mr. Sumner was the tail-piece of Revolutionary claims, as of roads and canals; Mr. Wade was also appended to two—agriculture and claims. One recognizes the fitness of placing both Chase and Sumner on revolutions. One does not now care, save historically, what posts were assigned to the slavery leaders. Mason had the foreign relations, Douglas the second on this committee, and was chairman on territories—a sadly over-estimated man by his fellows. Intrepid, audacious, unscrupulous, he will be remembered as the breaker of the Missouri wall against slavery, when through the breach thus made rushed the border ruffians and all that followed. Soule had agriculture, Shields the army and District of Columbia

—*paddy* that he was ; Gwin the navy, Atchinson
the Indians, Butler of South Carolina the judiciary,
Bright the roads and canals, Houston looked after
the militia, and the others had second places.
The rule is, the majority take the first and larger
share of the places.   Mr. Chase was a pronounced
Democrat, as was Mr. Hale.   The violence against
decent usage in their cases marks the estimate
of them as anti-slavery men.   The judiciary is
a leading committee of the senate, next in
importance to the foreign relations.   The senate
was then strong in able lawyers ; the Whig, Berrien
of Georgia, was the only good lawyer on it—
whatever may be said of Butler the hero of
Sumner's famous phillipic later.

Considering the treatment of his colleagues and
friends, Mr. Wade had no cause of complaint.   He
was in his seat, had his place, would quietly and
silently study his fellows, correct his impressions,
let men find him out as they might, and bide his
days of usefulness—not of display, this self-reticent
descendant of the Bradstreets, Dudleys, Wigglesworths, this son of Mary Upham, born in the
bosom of the Feeding Hills of the Puritans.

He and Seward had met before.   Seward was
fairly the coming man.   Then slim, with marked
head and face, suave, a philosopher rather than a
man of action, he had a large personal following.
The two senators at once became fast friends ; each
did full justice to the fine, strong qualities of the
other.

The coalition by which Chase entered the senate lost him the confidence of Wade, as of all the older Whigs of Ohio. It lost him the one chance he might have had for the Presidency. For Wade there was a suspicion of arrogance, a flavor of sham, in the grand assumption of the splendid Sumner. He, too, came in by a Democratic coalition. Neither he or Chase ever had a personal following. Each was surrounded by worshiping young men and old sycophants, to whom condescension was grateful. Neither had many intimates of their own age and rank. Chase had fine social qualities; could inspire warm attachments. Sumner seemed to care for neither. Most men at each interview with him had to tell him who and what they were. Some grew weary of that. Each had great personal advantages, and were the most striking of the still youthful figures of the senate chamber.

Wade already knew Hale, who had all the qualities of good-fellowship—a handsome personable figure, rosy cheeked, with fancy and dash then at his best, he lacked the patient, persistent industry to realize the possibilities, the promise and prophecy, which attended his footsteps. He and our senator became well attached friends, remained such after the decline of Hale's popularity and efforts to sustain himself, and Wade had become one of the most prominent senators.

Congress is about the last body which should ever deal with private claims. It is in no sense,

by function or temper, judicial; is without the
means of verifying facts.   Under the care, skill
and industry of Elisha Whittlesey, chairman of the
house claims committee, dealing with them was
reduced to something like system, and his methods
were respected in the senate.   Succeeding to his
seat, Mr. Giddings succeeded him at the head of
the committee, and carried forward the business
on his lines until formally deposed by his
pro-slavery enemies.   Mr. Wade, the partner of
the one and pupil of the other, with his legal and
judicial ability, though last of his committee, in
labor, skill and usefulness, became in a single
session quite the first.   It was a post where a man
can do more work, render more real service, and
gain less reputation, perhaps, than in any other
senatorial position.

There was one case coming from the house not
referred to him, characteristic of the times and the
dominant party, growing out of the old Seminole
war.   It seems that certain Creek warriors, serving
in the Georgia contingent, captured some runaway
slaves — maroons — and claimed them as spoil.
To save them for their owners, really, General
James C. Watson, a Georgia general, advanced
fourteen thousand dollars and more to buy them
of the Creeks, and it was to pay his heirs this
advance and interest on it that this bill, in spite
of Gidding's war in the house upon it, was pending in the senate.   Chase thoroughly understood
it, and when Dawson of Georgia called it up, he

declared his purpose of debating it. It was laid over and should have come up on Friday—private bill day. In his absence it was called up. Wade made an earnest effort to have it take the usual course, seconded by Sumner, so that his colleague could be present. This was refused, and the bill passed without discussion.

Wade's only set speech of the first session was in opposition to the Collins subsidy for carrying the United States mails between New York and Liverpool. He evidently thoroughly understood the subject, and dealt with it in his direct western way. General Cass, still sore from his defeat by General Taylor, had made a speech it its favor, was especially worried by Wade's reference to his "noise and confusion" speech at Cleveland, made in response to an injudicious remark of Judge Reuben Wood, and insisted on an explanation, to which Wade good-naturedly yielded. It availed him nothing. He and his party were taunted with fifteen years of utter neglect of the lakes and rivers, and interposed again. He finally promised to vote for a properly framed bill for these improvements, knowing full well, as Wade told him, that, under his party management, no bill for such a purpose would ever be seen or heard of. The speech was a compact, vigorous statement of the whole question, from a western senator, sore under the chronic neglect of his section, and rapidly growing to strength and power to care for itself. It was not only impressive upon the

question, but made a good impression in the senator's favor.   Reticent, alway seen in his seat, not
before heard save for a terse statement or sen-
tentious explanation.

The provision passed, authorizing twenty-six
trips per year, at $33,000 per trip, approved
August 25, 1852.*   That session ended six days
later.   It was comparatively an unimportant session.   Its perfected labors fill four thousand and
forty-seven pages of the thribble-columned *Globe*.
It produced three large volumes of that tumid
work.   There were notable debates of the finished,
completed, settled work of the last congress, in
which leading men took part in both houses.   In
the senate, Cass, Chase, Foote, Hale, Mason,
Rhett and others.   Mr. Sumner occupies much
space in the *Globe* of that year.   The compromise
measures early, the fugitive slave act later.   Mr.
Seward remained silent upon the great and greatly
settled slavery issues.   This was the year of Kos-
suth's advent.   Foote introduced a resolution the
first day of the session to provide a fitting welcome, on which all the group of five, save Wade,
were heard.

The great Clay died the twenty-ninth of June,
and though the new issues had brought his just
fame under eclipse for the day, the Republic will
cherish his memory as one of its most valuable
possessions.

The first session of a congress is alway long.

---

* Subsidies for foreign mails were then Democratic.

The constitution limits the second. Usually as much real legislative work is accomplished by the second. The perfected laws in the second were larger in bulk than the first, the most of which, however, were largely the work of the earlier session. It is to be remembered that while the senate is in a way a continuing body, congress is not, and that all unfinished business falls at the end of the final session, not to be resumed by the succeeding congress, unless introduced by new bills. Congress has never invented a method of bridging the intervening chasm and saving itself much real and perfunctory labor and the Republic much expense.

The second session was a quiet period. It mourned the death of the great Webster and respectable Upham. Mr. Wade had a notable contest over a private claim, carrying it through against Mr. Broadhead, his chairman. Nobody debated the compromise measures at that session. The Whigs, meantime, had been beaten in the Presidential election. Their party was about to disappear. They were sober and subdued; the victorious Democrats forbearing and silent. Meanwhile the Galphin and Gardner claims had made their way, and Mr. Corwin was to be investigated, and with the addition of a rather swollen *Globe* and a supplement, that commonplace congress quietly subsided.*

---

* Many of the speaking men of both houses revise their speeches as they run through the *Globe* presses. This was the habit of our sena-

Something is to be said of this Presidential election of 1852, of great historical significance, and in the canvass receiving after the adjournment, the entire time and best efforts of Mr. Wade, whose seat in the senate gave him added influence. The struggle between the great parties was for the support of the south.

Reunited and confident the Democracy met in convention at Baltimore, June 1, 1852. Cass, though seventy, was a candidate, as was Buchanan. Douglas, not yet forty, was also brought forward, as was Marcy. A fear of the old dissensions of his state was fatal to the best man then prominent in the party. " Manifest destiny," supposed to be a doctrine of Douglas, was injurious to him. Buchanan never had personal popularity. Cass was old, had been unfortunate. Neither could command two-thirds of the votes under the inflexible rule. This condition of things had been anticipated and provided for, and the way carefully prepared for a purely spontaneous upheaval for the youthful Pierce. Caleb Cushing and B. F. Butler had the credit of manipulating this movement, and it succeeded. William R. King was nominated for vice-president.

The platform was eminently Democratic, none ever more so. It fittingly denounced the Abolitionists and all anti-slavery men, lauded the com-

tors. Such as are retained for more leisurely revision are collected and presented in the *supplement*. This volume of the *Globe* for the Thirty-second congress contains none of the labors of our group.

promise measures and gave the fugitive slave act " honorable 'mention " by name. "The Demo-cratic party will resist all attempts at renewing in congress or out of it, the agitation of the slavery question under whatever shape or color the at-tempt may be made," was its unanimous and em-phatic declaration.

Mr. Pierce was forty-six years old, handsome, accomplished, plausible, and not without talent in a small way ; had served in the house and in the senate, was one of Polk's political generals. That was before the invention of favorite sons. He was one in fact.*

The action of the convention was everywhere, north and south, hailed with Democratic acclaim. The sage of Lindenwold—what a state New York is for Democratic sages! Mr. Van Buren was taken to the Tammany wigwam, threw himself with abandon into the embraces of his whilom foes—forgiven and forgiving. His representatives, who secured his nomination at Buffalo four years before, were some of them in the Baltimore con-vention, and he and they placed unshod rejoicing feet on its platform.

Two weeks after the nomination of General

---

* His friend, Nathaniel Hawthorne, wrote a campaign life of him, and had the Liverpool consulate—certainly the best thing flowing from his elevation. Mr. Howells performed the like service for his friend, in 1866, and received the Venetian consulship. I always thought his much the better work, but it is to be remembered that he had more and better material to go on. His hero certainly never *fainted* in presence of the enemy. Both works were fortunate incidentally for American letters—safe precedents to follow.

Pierce, the Whigs met at the same city to select
their candidates and declare their sentiments and
policy.   In view of the catastrophe awaiting them,
to look back at now, it seems as if their assembly
must have been the saddest body of politicians
ever convened.   Not without strength, courage
and high hope did they meet.   Apparently the
party was strong and firm at the south.   This
canvass was to demonstrate that there was a
stronger common bond uniting that south than
one binding its people to any party.

The convention sat continuously five days. Mr.
Webster, Mr. Fillmore and General Scott were
the candidates.   Of course the President and his
secretary of state represented exactly the same
idea and issue.   Why some arrangement was not
had before the convention sat, is a mystery. From
the tenacity of the parties in the convention, this
was perhaps impossible.

General Scott was the candidate of the anti-
slavery Whigs, unpromising as he was.   On the
first ballot Mr. Webster received twenty-nine
votes—the largest number he ever received.   Mr.
Fillmore, one hundred and thirty-one ; and General Scott one hundred and thirty-three ; showing
an apparent ease for the administration to control
the nomination.   Certainly no administration ever
occupied such a position before a convention of its
own party.

Mr. Clay was then dying in Washington; as
will be remembered, did die a few days later.   A

letter from him was circulated, urging the nomination of Mr. Fillmore. The friends of Mr. Webster were a good deal embittered by this action on his part, and when Mr. W.'s warm, earnest, steady support of Mr. Clay, in 1844, is remembered, this seems little in accordance with his known character. He had never forgiven Mr. Webster for adhering to John Tyler, and in a way shielding him from his fierce assaults nine and ten years before. Unquestionably, his controlling motive was a vindication of his own course in the last congress. To have nominated any one but the President, would not have been a vindication, so dear to him in extremis.

The anti-slavery Whigs, under Seward's lead, could not be won to support the President, who had no votes from his own great state. Her delegation was solid against him. That alone would be fatal. The marvel-working Choate was at the head of the Massachusetts delegation, and exhausted his power of eloquence and persuasion to secure a complimentary vote, *one pro forma*, from the southern states, for the great expounder who laid down his life—all his lives for it. The charm was powerless. Not a man responded. · A crime never atoned.

So the struggle went on until the fifty-third ballot, when Scott was nominated with William A. Graham of North Carolina for second.

The platform in substance was a counterpart of the Democratic. It could not be less. It specifi-

cally declared the compromise measures were a
settlement, in substance and principle, of the great
controversy, including the fugitive slave act by
name, and as such accepted by the Whig party.
That its acquiescence was essential to its existence as a national party, and the integrity of the
Union.

There was a wide and general admiration of
General Scott; his nomination produced some
enthusiasm, and for the few first weeks the Whigs
were not without much hope and confidence.
The platform everywhere north was received with
derision and execration.   Horace Greeley deliberately *spat* upon it.   Indeed, *spitting* on their
platform by the Whigs became an amusing but
not a healthy exercise for them, though many of
them did little else.   I am certain Frank Wade
did a fair share of that, and he was a worker.   It
was fatal to them at the south; an attempt to run
the candidate north and the platform south, was
never so purposely attempted before.   It did not
work.   Neither run well anywhere.   General Scott
carried Kentucky and Tennessee south, and Massachusetts and Vermont north.   Pierce carried all
the rest, with two hundred and fifty-four electoral
votes, to forty-two for his opponent.   So far from
giving the Whig candidate any, the least, support,
the Whig administration, in some instances, openly
opposed in others more numerous, secretly betrayed him.

Mr. Clay died without the coveted approval of

his party, followed by his greatest rival in October. Mr. Webster was profoundly mortified at the result of the convention, and it was very generally supposed that the melancholy which darkened his closing days was due to this as a cause and helped to lessen their number.*

There remains an important part of the Presidential election to be mentioned. The Freesoil party of 1848 and the Liberty party of 1840, now merged, had tried to take the name of the Free or Independent Democracy. They put in nomination John P. Hale for President and George W. Julian for vice-president. They made a vigorous, enthusiastic campaign, and gave 156,000 votes for them. Of these Ohio cast 31,682; Massachusetts, 28,023; New York, 25,329; Illinois, 9,966; Wisconsin, 8,814; Vermont, 8,621; Pennsylvania, 8,525; Michigan, 7,237; Indiana, 6,929; Connecticut, 3,160; Iowa, 1,604; Rhode Island, 644; New Jersey, 350; Kentucky, 265; California, 100; Delaware, 62, and Maryland, 54. These figures were significant, not more in their sum total than in their wide diffusion, sufficient in themselves to secure the defeat of Scott in Ohio, New York, Illinois, Wisconsin, Maine, Iowa and Connecticut, although including many votes of Democrats.

Seemingly never was Democratic power so firmly established, and seemingly on such secure

---

* Whoever cares to see an elaborate, brilliant parallel and contrast of these great men, will do well to read Mr. Blaine's striking passages 'Twenty Years, etc.,' Vol. I, beginning at page 106.

foundations. Pierce's total was 1,601,478; Scott's 1,386,278; majority over Scott was 214,896; over Scott and Hale 58,747. An examination of his majorities in the southern states compared with them in the great northern, in the presence of Hale's vote, will show how deceptive that was, and the awful significance of the vote for Hale, as also the effect of a united south in solidifying a confronting north. Mr. Pierce placed Mr. Marcy at the head of his cabinet; Mr. Guthrie had the treasury, Robert McClelland the interior, and Cushing, who had been a Whig—a John Tyler man and now a Democrat*—was attorney general.

One may fancy the meeting of Seward and Wade at the capitol for the closing session of the current congress. Seward had lost New York only by 1,872 votes, while Hale had received 25,329, mostly Whig. Wade had seen Ohio go for Pierce, on whom he had been bitterly sarcastic, by 16,695, and cast her 31,682 for Hale. They had much in common, and there was great suggestiveness in these figures for them. Mr. Seward, politician and a statesman, was also a philosopher, an inveterate smoker, and found solace in an extra cigar. Wade was a moderate smoker, and clothed himslf in pungent and sarcastic sayings, as with a garment, for the benefit of the successful Democracy. Sumner could have found small comfort in Massachusetts' eight thousand for Scott over Pierce, though much hope in her twenty-eight thousand

---

* He became a Republican ultimately, and died a Democrat.

for Hale. Chase had made a vain effort to evangelize the Democracy, and though his state cast her electoral vote for his nominal candidate, upon the promulgation of the Democratic platform he wrote a strong letter to his friend and coadjutor at the Buffalo convention—the B. F. Butler of New York—repudiating the convention and its doings, and declared his purpose of adhering to the principles there set forth. This severed his nominal connection with the Democracy. Of our five, Mr. Hale certainly had most cause for self-congratulation. †

Three important accessions were made to the senate meantime, John M. Clayton of Delaware, ranking with Cass. Silas Wright and Marcy ; Robert Toombs of Georgia, swaggering, assuming and able—both Whigs—and Judah Peter Benjamin of Louisiana, able, artful, treacherous ; later, Mr. Davis' secretary of state, still later a subject of Queen Victoria, and a leader of the English bar.‡ Later came Edward Everett

---

† Mr. Hale and Mr. Giddings met some of the younger of us at Cleveland immediately after our state election of that year, at which we elected Edward Wade—the "Ned" of my opening papers—our representative in the thirty-third congress. Mr. Giddings had also been re-elected, and a great dinner in the open air was tendered him by that corner of Ohio, at Painesville, immediately after the election. I drove Mr. Hale, Mr. Giddings and Mr. Edward Wade, in the morning of the day, from Cleveland over the ridge road to Paineville. I had a splendid pair, a light carriage, the road hard and smooth, the country beautiful, the morning one out of Paradise. I was still young and knew horses. It was a drive, a ride, a day never to be forgotten.

‡ At the English bar he not only became famous and wealthy, but he contributed a learned and valuable book to the profession, a standard

and William Pitt Fessenden. Mr. F. came to remain. Everett's time would be limited. Thomas
Hart Benton reappeared in this congress as a
representative in the house.

Prince Charming sent his first annual message
to the thirty-third congress on its second day.
Full of gay promise, he declared that no promi-
nence should be given to any subject set at rest by
the compromise acts. The past should only be
recurred to for admonition and wisdom. " That
this repose is to suffer no shock during my official
term, if I have power to avert it, those who placed
me here may be assured."

This was December 6. January 4, Mr. Douglas
introduced the Nebraska bill " and all our woes."
Mr. Pierce's supporters had large majorities in
both houses ! What did he mean ?

The bill did not in terms repeal the Missouri
compromise of 1820, that Mr. Douglas said, in his
accompanying report, would disturb the late settlement—nice casuist ! He did, however, report
a section declaratory of the meaning of his bill.
First, all questions of slavery in the territories and
states to be settled by the inhabitants ; second, all
questions involving slavery to be adjudged by the
local courts, with right of appeal to the supreme
court of the United States ; third, the fugitive

work on sales ; a Jew of the Jews, as his name, qualities and push
indicated ; he was a native of San Domingo and then forty-one years
old.

slave act should be extended to the territories.
On the sixteenth of January, Dixon, Whig senator of Kentucky, gave notice that he would move
an amendment repealing the Missouri compromise
directly. Of course, Mr. Pierce was not responsible for him.

Mr. Douglas was not inventive, but quick to
avail himself of a suggestion. Some one advanced
the idea that the compromise of 1850 suspended
that of 1820. Mr. Douglas seized upon this,
brought in a new amendment and report, based
on this " new and useful " discovery. In his
amendment occurs the famous declaration—" this
does not legislate slavery into the territory or out
of it,"etc.—which Colonel Benton described as " a
section with a stump speech in its belly." The
amendment divided the territory into Nebraska
and Kansas.

The American world took alarm. The Free-
soilers were the first to take effective action.
They promptly issued one of the ablest addresses
—terse, compact, vigorous—ever issued by representatives to a constituency. It contains internal
evidence of being largely the work of Mr. Chase,
written with the aid of a paper prepared by Mr.
Giddings, whose hand is very apparent in it. It
was signed by Giddings, Chase, Sumner, Edward
Wade and Gerret Smith, then in the house, and
DeWitt of Massachusetts. It was printed in every
leading paper in the north, and fixed public opin-

ion unalterably against the bill.   This publication
appeared January 23 and 24.*

Mr. Pierce's organ, the *Union*, replied that the
Democracy were resolved, and the President would
provide for all the senators and representatives
who perished in this cause.

On the thirtieth of January, the day named to
take up the bill, Mr. Douglas, in stormy wrath,
fell abusively upon Mr. Chase as responsible for
the address.   With flashing face the Ohio senator
confronted and threw his imputation of misconduct
back.   Douglas retorted that he had made false
statements.   The president called him to order.
Chase said he should be answered.   Later, Wade
interrupted him and he answered civilly.   His
speech was an arraignment of the address and its
authors.

Mr. Chase arose fully wrought up, and his reply
was most effective and happy.   It appeared that
originally the address was intended for Ohio only,
and in its then form was signed by Senator Wade.
Before issued, its originators changed the form and
put it forth as from the Independent Democrats,
when they omitted Mr. Wade's name.   Mr. Wade
arose and confirmed this, and emphatically indorsed
every word of it.   Mr. Sumner got a moment to
acknowledge his signature, and declared his purpose at an early day to establish its entire verity.
Mr. Seward moved the adjournment that day.

---

* Mr. Hale had lost his seat and was in New York city practicing
law.

There was spirited and angry exchange of person-
alities between the Ohio and Illinois senators the
next day, in which both were called to order.
Whatever may have been their relations, this was
an end of amity. Mr. Chase finally had great
deliverance on the fourth of February—speaking
two and a half hours. Ohio had given the largest
direct vote against slavery. She had taken decided
lead against the Nebraska bill. Her senior senator,
as longer in the service, spoke on the third. On
the sixth he was followed by her second champion,
who declared that his colleague had left not even a
dust of Douglas.

It is to be remembered that the region then
vaguely called Nebraska, was what was left of the
Louisiana purchase, north of thirty-six degrees
and thirty minutes, extending to the dividing line
with England, and from the west line of the states
to the comb of the Rocky mountains.

" Here is a territory as large as an empire,"
said Mr. Wade—" as large as all the free states—
pure as nature, and beautiful as the garden of
God." The area equalled all the free states, with
Virginia added. He began with modest self-
depreciation, quite common in really diffident men,
but of doubtful taste, and launched upon his theme.
Evidently the whole subject lay closely within his
mental grasp, and well arranged. He reminded
the southern Whigs what it cost their northern
friends, under the pressure of a growing public
opinion, to maintain the integrity of their common

party, to which was mainly due the prosperity of
the country, and upon which its dependence to
arrest misrule entirely rested. . He then turned to
the authors of the new measure, received everywhere with indignant surprise, terror and horror.
He demanded to know what visitation they had
enjoyed ; what new light had reached them hidden
from the world, as to the effect of the compromise
of 1850 upon that of 1820? He went over with
the later, showed its constant reference to the
older as subsisting, and which its framers with
studious care did their best to respect but which
it was now found they had entirely abrogated, in
spite of themselves. A hard, well-considered, fixed
enactment of congress, solemnly passed, recognized
by the nation and world, had been repealed by an
abstract principle, recently discovered in other legislation. This he unsparingly ridiculed. Douglas
explained and restated. Wade reiterated with
scorn and contempt.

It was said that in adjusting boundaries, New
Mexico, a territory under protection of the acts
of 1820, had been slightly cut into, and thereupon
it is now proclaimed that the acts of 1820 were
repealed as in the whole, notwithstanding the
declaration of the New Mexican act that it did no
such thing. Two owners of adjoining land re-run
their lines. It is found that A has by this received
an inconsiderable slip of B's domain, and thereupon
A claims that both parties have recognized a
principle which has abrogated, repealed, B's title

to the whole, and all A has to do is to take possession of the whole of it. He showed the effect
upon the northern immigration of the presence of
slavery in any region. No northern man, no
foreign born, migrated to a slave state. A freeman
would not make his home in the tainted region of
slave quarters. No freeman would labor by the
side of one degraded by being the mere chattel of
another. The work of a slave was servile, because
done by a slave. No free man would share in it.

He was severe on Dixon, a pupil and the successor of the great Clay, whose last work he was
impiously rending. While going on, Dixon and
Butler of South Carolina were noisily talking, after
the fashion of the south. Butler said Wade believed in the declaration of July fourth, which made
the slave his equal, and why should not equals
work side by side? Wade caught it up with a
flash. Dixon wished to know if he might ask him
a question. He replied that he would cheerfully
permit him and his associate (Butler) to ask him
any question. Dixon wanted to know if he believed the slave was the equal of a free man.
Wade told him he believed he was the born equal
of any man. "By the law of God Almighty your
slave is your equal, and so you will find out at the
day of judgment, though probably not before, at
your rate of progress," was his reply.

This brought up slavery directly, and he rapidly
sketched its effects on the people and country,
which he illustrated by a graphic drawing of Vir-

ginia, and it was proposed to thus Africanize the whole of the new great territory, after the Virginian pattern. He warned all parties north and south, that this would never be submitted to. He thought all compromises were mistakes ; wiser men thought differently, and made them. He acquiesced in them. With this instance of *punic faith*, there never would be another, there never should be another. This ruthless disregard of the compromise of 1820 left that of 1850 open to assault. Let the slaveholder beware.

He began without formal opening and finished with no prepared phrases. He was strong, brave, impressive, and listened to with profound attention.

The speech, as a whole, was one of the best specimens of the strong, plain, direct, vigorous putting of things by the clear, hard-headed, honest intellect of the New England type, to be found in the records of congress, and did much to strengthen Mr. Wade in the senate and through the country. It admonished men to beware of a close struggle, where fibrous pluck, hard muscle and manhood would tell.

The debate ran on, all the senators took voice in it, and on the morning of fourth of March, as the gray outer light mingled with the lights of the senate chamber, the vote was taken. Houston of Texas closed the debate with a strong speech against the bill. It passed—thirty-seven for to fourteen against it, and salvos of cannon, as on the

passage of the ten million Texas bill in the house,
advertised the still sleeping city of the deed.
Pearce of Maryland, even Clayton, who had voted
for the Wilmot proviso, voted for it. John Bell
stood with Houston against it. It was carried
through the corridors across the rotunda to the
house, where after nearly three months of stormy
debates, the cannon again announced its passage.
One hundred and fourteen voted for, and one
hundred against it. Forty-four northern Democrats voted against it; no northern Whig voted
for it. Seven southern Whigs voted against it,
and three southern Democrats, Houston, Thomas
Hart Benton* and John S. Millson of Virginia.†

George E. Badger of North Carolina was an
able man, a facile speaker, and, like many such
men, took much oral exercise standing. In the
Nebraska debate he made a pathetic, moving appeal to the opponents of the bill—personal really.
He described himself as wishing to emigrate to the
new territory, and carry his old colored *mamma*
with him—the woman who had nursed him in infancy and childhood, and whom he loved as a real
mother—and he could not take her. The enemies
of this benevolent measure forbade him. "We
are willing you should take the old lady there—"

---

* Colonel Benton passed from public life with that congress.
He devoted his remaining years to his work—'Thirty Years in
the Senate,' and died at Washington, April 10, 1858, at seventy-six.

† John S. Millson was re-elected to the thirty-fourth, thirty-fifth and
thirty-sixth congresses, was steadily devoted to the Union, and died at
Norfolk, his native city, February 26, 1873.

interrupted Wade, "*we are afraid you'll sell her when you get her there.*" It settled the tender senator, followed as it was by a universal roar of laughter. He made an ineffective effort to recover, and closed most abruptly. It was one of those stinging things that reduce an issue to a killing point, that precludes reply, escape or farther argument.‡

The session ran on till August 7, when the misrulers returned to meet their still amazed and indignant constituencies.

I have now with much breadth traced my Feeding Hills boy to a prominent, soon to be a leading, position in the senate, where his history is part of the history of his time. I have also rapidly sketched the rise and progress of the great struggles against slavery, to the passage of the Kansas–Nebraska act, when its history becomes the history of the country. My theme must now be subjected to a more rapid treatment, a more condensed grouping of events and men.

---

‡ The late Judge Jerry Black always spoke of this as the most effective single blow ever dealt a man, a cause or an argument, in the history of congress. It was rare, he said, that the conditions for such a reply could exist, and rarer still that a man was present equal to making it To fully appreciate it requires a study of the whole field and an apprehension of all the factors involved.

CHAPTER VIII.

WHATEVER may be the faiths of men, there are no indications of God in the affairs of modern nations or peoples. That their moral qualities, alike of men and methods, do directly work in the line of the elevation or depression of a people, carry them forward or backward, is abundantly apparent, without the supposed agency of an overruling Providence. A religious faith influences only as it helps to form individual character.

One of the most potent of human forces, the ruler who takes no account of it, is reckless or badly equipped. The profoundly religious man who acknowledges his daily obligation to a higher power, will see God in the affairs of men, whether his rulers take account of it or not. That faith in

God, whether enlightened or merely blind, had a large share in the causes of the great pending revolution is too obvious for proof, as its influence was too subtle to be segregated and discussed, even by a historian of philosophical tendency.   In the great congressional struggle just closed—interrupted for a day really—the most striking phenomenon was the memorial of the three thousand New England clergy, presented in the senate by Mr. Everett.   That it made a profound and wide, probably a lasting, impression is undoubtedly true.   It was at once debated, denounced and deferred to. That it called forth countervailing clerical labors on the part of the southern pastorate, was well-known. That men usually manage to believe what they wish to be true, is a law of the human mind, and the peoples of both sides were unconsciously prepared to secure the aid of the God they severally worshiped, when his help would be most needed.

Just when the southern leaders formed the resolution of secession is not known.   The idea was long a familiar one.   They lost in the admission of California as a free state, due mainly to Mr. Clay, the one thing gained by the north.   That they hoped to regain the lost balance in the senate by new states carved from Nebraska, won from the north, is unquestioned.   Failing with a connecting slave state, Kansas, California would secede with them.   True, so long as the Democracy of that hemisphere were false to their position as

northern freemen, they were safe. They were
soon to see Douglas repudiated in Illinois and
Cass in Michigan. True, the besotted Whigs would
aid in ridding them of Chase in Ohio for the time.
The struggle would be for the final possession of
Kansas. They formed their "Social Bands," "Blue
Lodges," and "Sons of the South," gathered up
two or three hundred slaves, and crossed the Missouri in the spring of 1854. The north was astir
with her " Emigrant aid societies, " and later her
Springfield rifles. Of all the forms of human association, slaveholders are the feeblest of colonizers.
In but one, the old way of the barbarians, was the
dominion of Kansas possible to them. They must
go in a body—a whole people—abandon their ancient seats, take homes and hovels, leave their older
domain a solitude, and thus secure the new. Of
all forms of property in the wide, empty plains,
slaves would be the least certain, the most fuga-
cious, beyond the utmost reach of fugitive slave
laws. Mr. Pierce at once appointed A. H. Reeder,
"a sound, national, constitutional, Conservative
Democrat"—it took a good many adjectives then
to name a Pierce Democrat—governor of Kansas.
He was an upright man. He ordered an election.
The wild riders and raiders of Missouri camped in
Kansas, elected themselves, assembled in legislature, and made it felony to deny the divine existence
of slavery in Kansas. Reeder repudiated their
legislature and vetoed all their bills. Pierce repudiated and vetoed him, and sent Wilson Shannon

—mellifluous name—to misrule in his stead.　I am only to send the younger generation to read up the tradegy of Kansas—" Bleeding Kansas " as the Democrats derisively called it.*

The transition period intervening between the fall of the Whig party and the rise of the Republican was brief.　The southern wing disappeared in the Democratic.　The northern reappeared in the Republican, save a few fossilized and very respectable elderly men, known as Silver Grays of the John Bell and Edward Everett school.†　That short time was one of conventions, arrangements, fusions and the reign of the Knownothings north, and which extended into the south, where it was under the lead of Henry Winter Davis, Humphrey Marshall, and the alway melancholy Horace Maynard.　Its leaders north were many.　Its stay so brief that it would be now useless and difficult to identify them.‡　They were largely the disappointed —the failures of the old parties, of course.　A successful man never leaves his party or sighs for a new one.　Nor does a successful party dissolve.　A new question sometimes arises to which existing

---

*They will find the latest an admirable account of it in Professor Leverett W. Spring's Kansas, of Houghton, Mifflin & Company's, ' American Commonwealths,' recently published.

+ A Silver Gray Whig was aptly described as an eminently respectable gentleman who took the *National Intelligencer* (of Gales & Seaton), drank the best brandy and voted the Democratic ticket.

‡ Called itself the American party, as one sung of the autumn leaf,
　　　" Its hold is frail, its stay is brief ;
　　　Restless and quick to pass away."
　　　　　　　　—*Wild's Southern Rose.*

parties are unequal. If of pressing moment, it makes for itself a new party ; when the remnants of the old unite against it. There never can be but two. This is a time of many factions, ere new formations appear with crystallization and growth. This was such a period of our national history, of which some thoughtful man will some time give us a most interesting study, which will involve the law of the rise, rule, and fall of political parties. Our history is rich with the material.

Mr. Chase failing of reëlection to the senate was nominated by a Fusion body and elected governor of Ohio by over fifteen thousand in 1855. A state convention of Michigan first took the old name Republican, assumed by the first national convention at Philadelphia.

Meantime another Presidential election was approaching and Florizell, the President, must " face a frowning world," and as so many men of his brief day had, will find himself utterly devoured by the relentless power he so weakly and willingly served—men who learned nothing from what they saw and who, save as examples, did not survive their experiences.

Some new names appeared in the Thirty-fourth congress. The most conspicuous in the senate were Lyman Trumbull from Illinois and Henry Willson of Massachusetts. J. J. Crittenden reappeared, as did Mr. Hale. Ohio contributed not only a new senator, Pugh, but John Sherman,

John A. Bingham, Samuel Galloway and Phile-
mon Bliss to the house, which now had the three
historic brothers Washburn from three states.
Francis E. Spinner and Justin S. Morrill both
appeared there for the first time, as did Colfax.
Preston S. Brooks was there from South Carolina
—was in the last house. Anson Burlingame was
elected to this house, a Knownothing from Boston.
That was the house which elected N. P. Banks*
speaker after a protracted struggle. He was
voted for exclusively by the north ; not a southern vote was cast for him. This was the first
purely sectional election. As in the greater
ensuing Presidential elections, the south refused
to vote for either northern candidate, and made
this refusal a pretext for denouncing the elections
as sectional.

The first thing now was "Bleeding Kansas."
Hitherto the great ulcer had produced irritations,
sores, eruptions in various other parts and forms.
The presence of the slave was everywhere, and
everywhere north it was offensive. It had now
transplanted itself north. The feet of nearly three
hundred slaves were burning the soil of Kansas,
profaning her bosom and polluting her air.
Henceforth she was the one cause, the field of

---

* Banks entered the Thirty-third congress as a coalition Democrat,
to the present as a Knownothing. Had been speaker of the Massachusetts house of representatives, and president of her last constitutional convention. His defects of character defeated the prophecy of
his young manhood.

strife. As fared slavery in Kansas, so fares slavery in the Republic.

> Who foremost sheds a foeman's life,
> That party conquers in the strife,

though none foresaw it.

Kansas of the many constitutions—four, at least, voted upon by her people, and others, in cluding that of Lecompton, the pure product of slavery, which were finally submitted. She was the one thing to dissolve and reconstruct parties north, solidify the south, create and destroy men, strip the thin veneering of civilization from slaveholders, their servitors and lackeys in congress, convert and con duct the two sections to armed hosts confronting each other in war actual.

The bondmen's masters who sought by outrages to possess the youngest of the daughters, were strangled by her, sustained as she was by her northern sisters, and she took her proper place with them under the Wyandotte constitution January 29, 1861, seven years and a few days from the fatal introduction of the Nebraska bill by Stephen A. Douglas—seven years of chronic war thus initiated, to serve the vulgar ambition of an arrant dema gogue, was the fitting, educating process leading up to the contest instantly to follow, which yet no one saw or suspected.

A rapid survey, a glance at some of its inci dents and salient points, with which Mr. Wade was personally connected, must be taken.

Kansas thus at once became the subject of

stormy debates in both houses, in the course of
which Butler, of South Carolina—who to his
graces as a chivalrous Carolinian often added the
inspiration of wine, its distilled spirits and of
vulgar whiskey—made a speech quite under the
usual elevating influence.   The southerners
were so accustomed to vituperative abuse of the
north and its delegates that they were unconscious
of the force of the terms and manner they indulged
in.   Butler made a bad exhibition of himself,
"scattering the loose expectoration of his speech,'
as Sumner described it, over his person, desk and
surroundings.   Some time elapsed when Sumner,
in the fullness of his own time and preparation,
also discussed Kansas, under which head, as all
on both sides had done, he discussed the whole
subject of slavery, and for quite the first time discussed slaveholders and their bearing in the
senate *ad hominem*.   In the course of his speech
he made contemptuous—not unjust—reference to
Senator Butler and his performance.   It was a
graphic, condensed, painful speech.*

At the recess the northern senators went out,
leaving Sumner in his seat, with many of the
southeners sitting about him—as if the whole

---

* It is said that both Wade and Seward regretted it—as much of
the speech. It was said also, and among Republicans, that Sumner
was dissatisfied with his position before the country, and that this lent
bitterness and acrimony to his speech of that twenty-second of May.
It certainly was the most awful phillipic ever pronounced against
slavery, and in the senator's thunderous voice and face aflame, little
wonder that its effect was so maddening on the chronic exacerbated
southerners and their allies.

thing was not over, when Preston S. Brooks of
South Carolina, a kinsman of Butler, approached
him, bent over his writing-desk and dealt him a
heavy and stunning blow upon the head with a
stout cane. Sumner was in his prime, and, though
a student, was of large mould, healthy, and must
have had great strength. With one mighty, instinc-
tive effort he wrenched the solid oaken desk from its
fastenings, nearly gained his feet, when a second
furious blow felled him, where his cowardly assailant
continued to beat him until he shattered his heavy
bludgeon. Toombs and other southern senators
were near. Douglas was not remote. Not a man
went to his rescue or made sign or note of disap-
proval. The senate chamber was a part of Kansas.
E. B. Morgan of Aurora, New York—of the house—
happened to enter the senate chamber and ran to
the nearly insensible, bleeding man's aid, when
Brooks prudently desisted. Sumner was borne
out from the presence of his scowling, rejoicing
foes. What they said to each other after he departed they never reported. Brooks made the
only reply to him ever attempted in the senate.

On the next day a committee of five was raised
by ballot in the senate, consisting of Pearce of
Maryland, Cass, Allen, Dodge and Geyer—all
Democrats, all enemies. Mr. Cass had the smallest
number of votes. Mr. Pearce reported without
much delay. The assault was by a member of the
house. The senate was without jurisdiction.
There was a studious silence of the quality of the

act, though committed in the senate chamber during a session, and in the presence of many senators
—a silence sufficiently expressive.   A pure *negative pregnant*, of the old lawyers, not misunderstood.   Nor did the committee intend that it
should be.   The house promptly sent Mr. Brooks
to a committee.   Mr. Sumner's deposition was
taken at his lodgings.   The publication of it
called out explanation on the part of Messrs.
Slidell, Douglas, Toombs and Butler.   The severest condemnation of these men rests on the page
of the *Globe*, which preserves their preconsidered
statements.   Mr. Slidell denied the statement that
he was in the senate chamber at the instant.   In a
room adjoining a page rushed in and said Mr.
Brooks was beating Mr. Sumner.   He had no interest in the Massachusetts senator.   Later the
boy came back and said it was over, and he went
out, saw Mr. Sumner borne by him — was
the substance in very many words, contrived
to express satisfaction without saying it.   The
most humiliating to an American was the
column of words uttered by Douglas.*   He
said he was present, knew Brooks assaulted
Sumner, a crowd gathered about them, and he
could not see exactly what occurred, and *soon went*

---

* It is impossible almost to find Douglas anywhere in the *Globe*
where he appears to advantage. I know it is said he redeemed himself
in 1861.   What was left for him—repudiated north, maltreated south ?
He doubtless felt the sting of humiliation and resentment.   He was
not needed.   He received twelve electoral votes in 1860 ; and died
June 3, 1861.

out. The bold, bad Toombs, referred to by Slidell, corroborated him. Said he was present, saw the whole transaction, *and approved it.* Four lines give his speech. Space too much. Wade arose within arm's length of the savage, face livid, eyes flashing, hands clenched:

Mr President—It is impossible for me to sit still and hear the principles announced which I have now heard here. I know nothing, say nothing of the facts ,involved. I am here in a lean minority. Not a fifth of the senate entertain my views. They are very unpopular here; but when I hear it stated on the floor of the senate, that an *assassin-like, cowardly* attack has been made on an unarmed man, powerless to defend himself—was stricken with a strong hand, and almost murdered, and that such attacks are approved by senators, it becomes a question of interest to us all, and especially to the minority. It is true that a brave man may not be able to defend himself against such an attack. A brave man may be overpowered by numbers on this floor, but sir, overborne or not, live or die, I will vindicate the right and liberty of debate and the freedom of discussion upon this floor, so long as I live. If the principle now here announced prevail, let us come armed for the contest, and although *you are four to one* I AM HERE TO MEET YOU. God knows a man can die in no better cause than in the vindication of the right of debate on this floor. and I only ask if the majority approve the announcement made, make it a part of our parliamentary law, that we may understand it.*

The world held its breath or drew it with tremors. Here were the sons of chivalry defied

---

* Real lightning—God's article—had never before flashed in the senate chamber and struck senators in their curule chairs. I am permitted here to give a private note of James C. Welling, LL. D., president of Columbian college, distinguished for scholarship and an accomplished historical writer. I am glad to have a graphic account of the same by such an eye witness :

WASHINGTON, May 6, 1886.

MY DEAR MR. RIDDLE :—Many thanks for a copy of the April number of the Magazine of Western History, containing the contribution of your interesting biography of "Brave Ben Wade." I have read this installment with the greatest curiosity and interest, because the earlier part of it relates to the time when, as an enthusiastic boy shouting for "old Tippecanoe," I first began to watch the drift of

with the terms assassin and cowardly, applied by a
man of the north.   It was known that he was of
heroic descent.   Of course it devolved on Toombs
to call him to account.*

American politics. And that humorous speech of Tom Corwin, "the
user-up of Crary," as the boys loved to call him in 1840! Why, I
could then repeat whole paragraphs of it for the confusion of the Van
Buren boys in the Ironton academy, where I was preparing for college.

I shall never forget the defiant atitude of Mr. Wade in the senate of
the United States a few days after the assault of Brooks on Senator
Sumner. In the course of some "personal explanations" made by
Senator Slidell and others who had witnessed that outrage, Toombs of
Georgia openly avowed that he had witnessed the assault, and that he
approved it, too! This was more than Wade could stand. I can see
him now as he rose in his place, while Toombs was in the act of
sitting down—his seat was very near to that of Toombs—and he began
at once, with great vehemence of speech, to throw down the gage of
personal combat, then and there to the southern senators, if the
bludgeon was to be their weapon of argument in that stage of the controversy. Alternately rising on the tips of his boots and sinking with
all his weight on his heels, he thundered defiance alike with voice and
eye as he gave emphasis to his periods with his sturdy fist pounding
on the desk before him. Turning to Toombs he exclaimed : "If the
principle now announced here is to prevail, let us come armed for the
combat, and although you are four to one, I am here to meet you."
The very air of the senate chamber was tremulous with passion.

The fiery speaker cast a withering look at Toombs as he resumed
his seat, yet that thrasonical statesman did not adventure a word in
reply.

But I am trenching on an episode in the life of Senator Wade to
which you can do better justice in all its aspects, and so I will forbear,
simply pausing long enough to repeat the thanks, with which I am, my
dear Mr. Riddle,

Very truly yours,

James C. Welling.

As Dr. Welling advises me the *Globe* index contains no reference to
Wade's speech, I found it by going through the *Globe* bodily.

* James Watson Webb, founder of the once great *Courier and En-
quirer*, who had an affair with Tom Marshall, a friend and admirer of
Wade's, sought him, in company with J. A. Briggs of Ohio, another
friend and admirer, the evening after the speeches, to be of service if
required. They found him in his usual pleasant state, and Colonel
Webb was amazed that no challenge had been received. He was
certain Toombs had been in council with his friends, who would require it of him. He wished to know his intentions if one came. Wade
said his constituents to a man, perhaps, were opposed to the code. This
was his affair. It was an exceptional time. In his judgment nothing

Mr. Wade's personal matter with Senator Clayton occurred this season. It grew out of all fruitful Kansas, on which the Delawareian made a speech. Mr. Wade detected matter reflecting upon himself personally, which he was sure had not been spoken. On reference to the reporter, who had not destroyed his character notes, his suspicion was confirmed. He quietly called the senator's attention to it, and, failing to have the matter set right, took notice of it in a way to provoke much comment. It is said the diplomatic senator had the address to ascertain how an invitation to the field would be received by this descendant of the Puritans. The result did not incline him to send

---

could be more salutary than the firm punishment of one of these southern braggarts. He was asked what would be his terms. He replied, "The rifle and thirty paces." He was cool, determined ; was a dead shot, and had his rifle in the city. His position was painful to the last degree. He betrayed no signs of it. The few intimates about him expected a meeting, and fatal to the southern. They said, "Pin a paper to Toombs' bosom the size of a quarter coin and Wade's bullet would certainly cut it." The next and the next day passed and no call. On the third both were in their seats. Toombs reached his hand over and placed it on Wade's shoulder saying : " Wade, what is the use of two men making damned fools of themselves?"

"None at all—but it is the misfortune of some men that they can't help it," was the good-humored reply ; and they were really good friends from that day on. Once later the fiery southern made an onset, this time coupling Wade with Seward. The philosophic New York senator went to the cloak-room at its commencement, lit a cigar, and stood in the door enjoying it. Wade took the floor and flashed back a few caustic words.

Toombs boasted in the senate of being "as good a rebel as ever sprang from revolutionary loins." He was at feud with Jefferson Davis, and made small figure after leaving the senate—one of the few blustering men of very great ability. His death occurred recently.

a missive. The matter lingered with a flavor in
the atmosphere. Mr. Clayton found an opening to
an interview, in which Wade good-naturedly said
that "it ought to be regarded as barred by the
statute of limitations." Mr. Clayton died the following November.

It may be stated that Brooks was saved expulsion by the south—the majority against him being
less than two-thirds.*

It was a little after this time that the chronic insolence of the slaveholders in both houses, and
especially in the senate, led to the conviction and
determination on the part of three conspicuous
northern senators to resent these aggressions, and
meet the foe on their own favorite field, a determination which took the form of a league, "a compact." Years afterward the senators as a testimo-
nial of the times, and their final method of dealing
with some of the difficulties besetting them, executed the memorandum given in the note below,
now first made public. Its language and structure
would lead to the inference that it was to some

---

* He resigned, was unanimously re-elected—also a second time.
The last to the thirty-fifth congress. He is said to have been presented several hundred canes. He died very suddenly of diphtheria, at
Washington, in January, 1857. He challenged Burlingame for words
spoken on his case, but declined to follow him for the meeting—"across
the enemy's country " to Canada, the place named. It will be remembered that Mr. Sumner's condition was jeered and sneered at by the
southern senators until he returned to his seat. He undoubtedly received a severe spinal injury, which soon developed, and he went abroad
for treatment, where he remained for years, Massachusetts keeping
him nominally in the senate. He never fully recovered. His attitude
was infirm, his step shaky.

extent dictated to a secretary by Mr. Wade, the
only paper deliberately made by him to perpetuate
historical matter that has come to my notice :

MEMORANDUM. — During the two or three years preceding the
outbreak of the slaveholders' rebellion, the people of the free states
suffered a deep humiliation because of the abuse heaped upon their
representatives in both houses of congress by their colleagues from the
slave states.

This gross personal abuse was borne by many because the public
sentiment of their section would have fallen with crushing severity
upon them if they had retorted in the only manner in which it
could be effectively met and stopped, by the personal punishment
of their insulters.

Mr. William H. Seward was the especial object of these insults,
and, he being the admitted leader of the Republicans in the senate,
all men were insulted through him. Whether from philosopical
serenity of temper, or from a positive lack of physical courage, he
took these premeditated insults with a calmness which set many of
his followers frantic with rage and shame. On one noted occasion Mr.
Robert Toombs indulged in such terrible unjust denunciation of Seward
and his followers, that the undersigned felt themselves forced to do
something to vindicate themselves and their constituents, threatened
by these means of a denial of equal representation in the senate.

We consulted long and anxiously, and the result was a league by
which we bound ourselves to resent any repetition of this conduct
by *challenge to fight*, and then, in the precise words, the compact " *to
carry the quarrel into a coffin.*"

After the lapse of half a generation the statement of this arrangement of this measure may have the appearance of bloodthirstiness, but
it should be remembered that the causes which led to it were extremely
grievous. Our constituents were well nigh deprived of their rights in
congress by the insolence of our political oponents. Our very manhood was daily called in question. Only one method of stopping the
now [then] unendurable outrage was open, and that method required
us to submit (because of the sentiment against duelling at home) to an
ostracism if we defended ourselves, as galling as the endurance of the
insults we encountered in the pursuit of our public duties. Nevertheless this arrangement produced a cessation of the cause which induced
us to make it, and when it became known that some northern senators
were ready to fight for sufficient cause, the tone of their assailants
were at once modified.

We have drawn up and signed this paper as an interesting incident for those who come after us to study, as an example of what it once cost to be in favor of liberty, and to express such sentiments in the highest places of official life in the United States.

This is a confidential memorandum. Only three copies exist, and we have each placed the copy we [severally] possess in our private and confidential papers, subject only to our order.

(Signed)   SIMON CAMERON,
B. F. WADE,
L. CHANDLER.

WASHINGTON, May 26, 1874.

Though in terms confidential the paper was intended to be at some time made public. Obviously no harm can now accrue to the dead or living by permitting it to transpire. It is given here as written, with slight change in punctuation.

The year 1856 was memorable for the Fremont campaign—Fremont the Pathfinder, whom brave Jessie Benton ran away with, bless her eyes! Fremont, the eighteen-day senator of Free California—a half myth alike of history and romance—one of the badly-used generals of the war.

Mr. Seward was unquestionably the leading man. His sagacious adviser, Thurlow Weed, thought his day was not yet. His candidacy that year would have secured it in 1860. Mr. Chase did not care for it. Judge John McLean alway wanted it. He was old, too old for fresh, rosy *Republica*. The Blairs brought forward Fremont. He was nominated at Philadelphia in June. Wm. L. Dayton of New Jersey was placed with him on the ticket. New Jersey has furnished several defeated candidates for vice-president.

The Democrats were obliged to pass their really

best man, stout Sam Houston. His nomination
would have been a rebuke to their entire brood south.
Pierce and Douglas made persistent efforts. Pierce
sent Buchanan on the English mission, and this
brought him the golden opportunity to become the
saddest, the most unhappy figure of American history. He received 135 on the first ballot to 122
for the President, and 33 for Douglas. Pierce ran
down to half of one and was withdrawn. On the
sixteenth, Buchanan was nominated, and Breckenridge had the second place with him.

The Knownothings (American) had speedily
split on slavery. The adherents of "the peculiar,"
and the shadows remaining of the Whigs, placed
Fillmore and A. J. Donaldson in nomination also.
What a ghostly business was that! There was
never such a mingling of the present with the past
and future, as that campaign presented.

Mr. Buchanan carried every southern state but
Maryland; and New Jersey, Pennsylvania, Indiana,
Illinois and California, 174 votes. The remaining
free states, eleven in number, from Maine round
to Iowa, cast their votes for Fremont—114.
Maryland, in the realms of shadow, gave her eight
to Fillmore. The popular vote was—Democrats
1,838,169; Republicans, 1,341,264; Americans,
874,534. Buchanan thus reached the Presidency
with a majority of 407,629 against him. The
Democrats were greatly chagrined by the result.
The Republicans were entirely satisfied. They were
fully aware that they at the time were not ripe for

power. The future was theirs as they belonged
to it by aspiration. Under the emphasis of the
results of the election, the remaining session of the
Thirty-fourth congress assembled and wore and
warred Kansas through to March 3, 1857.

Mr. Buchanan had a good deal of dead wood
lying about all over the north, from which a cabinet might be constructed. He naturally, almost
necessarily, placed Cass—then seventy-five years
old—at the head. From his own state he selected
Jeremiah S. Black for attorney-general—by no
means dead wood—the ablest man, with the widest
acquisition, of his party. Of almost wonderful
force and energy of character, he was still without
perceptible personal following. From the south
he took Cobb and Floyd and Jake Thompson,
with Toucy for the navy. Toucy was dead enough.

That was also the year marked by the Dred Scott
decision. That should have surprised no one.
The judges, not walled in by precedent, were left
to the influence of unconscious bias—as in the electoral commission of 1876. It was expected that
slavery would greatly profit by this judicial aid.
Its besotted advocates could not see that whatever strengthened it south, where it was resistless, must weaken it north ; that the united north
would depose it, and that deposed, it would die—no
matter what immediate agencies were employed by
them. The Dred Scott decision equalled the fugitive slave act as an exciting cause. These and
Kansas would be all sufficient. This, the first

judgment of the supreme court that became an exciting popular theme, was added—a fresh emphasizing cause of contention in the ensuing congress. The court sat in the half beehive-shaped room below—east-front, at the right as one passes the main lower entrance, now occupied by the Congressional Law library.* It sat quite under the senators, who with great freedom called in question its decision, arraigned and condemned it, and almost within hearing of the tribunes of the people in the other house, who consecrated it to derision and ridicule.

If we glance at the Thirty-fifth congress we shall discover some noteworthy changes and additions. Broderick was there in the senate from California, and Harlan from Iowa. Cass had yielded to Chandler. Preston King succeeded Hamilton Fish. Simon Cameron entered that senate, as did . Simmons from Rhode Island. So also came Doolittle from Wisconsin. In the house Owen Lovejoy, Farnsworth, Henry L. Dawes, L. Q. C. Lamar and Frances C. Blair, jr. New York contributed an unusual number of new names to become notable. Among them Corning, Fenton, Olin and Sickles. Ohio's new names to grow conspicuous were several, Cox, Groesbeck, Pendleton, Vallandigham—all Democrats, of course, while William Lawrence was added to the Republicans. Maynard made his first appearance there at this congress. Houston found a seat in that house now, where he had been be-

---

*Said now to be the largest law library of the world,

fore. Seven territories were represented in that body also.

The long session began December 7, 1857, and ended the fourteenth of June, 1858. A notable incident of it was the presentation by Pugh of the resolutions of the Ohio legislature (by the majority, of course), crouching, like Issachar, between two burdens, now glorifying the Cincinnati platform, on which Buchanan was elected. Pugh, on their presentation, delivered one of the finest of his finished orations, quite for the hour enchaining the galleries. Wade, who had meantime been reëlected, came down upon the impudent and impertinent contribution of the Ohio Democracy with good-natured contempt. He showed the value of this indorsement of the platform by Ohio, whose people, since its promulgation, had cast a majority of sixty thousand votes against it. For the rest, a few well-directed blows left the thing in ruins past patching. He had now, by steady attention to his duties, his practical good sense, freedom from mistakes, large intelligence, his clearness and certainty of vision, honesty and absolute sincerity, grown to a leading, a commanding and entirely independent position in the senate. He had come to be not one of the oftenest heard, but one of the alway listened to, debaters, never speaking unless to add something to the volume of the right understanding of the subject in hand. He might not alway say anything new, nor old things in a new way. His judgment was admirable. He saw quick and clear ; was capable of prejudices. His mind was honest. He was brave in the utterance of his convictions. Men came to have trust in his level, practical views. They alway gave weight to the side he took on all non-partisan things. There are many things national, common to all men, policies, courses, conducts, to be pursued, that occupy much time, involve real doubt, about which all men want to be right. On all these the question was, " What does old Ben Wade say about it ?" He usually came in late, with well considered views, and the thing was not regarded as thoroughly debated till he was heard. Men, after all, are more influenced by weight and strength of character. Men of these qualifications have alway been true governors. Thus estimated, our senator had few peers. He never referred to the people—his constituents —probably cared little what they thought. The thing he believed he said, the thing right he did. Time lapsed. Many things were considered— grave and numerous—the homestead scheme, a Pacific railroad. Many things, in the presence, under the shadow of the great coming events, so ominously cast before, and for which the discussions, the irritations of the great growing and ever growing great issues—the very brooding over which by the reticent northern mind, admirably and all unconsciously, fitted the people for, while they conducted them now rapidly to the battle's edge.

The year 1858 came with the state elections—
elections for the house of the Thirty-sixth congress. The second session lapsed, and the spring
and summer of 1859, with incipient steps for the
decisive contest of 1860, in which empire was to
be lost and won—the Republic's fate for good or
ill to be cast.

The old causes of political war with new features and incidents constantly recurring, had
become chronic. Comparative peace and quiet
were the rule over the northern states, as at the
south. Summer ripened, passed September, and
the season lapsed to serene October, ran to its
middle, passed that. Can any man now tell how,
of whom he first heard it—the strangest thing in
American history? It stole upon men's con-
sciousness in a day of absolute serene repose, that
seventeenth of October, 1859. John Brown at the
head of an armed band—seventeen—was in possession of the armory—the arsenal—at Harper's Ferry,
had fortified it, was besieged by a Virginian army
there. Never such a prodigy dropped from the
serene heavens on the unexpectant earth, nor
ever one of more awful portent. Men did not
believe it. It grew upon them—was true. The
north had heard of John Brown. What they had
heard came warped, refracted by the Kansas atmosphere. They knew nothing of the darker lines
and shades, if not stains, which, estimated in the
white light of to-day, make men wish to account
for as the product of a sadly unbalanced intellect.

That really was the tocsin ringing out through the land—heard through all lands—the foe is coming! Arm! Arm! On the reassembling of congress scarcely had the senate come together on call, when Mason of Virginia offered his resolution of investigation into that deplorable affair.

It was the hope, the expectation, to fasten at least the odium, probably the responsibility, of this hair-brained adventure upon anti-slavery Republican north. Mr. Trumbull moved an important amendment. No Republican opposed investigation. The southern leaders were first heard—bitter, denunciatory, yet with a common air of self-gratulation, of incipient triumph. Abolitionism was about to be delivered into their hands. The account of blood scored against them in Kansas would now be set off, balanced. Mr. Wade addressed the senate early in the debate. He would not speak but for the extraordinary language of the Virginia senators. Obviously the intention was to swell the present great volume of public excitement. He had been specially referred to. It was declared that one purpose was to ascertain the feeling of the north in regard to the act. The purpose to make it *particeps* in sympathy. Mr. Mason explained. His colleague, Hunter, may have said some such thing. Mr. Wade cared little which of them said it. He sketched the career of Brown in Kansas, spoke of his personal qualities, of his march on Harper's Ferry, quoted Governor Wise's encomium of him, and showed the absurdity of attempting to make the north responsible for him ; quoted the declarations of the older great southern men from Jefferson to Clay against slavery, to show how widely and fatally the south had departed from their teachings. The tone of the whole was moderate, the temper admirable. I quote an average passage :

Do I stand here to accuse a gentleman who is a slaveholder of the south with crime? I have never done so. You may say that if we regard slavery as wrong, and as a robbery of the rights of men, we should accuse you of being criminal. Well sir, the logic would seem to be good enough, were it not modified by the fact that with you it is deemed a necessity. I do not know what you can do with it ; I was almost about to say that I do not care what you do with it ; I will say, it is none of my business what you do with it, and I never undertake to interfere with it. To be sure, believing it to be wrong—wrong to yourselves and wrong to those whom you hold in this abject condition —I wish that you could see the light as I see it ; but if you do not, it is a matter of your own concern, and not of mine. I can very well have charity towards you, because with all my opposition to your institution, I can hardly doubt that if we had changed places, and my lot had been cast among you, under like circumstances, my opinions on this subject might be different, and I might be here, perhaps, as fierce a fire-eater as I am now defending against fire. I can understand these things, and I accuse no man.

This was the man who defied Toombs. He was in the ascendant now.

John Sherman had already gained the enmity of the southerners. Had been assailed on the floor of the senate. Thus Mr. Wade defended him :

There is one thing more which I will notice in passing. The senator from Georgia [Mr. Iverson] saw fit, in his place in the senate, to assail my colleague in the house of representatives (Mr. Sherman), and to impeach him because of a transaction which he characterized as exceedingly dishonorable, and which he thought should go to destroy

that confidence that is reposed in one so situated. When I heard his
denunciations I was happy to find that the senator did not accuse Mr.
Sherman of any erroneous vote, or of any wrong action. Mr. Sherman's course, in the other branch of congress, has been known of all
men for some four years past. He has been a very active and a very
worthy member ; and if there is anything wrong in any principle that
he had advocated or any vote that he has given, I am sure that the
vigilance of that astute senator would have found it out. I say, then, I
was exceedingly gratified to find that my friend in the other house was so
little assailable upon this floor, or anywhere else. We consider him as
one of the brightest ornaments of the state of Ohio. That great state
seeks to do him honor, and I rejoice to know that the great party to
which I belong repose in him the utmost confidence. They have found
nothing in him but what they approve ; and the senator, after all his
investigations, could not find more than this, that Mr. Sherman had
recommended the circulation of a certain book.* Now, I want to ask
the senator if there is anything in that book that he thinks dangerous
to the people of any section of this country? I want to know from that
senator if he believes that book cannot safely be intrusted to the hands
of any freeman in this government? The senator does not choose to
answer me.

Mr. Iverson. Mr. President, I do not choose to stultify myself by
answering any such question as that. It is too apparent to any man
of common sense who has read the book, what would be the effect if
its recommendations were carried out.

Mr. Wade. Well, sir, since the question has been up, I have taken
some pains to look through that book, and I find nothing there but arguments addressed by a non slaveholder of a slaveholding state to his
fellow non-slaveholders in those states, laying down rules and regula-
tions for their proceedings, and arguing this great question of slavery
as it affects the interests of non-slaveholders in the slaveholding states.
Unless such arguments are unlawful there, I see nothing in the book
but what is proper for the consideration of all men, who take an interest in these matters. Why, sir, has it come to this, in free America,
that there must be a censorship of the press instituted—that a man can

---

* 'Impending crisis of the South,' by Hinton Rowan Helper of North
Carolina—must be the book—presenting a sharp and startling eco-
nomic view of slave and free industries contrasted, now forgotten. Mr.
Helper secured a recommendation of it by many members of the house.
He and his book were banished the south, and the gentlemen indors-
ing it, one and all, tabooed by southern men.

not give currency to a book containing arguments that he thinks essentially affect the rights of whole classes of the free population of this nation? I hope not, and I believe not.

Why, sir, the great body of the statistical information in that book, as I read it, is drawn from the census of the United States, from your public documents, and from the archives of the nation. Is it improper that arguments deduced from these sources should be addressed to the free population of this country anywhere? If they may not be, it is the hardest argument against the institution I have yet heard. If we really have an institution that we cherish—are seeking to spread over our land, so delicate in its texture that the free people can not have information that they themselves claim— I say again, it is fraught with an inference more fatal to that institution than any I have heard of yet.

The following, the closing paragraphs, are a fair specimen of his method and style of speech, as of his dealing with the southerns:

Mr. President, I have pursued this subject much further than I intended when I arose. I have heard the muttering thunder of disunion greeting my ears through all the southern hemisphere. . All your principal papers have already fixed upon a contingency when this Union shall end. In some of the southern states, if I read aright, proceedings are pending now, having for their object an overturning of this government, and the erection upon its ruins of a southern Confederacy ; and this idea is brought into the halls of congress, and we are compelled to listen by the hour to speeches, filled with denunciations of our party, telling us that the Union is to be dissolved if the people elect as President an honorable man, of a great predominant party, holding to principles precisely such as the old fathers of the government held. The Republican platform is nothing more nor less than the old Republican platform, marking the land-marks of the government as laid down by them. We claim no more ; we claim to live up to those doctrines ; we claim not to harm the hair of the head of any section of this Union; and yet we are to be told by the hour that if we succeed in wresting this government from your hands, and placing a constitutional man in that great office, according to the forms of the constitution, you will nevertheless make this a contingency on which you will disrupt and destroy the government.

I say to gentlemen on the other side, these are very harsh doctrines to preach in our ears. What, sir, are you going to play this game with go into the election with us, with a settled purpose and design, that if you win you will take all the honors and emoluments and offices of the government into your own clutches ; but if we win, you will break up the establishment and turn your backs on us? Is that the fair dealing to which we are invited ? I am happy to know that you propose to make that contingency turn upon an event that will make it impossible to be consummated. The government, to-day, is all in your hands ; it has been in your hands for years ; you are partaking of all its emoluments, all its measures you have moulded, and you have designated the men who receive its honors. Year after year you have done this, and men have come here from the free states, men holding our opinions; we have sat here patiently, but we have been deprived of all the honors and emoluments that flow from this government, as though we were its enemies ; but did we ever complain ? Not at all. We did not expect that we should share any of those favors, unless it should be so that our glorious !principles should commend themselves to a majority of the people of these United States.

But, sir, if it should turn out so—and Heaven only knows whether it will or not—I give gentlemen now to understand, this Union will not easily be disrupted. Gentlemen talk about it in a very business-like way, as though it were a magazine to be blown up whenever you touch the fire to it ; as if, on a given day, at a moment's warning, at your own election, at any time and in any event, you can dissolve the bonds of this great Union. Do you not know, sir, that this great fabric has been more than eighty years in building, and do you believe you can destroy it in a day? I tell you, nay.

Sir, when you talk so coolly about dissolving this Union, do you know the difficulties through which you will have to wade before that end can be consummated ; have you reflected that between the north and the south there are no mountain ranges that are impassable, and no desert wastes which commonly divide great nations one from another ? Do you not know that, whether we love one another or not, we are from the same stock, speak the same language ; and although institutions have made considerable difference between us, the great Anglo-Saxon type pervades the whole. We are bound together by great navigable rivers, interlacing and linking together all the states of this Union. Innumerable railroads also connect us, and an immense amount of commerce binds all the parts, besides domestic relations in a thousand ways. And do you believe you can rend all this asunder without a struggle? I tell you, sir, you will search history in vain for a precedent ; there has been no such government as this that was ever rent asunder by any internal commotion. I know that Poland was broken up and divided, but it was by external force. We are found in the same ship ; we are married forever, for better or for worse. We may make our condition very uncomfortable by bickerings if we will, but nevertheless there can be no divorcement between us.   There is no way by which either one section or the other can get out of the Union. I do not say whether it is desirable or not.   There is no way by which it can be effected, but least of all on the contingency that you have spoken of.   I tell the senator from Georgia, if you wait until a Republican President is elected, you will wait a day too late.   Why not do it now, when, I say again, you have the government in your own hands? Why tell us that it is to be done when our candidate is elected ?   I say to you, Mr. President, he would be but a sorry Republican who, elected by a majority of the votes of the American people, and consequently backed by them, should fail to vindicate his right to the Presidential chair.   He will do it.

No man in the north is to be intimidated by these threats of dissolution that are thrown into our teeth daily, and I ask senators on the other side, why do you do it ?   I know not what motive you can have in preaching the dissolution of this Union day by day.   If you are going to do it, is it necessary to give us notice of it ?   There is no law requiring that you should serve notice on us that you are going to dissolve the Union ; [laughter] and I should think it would be better to do it at once, and to do it without alarming our vigilance.   It grates harshly on my ears ; and I say to gentlemen, that if a Republican President shall be constitutionally elected to preside for the next four years over this people, my word for it, *preside he will.* Do not senators know that an attempt to dissolve this Union implies civil war, with all its attendant horrors ; the marching and countermarching of vast armies ; battles to be fought, and oceans of blood to be spilled, with all the vindictive malice and ill-will that civil war never fails to bring ? And do gentlemen believe the wild tumult of such a struggle peculiarly favorable to the growth and perpetuity of this *delicate* institution? Why, sir, if it can not stand the mild arguments of Helper's book, how can it abide the ultimate shock of arms?   But, Mr. President, such things shall never be.   The souls and bodies of traitors may dissolve on the gibbet, but this Union shall stand forever.

Mr. President, I have said all and more than I intended, and I regret that it has become necessary for me to say anything on account of what has been said on the other side.   I regret that at this early period of the session we should get interlocked with this old controversy.   I wish it might have been postponed.   I shall vote for this resolution most cheerfully, and will give it the furthest and most extended sweep that you may desire, because it is my wish, if there is any misunderstanding with regard to the participants in this affair, that you should have the greatest latitude that you can desire to ferret them out, and make them known to the public.

One of the most extended of Mr. Wade's earliest speeches, was that on Senator Brown's resolutions, that the territories were the property of all the people alike, to be enjoyed by each with his property of every species alike, delivered January 18, 1860. It covers the whole field, was one of his best considered, compact, sustained level efforts; without flights, without depressions or weak places. A deliberate, calm speaker, glowing only with mind at full play, he alway extemporized, without note or memoranda of any kind. It will even now well repay perusal. The moral right of slavery had been stoutly contended for. I quote what he says of this with the residue, from the bottom of p. 12 of a popular edition.

I have nothing to say of slavery in the states. I do not wish to say, and would not say, a word about it, because I am candid enough to confess that I do not know what you can do with it there. I want no finger with it in your own states. I leave it to yourselves. It is bad enough, to be sure, that four millions of unpaid labor now is operating there, in competition with the free labor of the north; but I have nothing to say of that. Within your own boundaries, conduct it your own way; but it is wrong. Your new philosophy cannot stand the scrutiny of the present age. It is a departure from the views and principles of your fathers; yea, it is founded in the selfishness and cupidity of man, and not in the justice of God. There is the difficulty with your institution. There is what makes you fear that it may, sooner or later, be overturned; but, sir, I shall do nothing to overturn it. If I could do it with the wave of my hand in your states, I should not know how to do it, or what you should do. All I say is, that, in the vast territories of this nation, I will allow no such curse to have a foothold. If I am right, and slavery stands branded and condemned by the God of nature, then, for Heaven's sake go with me to limit it, and not propagate this curse.   I am candid enough to admit that you gentlemen on the other side, if you ever become convinced, as I doubt not you will, that this institution does not stand by the rights of nature nor by the will of God, you yourselves will be willing to put a limit to it.   You have only departed because your philosophy has led you away.   Sir, I leave you with the argument.

And now Mr. President, in conclusion, I would ask senators what they find in the Republican party that is so repulsive to them that they must lay hold of the pillars of this Union, and demolish and destroy the noblest government that has ever existed among men?   For what ? Not certainly for any evil we have done ; for, as I said to start with, you are more prosperous now than you ever were before.   What are our principles?   Our principles are only these : we hold that you shall limit slavery.   Believing it wrong, believing it inconsistent with the best interests of the people, we demand that it shall be limited ; and this limitation is not hard upon you, because you have land enough for a population as large as Europe, and century after century must roll away before you can occupy what you now have.   The next thing which we hold, and which I have not time to discuss, is the great principle of the homestead bill—a measure that will be up I trust this session, and which I shall ask to press through, as the greatest measure I know of to mold in the right direction the territories belonging to this nation ; to build up a free yeomanry capable of maintaining an independent republican government forever.   We demand, also, that there shall be a protection to our own labor against the pauper labor o Europe.   We have alway contended for it, but you have always stricken it down.

These are the measures, and these are the only measures, I know of that the great Republican party now stand forth as the advocates of.   Is there anything repulsive or wrong about them?   You may not agree to them ; you may differ as to our views; but is there anything in them that should make traitors of us, that should lead a man to pull down the pillars of his government, and bury it up, in case we succeed?   Sir, these principles for which we contend are as old as the government itself.   They stand upon the very foundation of those who framed your constitution.   They are rational and right ; they are the concessions that ought to be made to northern labor against you, who have monopolized four millions of compulsory labor and uncompensated labor, in competition with us.

There is one thing more that I wil say before I sit down ; but what I am now about to propose is not part and parcel of the Republican platform, that I know of.   There is in these United States a race of men who are poor, weak, uninfluential, incapable of taking care of themselves. I mean the free negroes, who are despised by all, repudiated by all ; outcasts upon the face of the earth, without any fault of theirs that I know of ; but they are the victims of a deep-rooted prejudice, and I do not stand here to argue whether that prejudice be right or wrong. I know such to be the fact. It is there immovable. It is perfectly impossible that these two races can inhabit the same place, and be prosperous and happy. I see that this species of population are just as abhorrent to the southern states, and perhaps more so, than to the north. Many of those states are now, as I think, passing unjust laws to drive these men off or subject them to slavery ; they are flocking into the free states, and we have objections to them. Now, the proposition is, that this great government owes it to justice, owes it to those individuals, owes it to itself and to the free white population of the nation, to provide a means whereby this class of unfortunate men may emigrate to some congenial clime, where they may be maintained to the mutual benefit of all, both white and black. This will insure a separation of the races. Let them go into the tropics. There I understand, are vast tracts of the most fertile and inviting land, in a climate perfectly congenial to that class of men, where the negro will be predominant ; where his nature seems to be improved, and all his faculties, both mental and physical, are fully developed, and where the white man degenerates in the same proportion as the black man prospers. Let them go there ; let them be separated ; it is easy to do it. I understand that negotiations may easily be effected with many of the Central American states, by which they will take these people, and confer upon them homesteads, confer upon them great privileges, if they will settle there. They are so easy of access that, a nucleus being formed, they will go of themselves and relieve us of the burden. They will be so far removed from us that they cannot form a disturbing element in our political economy. The far-reaching sagacity of Thomas Jefferson and others suggested this plan. Nobody that I know of has found a better. I understand, too, that in these regions, to which I would let them go, there is no prejudice against them. All colors seem there to live in common, and they would be glad that these men should go among them.

I say that I hope this great principle will be engrafted into our platform as a fundamental article of our faith, for I hold that the government that fails to defend and secure any such dependent class of freemen in the possession of life, liberty and happiness, is to that extent a tyranny and despotism. I hope after that is done, to hear no more about the negro equality or anything of that kind. Sir, we shall be as glad to rid ourselves of these people, if we can do it consistently with justice, as anybody else can. We will not, however, perpetrate injustice against them. We will not drive them out, but we will use every inducement to pursuade these unfortunate men to find a home there, so as to separate the races, and all will go better than it can under any other system that we can devise. I say again, I hope that the demand of justice and good policy will be complied with ; and by the consent of all, this will be done ; and if it is not done with the assent of all, I do hope it will be part and parcel of the great Republican platform ; for I think it consists with right, with justice, and with a proper regard for the welfare of these unfortunate men.

Many new men appeared in the thirty-sixth congress, especially in the house. Among them Charles Francis Adams, Roscoe Conkling, William Windom, Holman and Porter of Indiana. Corwin reappeared there, Ashley and Hutchins with him from Ohio—her people exchanging Joshua R. Giddings for John Hutchins. Van Wyck came in with Conkling and Reagan from Texas, Roger A. Pryor from Virginia and John F. Potter from Wisconsin.

The house had an extraordinary experience in reaching that parliamentary form. Mr. Sherman had exhibited in his Kansas mission unusual high qualities of courage, tact and coolness. The Republicans placed him in nomination for speaker— if possible a more trying position through the protracted struggle, and, though he failed in reaching the desk and gavel, he was not defeated in the higher sense. Such men seldom are. His party finally withdrew him and succeeded in electing Pennington of New Jersey.

1860—characters of fire inscribed on its page of the American chronicle. It saw the mar-

shaled forces of the great antagonists, in citizens'
panoply, in the ordained forms of the law, on the
national field, to determine, by sheer weight of
numbers, the great contest, so far as political action
could settle it—so far as a continuance or transfer
of the legislative and executive power of the government could determine it. Beyond was acquiescence or armed aggression. The contest of '56 was
but a test of strength and skill on the part of the
youthful party. Now mature and confident, it selected its leader with the utmost care and confidence. Defeat to it, postponement only. To
the host of slavery defeat was destruction. So its
leaders regarded and proclaimed. Destruction of
the old and a recasting in new forms was the
translation.

Mr. Douglas acted in character throughout the
great struggle. Mr. Buchanan sent Kansas with
the Border Ruffian Lecompton constitution to congress for admission. Stimulated by Broderick,
there occurred the fatal parting. The south were
imperious for a slave state. Douglas was not ready
for that. It would assuredly lose him Illinois, cut
the political earth from under his feet. Lecompton
was carried through the senate, thirty-three to
twenty-five. Broderick, Pugh and Stuart, with
Douglas, Crittenden and Bell were with the Republicans on this. The administration was powerless in the house. Then came the infamous English* scheme to bribe the settlers of Kansas to

---

* The late Democratic candidate for vice-president, English.

adopt the Lecompton constitution—it had of
course never been voted upon, even by the Border
Ruffians—by a huge land grant. Notwithstanding
the defection of ten or twelve Democrats, this
scheme passed the house, one hundred and twelve
to one hundred and fifty-three. Of course it
passed the senate.†

One fair vote was accorded Kansas, and she rejected the offer by a majority of ten thousand. With
prestige somewhat regained at the north, Douglas
made the great contest with Lincoln of Illinois.
It was a struggle for the Presidency. Douglas
retained his seat. He lost the south, divided the
Democratic party, and it was thus that the north
and south came to stand in array against each
other. In his absence he was in effect cut off by
a set of resolutions passed in the senate. Douglas
replied by letter. All this preceded the actual
arraying of forces on the field in 1860.

The struggle between the Democratic factions
came off in April at Charleston. On the great
test question Douglas beat the south. It seceded
as usual, and nominated Breckenridge and Lane.
The Douglas wing adjourned to Baltimore and
nominated him and Johnson, Hershel V.

Meantime the fossilized Whigs, the remains of
the American Knownothing—do nothing men,
who would not act with either wing of the Demo-

---

† Mr. Cox makes much of his vote *vs.* the Lecompton constitution.
He says nothing of his vote for the English bill. See his ' Three Decades in Congress.'

crats, and stood still while the Republicans went on—put Bell and Everett in nomination at Baltimore. There are men with their faces ever toward the past, who, like the fabled gnomes said to haunt and linger about the place where their dead treasures are buried, never can be induced to go forward with their age—Conservatives.

The story of the Chicago convention of 1860, its men and doings, is not even to be glanced at. It is everywhere written in word and deed. Nor yet of the great campaign it inaugurated. Men see the hand of providence, luck, fortune, as their temperaments or habits of mind may be, in the division of the Democratic party. It rendered the success of the Republicans certain. Suppose the Democrats had taken the Douglas platform with himself and Breckenridge on it. The south would have been as certain. On his platform north, what would have been the result? Fortunately the question is without practical interest. It is probable that the Republicans would then have beaten Douglas. Many Democrats, more Know-nothings, would then have voted for Lincoln.

The popular vote stood: for Lincoln, 1,866,352; Douglas, 1,375,157; Breckenridge, 845,763; Bell, 589,581.

Lincoln received one hundred and eighty electoral votes, Breckenridge seventy-two, Bell thirty-nine, Douglas twelve.

These figures furnish the factors of curious problems under our complex system of election.

Under constitutional sanctions, the Republicans prevailed. The south, still in full possession of all the departments of the government, executed her threat. Her senators departed from an open session, and, through the door thus opened, way-worn, heroic Kansas entered the indissoluble Union.

The hands of one of the great orators of Greek tragedy, wielding the forces of destiny, could have wrought nothing historically more dramatic than this closing scene, indeed than the whole of this great first act, from the formation of the conspir-acy, the gathering of the forces, the confusion and divison of the more powerful, to defeat and flight —historically, the whole is eminently dramatic.

These wise, poetic, true-born artists never ex-hibited blood and death on the stage. That was always within. The chorus in their actual pres-ence, saw and interpreted to the outside world. In no sense shall I become even a chorus. Out-side scenes will have but scanty mention.

The Thirty-sixth congress was a stormy, not to say a quarrelsome body of men, with many attrac-tions and personal scenes. Conspicuous was the Pryor–Potter episode. The Virginian challenged the western, who promptly accepted and named *bowie knives.* The southern declined. The weap-ons were not the arms of a gentleman, though eminently southern.*

Prior was more fortunate with Edgerton.

* Thad Stevens thereupon suggested *dungforks.* The meeting never took place.

CHAPTER IX.

THE first Continental congress was the natural
product of its time, convened to give expression
to its sentiment, and take counsel of its exigencies.
Washington and the first congress under the new
constitution were elected to put its new machinery
in motion, adjust, superintend and impart life and
vigor, steadiness and courage to its infant
processes. Mr. Madison was elected, as was the
Twelfth congress with him, in the midst of the then
chronic irritation between the Republic and Great
Britain, and with the expectation of war between
the two countries. They declared and fought it.
Each body, each President knew what he was elected
to do. Mr. Lincoln, his cabinet and the Thirty-
seventh congress were elected to do anything,
everything, except what fell upon them to do—
fight the greatest civil war of all history—one of

the hugest wars of modern times, involving larger
armies, a wider theatre than any of the Napoleonic
wars.   It came upon them by surprise utter.   As
we have seen, mentally, morally, but unconsciously, the people of both sides, with all the
leaders of the north, pressed forward blindly to
the inevitable.   The great contest passed logically
through all stages, moral, political, legislative,
judicial, and no man of the north, few of the south,
were in the least aware of it, until armed they
confronted each other, and then neither believed
the other intended very war.   It amazes us now to
recall how utterly we misunderstood each other—
one and all.   On the morning of February 11,
1861, the President-elect started on his memorable
progress through the northern states to the capital.
He reached it to find seven states of the Republic
with an organized government, a President and
congress, its seat at Montgomery.   Its congress convened there the fourth of the same
month, organized, adopted a constitution the seventh, and elected its executive the eighth—three
days before he left his home at Springfield.   Mr.
Lincoln was inaugurated in due form, in the
midst of secretly armed friends, who were greatly
relieved when they saw him in possession of the
executive mansion.   They feared assassination
and armed riot, to suppress which General Scott
made the best disposition of his scant force possible, and with his officers remained in command of
them.   Still war was not believed in.   Nor yet

when the forts in Charleston harbor were reduced,
even then the assembling of congress was delayed
till July Fourth.

That body convened to find over three hundred
thousand Union soldiers in the field. On the day
of its opening there were twenty-five thousand
marched through Pennsylvania avenue. At that
time quite one-third of the available military population of the south were under arms, from its then
eleven states, with its capital not a hundred miles
from Washington. How much time and blood it
cost us to get there !

At that time position in the government, executive or legislative, did not indicate the real position
of the man in the incipient, rapidly developing
contest. That depended entirely upon the personal qualities of the individual. In such times
the occasion finds them out ; elects and conducts
them to their places. Mr. Lincoln was not elected
to carry on a war, had few of the qualities save
courage, firmness, purpose, that make warriors.
Nor had any of his cabinet larger endowments in
that direction save Montgomery Blair.*

In the senate Wade, Chandler, Baker and one
or two more were the warriors. Thad Stevens and

* He not only had enough belligerency for the cabinet—if his colleagues would share it—for the war, but to conduct many private and
personal wars at the same time. "The Blairs," said he to me, "when
they go in for a fight, go in for a funeral." He was at feud with Stanton before the rebellion—they were not on speaking terms. He
soon reached the same stage with Chase, in which Frank Blair was his
ally.

a very few of the house had fighting qualities.
Stanton, when he reached the war office, developed
the native elements which find exercise in war.
He and Blair agreed in two things, boundless admiration and confidence in Wade and determination to extinguish the rebellion.   Blair was the
only man who had a just conception of real war.
He was a graduate of West Point, and why he and
Cameron did not have each other's places doubtless was because Mr. Lincoln did not expect war.
Mr. Wade, Stevens, the President, Stanton, and
the average man then supposed war meant to
march upon the enemy by the shortest route, assail, hang to him, and *lick* him in the most direct
way and in the shortest possible time.   I fear all
the men of that opening day had the same idea,
and hence the " on to Richmond " cry.   Warriors
are born.   War makes soldiers, and by a slow and
awfully expensive process.   The Indians assemble
the warriors of the tribe, fight a battle and go
home.   The war is over.   We were *aboriginal*.
By strength and force of character, indomitable,
inflexible, never in doubt or wavering, with a fixed
purpose to start with.

\ Mr. Wade soon came to be the first man in the
senate.   His qualities, experience, temper, even
level headedness, made him that.   The American
people knew little, saw little of the men in congress during the entire war, and cared nothing for
them   so   that   they   created   and   supplied   the

money and backed Mr. Lincoln and the secretary of war.

Thad Stevens, "Old Thad," as the leader of the more popular house—nobody cares much for the senate, save to get into it—was the popular congressional idol of the war. Next him ranked Wade—"Old Ben Wade," as he had already become. Of these two men, with Edwin M. Stanton, it may truly be said they were the most revolutionary men on the Union side of our history since the days of the Adamses and Jefferson. They had one purpose—the extinction of the rebellion. Whatever at hand seemed best fitted for that, they used. No scruple of the written constitution troubled either. The conservative notion of preserving the constitution, as next to slavery, the thing not to be touched, always provoked their derision. At the first, the rebels depended on the constitution to ward us off.

The Thirty-sixth congress, although it organized territories without excluding slavery, had yet the courage, under the lead of Seward, Wade and Fessenden, in the senate, and Stevens, E. B. Washburn, Corwin, Conkling, Kelley and others, to reject the Crittenden compromise—an amendment of the constitution prohibiting the abolition of slavery, did many things subservient in its desire to propitiate the south—it may well be questioned whether that body ever went so far in that direction as did the Thirty-seventh, at the called session of July Fourth.

Mr. Crittenden, then seventy-five years of age, had been transferred to the house, to make room for Breckenridge in the senate, produced his scarcely less famous resolution in the house the day after the first Bull Run battle. The first part stated that the war existed by the act of the south. It then declared its purpose and limit, on the part of the Union, as follows :

That this war is not waged on their part in any spirit of oppression, or for any purpose of conquest or subjugation, *or purpose of overthrowing or interfering with the rights or established institutions of those states*, but to defend and maintain the SUPREMACY of the constitution, and to preserve the Union, with all the dignity, equality and *rights of the several states unimpared* ; and that as soon as these objects are accomplished the war ought to cease.

On the full house this without a word, under the previous question, passed, one hundred and seventeen for to two against it. The two were John F. Potter of Wisconsin, and one of the younger of Ohio's new men. Lovejoy, though in his seat, remained silent. It was passed in the senate after full discussion, by thirty for to five against it. All the northern senators voted for it, save Sumner, who spoke, but *did not vote*, and Trumbull, who voted against it on *verbal* grounds with the rebel Breckenridge, and Polk, and Johnson of Missouri, and Powell. Wade and Chandler remained silent and voted for it. Hale did not vote. The slaveholders voted against it because it charged the war upon them.

The Republicans, with Stevens and all of the

house, would then so wage the war as to hurt the south the least, and slavery not at all.*

The resolution as the unanimous declaration of congress, so significant and so amazing, which no man of that majority now speaks of, and is now a curious study, was everywhere not only accepted north but constituted the state platform entire of the Ohio Republicans in 1863. It is probable this was the prudent, the wiser course. Perhaps the cooler-headed Wade, Fessenden and Stevens saw clearly enough the real objective point of the war, but knew very well that the declared purpose of the war at that time, to abolish slavery, would greatly diminish the northern ardor and weaken the hands of the government, if it was not fatal to the cause of the Union. In the old war we struggled to maintain the birthright of Englishmen; contending for that, we came directly upon the birthright of Americans. In this we took up arms to enforce the constitution—whatever it meant—as to slavery. We very soon proclaimed the abolition of slavery, and amended the constitution finally. The most of human goods are reached thus collaterally, incidentally, from the astrologers, alchemists, to Columbus.

---

* The two opponents were called to account, and boldly declared that slavery having thrust by the protecting constitution should be extinguished. One of them was emphatic. He declared his associates were after all afraid of slavery. They went about silent and tremulous lest, like a she dragon, it would come and devour them. There was something of this in both houses then. It will perhaps please the enemies of these gentlemen to be reminded that each was defeated for the next congress.

The session closed August 6. Congress was called to provide for the war. Its session was but a giant committee of ways and means. It called for five hundred thousand volunteers, and twenty-five thousand regulars. It appropriated five hundred million dollars for the army alone. The navy was augmented by immense appropriations. The repairs of old and the building of new, strong, powerful ships, the improvement of arms, invention of new ordnance, new projectiles, all calling into play the native creative genius of our northern people. Duties on imports were increased, a loan of two hundred and fifty million dollars authorized, an issue and re-issue of fifty million of treasury notes provided for ; the President's acts — his past indemnified, his future assured against ; and so that congress in that month launched the huge war.

Meantime Bull Run*—that dead sea victory to

---

* MR. WADE AT BULL RUN. Never was a battle so really and persistently misapprehended. We ran away and so were defeated. We were not beaten on the field. At the most it was a draw. We made the assault, and, as raw troops might, went off from the field, leaving . the amazed foe there. *They never pursued us an inch.* Governor Sprague went and brought off his guns the next day. A party brought off the body of Colonel Cameron the second day after. No rebels but dead ones were met with. Senators Wade, Chandler, Brown, sergeant-at-arms of the senate ; and Major Eaton in one carriage, Tom Brown of Cleveland, Blake, Morris and a colleague of theirs, of the house, in another, were at the battle—some of them on the field and saw men fall. On their return, near the extemporized hospital, Ashby's "Black Horse" swept down upon them and caused a panic. I quote from Cox's ' Three Decades ' a descriptive passage there credited to another.

"Mr. —— relates how his company were charged upon by wild riders of sable horses. ' It seemed,' said he, in a deliberately penned

the south like so many seeming triumphs—so
fruitful in far-reaching profits to the north, like so
many seeming defeats—had been fought, won, and
for the time lost.

---

description, 'as if the very devils of panic and cowardice seized every
mortal officer, soldier, teamster and citizen. No officer tried to rally a
soldier or do anything but spring and run toward Centerville. There
never was anything like it for causeless, sheer, absolute, absurd
cowardice, or rather panic, on this miserable earth before. Off they
went, one and all, off, down the highway, across fields towards the
woods, anywhere, everywhere to escape. The further they ran the
more frightened they grew, and, though we moved as fast as we could,
the fugitives passed us by scores. To enable themselves better to run,
they threw away their blankets, knapsacks, canteens, and finally
muskets, cartridge boxes—everything. We called to them, told them
there was no danger; implored them to stand. We called them
cowards, denounced them in most offensive terms, put out our heavy
revolvers, threatened to kill them, in vain. A cruel, crazy, hopeless
panic possessed them and infected everybody in front or rear.' Mr.
Cox gives much more, describing the awful pack at Cub's Run, pp.
158-9. From a letter of one of Wade's party, written the morning •
of his return—not deliberate, as its rush of language shows: 'The
two carriages of the party, which were blocked up in the awful gorge
at Cub's Run, had become separated. They, united after passing
Centerville, where the left wing of our army were still in position with
their batteries, not engaged during the day and not seeing an enemy.
They passed the drift wreck and ruins of abandoned arms and material
until within a mile or so of Fairfax Court House, where in a good position, under Wade, armed with his famous rifle, as were the rest with
heavy revolvers, they formed across the pike, Wade, his hat well back,
his gun in position, his party in line, facing the onflowing torrent of
runaways, who were ghastly *sick with panic*—it is a disease—called
out, "Boys we'll stop this damned runaway," and they did, for the
fourth of an hour not a man passed save McDowell's bearer of dis-
patches, and he only on production of his papers. The rushing,
cowardly, half-armed, demented fugitives stopped, gathered, crowded,
flowed back, hedged in on either side by thick, growing cedars that a
rabbit could hardly penetrate. The position became serious. A revol-
ver was discharged, shattering the arm of Major Eaton, said to be in
the hand of a mounted escaping teamster, whom he had arrested. At

Early at the ensuing—the regular session—Mr. Chandler introduced a resolution to inquire into the causes of the disaster of the twenty-first of July, supplemented by the sad affair of Ball's Bluff, and the fall of Colonel Baker. The idea covered by it was most suggestive. That was the origin of the to become famous "committee on the conduct of the war," the most useful of the purely congressional agencies, in the hands of its own members, of the war. The ready house caught it up, passed a joint resolution, for a joint committee of seven—three of the senate, four of the house.*

Its efficiency, like that of all congressional committees, would depend entirely upon the qualities and conduct of its head. Nobody but Wade was thought of for chairman. Chandler and Andrew

---

that instant the heroic old senator and his friends were relieved, perhaps rescued, by Colonel Crane and a part of the Second New York, hurrying toward the scene of disaster, and the party proceeded. At Fairfax the gentleman in charge of the second carriage delivered to an officer seven or eight rifled muskets and other property, all his carriage could carry, and thus lightened moved on, reaching the capital just before dawn. Wade's exploit, so in character—seven citizens stopping a runaway army—was much talked of. Nothing better illustrates the rawness in matters of war than the presence of men of this position at this battle. They were there by the special permission of General Scott with imposing passes. Eely of New York, at an early hour, was captured and carried to Richmond. Wade would hardly have submitted to that fortune.'

* At the opening of the session, Mr. Conkling, who had been upon the ground (Ball's Bluff), and thoroughly investigated the whole affair, made on the floor of the house, a masterly exposè of the causes which led up to and produced that shocking disaster and attending incidents. One of the strongest of his many great congressional speeches—the first that congress or the north really knew of the facts. This led to the action of the house.

Johnson were with him and Julian, Covode, Gooch, and Odell from the house.* The committee by Mr. Wade, omitting Mr. Johnson's name, made their first report soon after the close of the Thirty-seventh congress, in April 1863, which made three heavy volumes of over two thousand printed pages. Their second, May 22, 1865, a trifle more in bulk —six volumes in all, of over four thousand pages. We may only mention some of the leading subjects committed to its care: "Bull Run," "Ball's Bluff," "The Missouri Campaign," and "Fremont," "The "Hatteras Expedition," "Port Royal," "Burnside's Beaufort Exploits," "Fort Donelson," "The Capture of New Orleans," "Invasion of New Mexico," "Expedition to Accomac," "The Battle of Winchester," "The Battle of the Monitor and the Merrimac," "The Army of the Potomac," "Battle of Petersburg," Bank's famous "Red River Cotton Raid," Butler's equally famous "Raid on Fort Fisher," which Terry afterward carried by assault, "Treatment of Prisoners," "The Sherman–Johnson Capitulation"—a great many more events and incidents of the war important then, forgotten long since. A large edition, many thousands, were printed, of these now scarce volumes, where is recorded so much evidence of generals and others, of value to the real historian, who will know the use of original evidence, when he comes—not referred to by the generals who are now so busy patching their

---

* I think Johnson never acted on the committee. It was no place for him. Wade and Chandler were the two great men of it.

fames. It is said that Wade seldom missed a session
of the committee. The most conscientious of known
men, never ill—he never neglected a duty, failed
of an engagement, was never waited for, and never
failed to meet his foe, one or many.*

Largely we are indebted to Mr. Wade for the
advancement of Mr. Stanton to the war office.
He strongly urged him upon Mr. Lincoln, who
soon came to estimate Mr. Wade at his true value.
Stanton had been the bitterest of Democrats.
The Republicans then knew nothing certainly of
his course in Buchanan's cabinet. His appoint-
ment surprised the senate. Wade knew and
indorsed him there. That was sufficient.†

The army, the American world, thrilled under
Stanton's first touch. At his word everybody
moved, but McClellan. I may but mention some
of the leading things accomplished by that great
congress :

The abolition of slavery in the District of Columbia, in April '62. The confiscation of rebel

_____

*So the kindest of men, the most obscure could command his instant
attention. If at leisure—listening to Mrs. Wade's fine reading—he
arose at once, with his cane, would stride up the avenue to a department where all the doors stood open to him, and at once advance,
if it was possible, the interests of his temporary protégé. No man's
voice was more potent. I recall his persistent effort to secure the ap-
pointment of a grand nephew of Washington Irving to the naval academy. When he succeeded he was shocked when told that the gifted
youth lacked a *half inch* of the required height. The most laborious
tasks of a kind-hearted senator or representative were in obedience to
the endless calls for every variety of thing, from all possible people
—mainly those having no claims.

† Senator Pearce of Maryland, was my authority for this statement.

property—slaves, maugre the Crittenden platform not nine months old, and on which McClellan waged war, keeping in its limits. The abandoned and captured property law, a title that tells nothing to a stranger. It was the act under which all the cotton was seized and sold. The great blockade and also the rebel intercourse law, under which we sought to secure cotton in the rebel lines to meet the frantic foreign clamor for cotton, and thus keep them from intervening. The important law, authorizing the seizure of the railroads and telegraphs for the public service. Early in July the great Pacific railroad scheme was perfected by law. Though the walls of the capitol where congress deliberated, vibrated in the roar of hostile cannon that would destroy it, that congress set at once about erecting its great dome. The needs of the war, in the fruitful hands of that creative congress, the great scheme of the national currency, the ingeniously wrought out internal revenue and direct taxation laws, that floated the 900,000,000 of paper we were obliged to issue. It was not the legal tender clause that did this. That was a pure compulsion, which at a certain point would be powerless. It was the national credit based on its immense actual revenues, which persuaded, that kept us swimming though water-logged and constantly sinking. Gold ceased to be money, it became a commodity, the price of which marked accurately how far below the surface our paper was. There were the conscription laws—all the acts of that congress cannot be named.

I recall for a moment the real position of this congress, of which none of the busy, covetous military historians (?) has yet said a word. Lincoln, by common consent, stands next Washington, then Grant, Sherman, Sheridan (saying nothing of the cabinet), in the common estimate. What would Lincoln have accomplished had there not been a brave, firm, wise, far-seeing congress to advise, create, compel, reward, punish, pay premiums, bounties, prizes. Where would have been the glittering hosts, with the gold-spangled, glory-bedazzling generals ? In the true sense, that congress made and sustained them all—the President but executed their will—hence all their fame and glory. Nothing of this was or is yet seen. In the eyes of the nation in the near foreground there were but two figures looming through the dense cloud of war — the ever present smoke of ceaseless battle. Lincoln colossal, Stanton appearing and disappearing, sustaining, supporting, inflexible, impersonation of one of the great inexorable forces of nature. People supposed Chase was awfully busy up there in his huge stone factory, creating money—paper mostly ; poor stuff it was showing, notwithstanding legal tender—treasury notes and bonds. They caught glimpses of Seward, diminished by the immense distance — little man ! standing on the sands of the sea, frantically admonishing, waving

off the eager crowd, English and French, who
thronged the other shore, hardly restrained from
jumping into their boats and pulling over to break
the blockade and help the rebs. "Congress! Congress! Well, ain't old Thad Stevens and old Ben
Wade there? They'll keep 'em at work!" was
the popular cry. Ah, yes, they kept themselves
at work, work all the time. We may see some of
the other things done, some of the difficulties in
the way.

Upon the resumption of its labors at the December session of 1862, the senate, with becoming
promptitude, expelled John C. Breckenridge, of
the old firm of "Buck and Breck," so sharply
handled by Baker at the extra session. He was
not present, and his associate Powell did what he
might to divert or soften the blow. The vote was
unanimous. On the sixteenth the first bolt struck
Jesse D. Bright, the greatest Indianian before the
late Mr. Hendricks. He wrote *a letter* early in
March, addressed to "His Excellency, the President
of the Confederate States," whose name it was
"Jefferson Davis," whilom a senator of the United
States, earnestly recommending another rebel,
who had *an improved arm to sell*, to his Confederate
excellency's kind consideration. His defense was
adroit. He hated to go. The Democrats stood
by him. The new senators—Harris of New
York and Cowan of Pennsylvania, Republicans
both—spoke and voted for him. The votes
stood thirty-two adverse and fourteen for

him, and he slept with his political fathers. This was the work of young Senator Wilkinson from younger Minnesota. December 18 Sumner moved the expulsion of Trusten Polk of Missouri; called him a traitor by name. Trusten had also *written a letter*—to an editor. Meantime his colleague, Johnston, was gotten ready and paired with him, two and two, like the unclean in Noah's time. The Democrats joined in their cordial send off. Mr. Wade, certain of results— he never spoke when he was—remained in grim silence through these proceedings, the tone of voice in which he expressed his hearty approval betraying the cordiality of his concurrence. The house took the lead in this " *Pride's Purge.*" On the first day Frank Blair moved the expulsion of his colleague, Reid. He was sent out on the *common counts*, as a lawyer would say, as was the ever ponderously truculent Burnett of Kentucky. The house did not expend the "ayes and noes" on them. It "agreed" on their cases by good-natured acclamation, which one acquainted with the already departed could appreciate. Brave white-haired, old Wickliffe made Burnett the occasion of some cheering words loudly applauded by the Republicans. He took the arming of slaves greatly to heart later.

Meantime the literal Wilkes had intercepted and returned Mason and Slidell. America never had two sons she could better spare. But here they were, and the house so noisily applauded the act

that it was heard across the Atlantic and added
much to the complicated and compromising position the exploit placed us in.   Mr. Seward saved
us.   His position was the most difficult and the
least appreciated of any of the three great secre-
taries.   He gracefully apologized to her majesty,
and we rewarded the old South sea explorer in
true British fashion by making him an admiral.*

There was the dismembering of Virginia—would
we do it again, under the same conditions and in
our then temper ?   Yes.   She was betrayed by
her sons on all sides.   Her great leaders abandoned
her and themselves.   Her small men found in this
their opportunity.   Not a man of them made any
reputation.   Their needs required her division.
We did it for them.   Her very bondmen reviled
her.   Her day is not yet.   She promised to submit her ordinance of treason to a fair vote of her
people.   Old bawd that she had become—she
cared for no sanction.   Shamelessly she rushed to
her harlot's couch to find a harlot's grave.   The
chariots of war cut her soil to their hubs.   She
was a wide, red mire.   In her return to life she
brings from her dead past its dead burdens to
dam the way of new progress, free to her southern
sisters. It may be that her nearness—lying so clearly
in our field of vision, her sufferings are more obvious
—they seem almost more than her deserving.   The

---

* After the war I came to know him well, of large frame, tall, grim,
forbidding of aspect, with an aptitude for trouble in business and
property matters.

law of retribution executes itself alike on peoples as individuals.   There is no escape for either.

Two things of that congress thus far finding small mention, of great temporary and some lasting influence, should be here noticed.

Early in the winter of 1861–2 it became apparent to the sagacious Vallandigham, one of the able, clear-headed men of his day, ardent, ambitious, of manly, honorable impulses, largely influenced by his unfortunate bias to the south, whence came inspiration and family origin, that to support the war, the administration, was to lose—merge the Democracy with the Republicans and thus efface the party.   True, as he must have seen, to oppose the war the administration was to make the Democracy the allies of the revolted south.   He probably did not regret that, in view of the end of the war at some time.   Hence the party in the house was reorganized under his lead, and a written basis signed by some thirty of that body.   Unquestionably to that action was due many added months to the period of the war.*

---

* Stimulated by his new determination, his givings out were of such pronounced character that he was arrested by Burnside's order, sent through the lines, went to Bermuda, thence to Canada, and re-appeared at the Democratic convention of 1864, at Chicago, having in the meantime been a second time martyred as the Democratic candidate for governor of his state.   When his return was reported to the President, it reminded him only of a little story of Sangammon county.   The messenger hurried eagerly to the despotic Stanton, who peremptorily denied Vallandigham's presence in the United States, and closed the superserviceable man's mouth by assuring him that no human testimony ever would convince him of Vallandigham's return while the war lasted.

Very early there came to be a difference in the
estimate of the President, his policy, capacity and
intentions, between the distant northern public and
the leading men of the two houses. He soon became the theme of criticism, reflection, reproach
and condemnation on their part. The New York
Tribune was largely the organ of these congressional critics, and, as was known, Mr. Greeley,
with a lantern, was diligently searching all the
summer, autumn and winter of 1863 for a man to
succeed him. To such extent did the condemnation reach, that, at the end of the thirty-seventh
congress, there were in the house but two men,
capable of being heard, who openly and everywhere defended him—Mr. Arnold of Illinois and
one of the Ohio delegation. Corroborative of
this, I quote from a speech of one of these on the
"Bill to Indemnify the President," in the house, on
the twenty-eight of February. He dealt first very
directly with the resounding clamor, denunciation
and vituperation of the President by the Democrats, and thus passed to and addressed himself to
the Republicans :

These outspoken comments here and elsewhere have at least the
merit of boldness ; but what shall be said of that muttering, unmanly,
yet swelling undercurrent of complaining criticism that reflects upon
the President, his motives and capacity, so freely and feebly indulged in by men having the public confidence ?—whisperings and
complainings and doubtings and misgivings and exclamations and
predictions. I have heard men complain that George Washington had
died, as if untimely, and feebly sigh for a return of Andrew Jackson to
life. What can be done with such puling drivelers ?—men who have a
morbid passion to exaggerate our misfortunes, and aggregate and riot
in our calamities ; and who are never so happy as when they can gloat

over the sum of our disasters, which they charge over to the personal account of the President. I am sick of this everlasting cowardice and pallor under reverses. Defeats must come, disasters must come, and still greater ones perhaps, and the end is not yet. These men would never have worked through the first Revolution ; but that, as this will be, was achieved in spite of them.

Sir, if we fail it will be wholly because we are unworthy to succeed ; because we will not with our whole heart and energy, might, mind and strength, give ourselves up entirely to this war as do the rebels ; study its portents and obey its demands alone. The task it imposes is for our human kind. Its work is the accumulated work of the dead centuries thrust upon our hands, and its hope is the hope of all the ages to be born. If we doubt, assail and cast down those who alone must lead us, we might as well now slough into any infamy that men will call peace, or skulk behind the mediating scepter of no matter what despot, and hide forever our dishonored heads amid the ruins of our nationality· If any man here distrusts the President, let him speak forth here, like these bad leaders, openly, and no longer offend the streets and nauseate places of common resort with their unworthy clamor. He may not have in excess that ecstatic fire that makes poets and prophets and madmen ; he may not possess much of what we call heroic blood, that drives men to stake priceless destinies on desperate ventures and lose them ; he may not in an eminent degree possess that indefinable something that school-boys call genius, that enables its possessor, through new and unheard of combinations, to grasp at wonderful results, and that usually end in ruin ; or, if he possesses any or all of these qualities, they are abashed and subdued in the presence of a danger that dwarfs giants and teaches prudence to temerity. He is an unimpassioned, cool, shrewd, sagacious, far-seeing man, with a capacity to form his own judgments and a will to execute them ; and he possesses an integrity pure and simple as the white rays of light that play about the Throne. It is this that has so tied the hearts and love of the people to him, that will not unloose in the breath of all the demagogues in the land. It is idle to compare him with Washington or Jackson. Like all extraordinary men, he is an original, and must stand in his own niche. He has assiduously studied the teachings of this war ; has learned its great lesson, and in full time he uttered its great word. He commits errors. Who would have committed fewer? Think of the fierce and hungry demands that incessantly devour him up. Remember the repeated instances in our own times when the ablest of our statesmen in that chair, with cabinets of their choice, and sustained by majorities in congress, in times of profound peace, have gone down, and their administrations have perished under the bare weight of the government.

And then contemplate, if you can, in addition to the burdens that have crushed so many strong men, the fearful responsibilities imposed upon this man. Is it not a marvel, a most living wonder, that he sustains them so well?

.   .   .   .

But these gentlemen now denounce the President's policy of the war. Sir, I remember that others, too, used to complain the same way, and just as if the President was responsible for it, and could furnish a policy for the war. The war is greater than the President; greater than the two houses of congress; greater than the people, *with the new Democracy thrown in ;* greater than all together, and controls them all and dictates its own policy ; and woe to the men or party that will not heed its dictation.*

To Mr. Wade's credit—where he could not approve and praise the President he remained silent—never praised any one much. Due allowance has never been made for Mr. Lincoln's position. Seeing all the most advanced saw, he also saw what they would not—the slow, the tardy, the reluctant. For these he must wait. It required all. To rush forward with the van, like an old prophet, to risk all mayhap was to lose all. In this and in his grand docility to be taught by each day of its needs, at the feet of the war itself, consists the real greatness of the man. Constantly he grew with the people, till he filled their entire vision.

As will be remembered, Mr. Wade did once appear openly to criticise the President—not to assail him, but to inform the people, warn the

* No one on the floor or elsewhere replied to or denied these statements of the extent and character of these Republican criticisms of the President. The speech had a wide circulation and became a campaign document through the north.

public.   Our success in the southwest, late in
1863, led Mr. Lincoln to look for a near end of the
war, and consider the course to be pursued with
the subdued states.   He outlined a scheme which
alarmed the sagacious men about him.   His mag-
nanimity, like many of his great qualities, extended
to the border of weakness ; as when, on the fall
of Richmond, he directed General Hentzleman to
re-convene the rebel legislature to resume its
forfeited functions.   The time seemed pressing,
the danger imminent, in the absence of most of his
associates.   The Thirty-eighth congress adjourned,
its members had gone home. \ Mr. Wade, in
concert with Henry Winter Davis, respectively the
chairmen of the committees of the senate and house,
on Rebel-States, and on Territories, to whom the
matter would belong, issued the famous Wade-
Davis manifesto, reflecting on the proposed policy,
which produced a most prodigious sensation and
excitement north.   At one with them, the New
York *Tribune*, dared not publish it, and it went
out as a circular.   It disposed of the intended
policy.   It brought Mr. Wade under a dense
eclipse—the first and only one of his life.   Fortunately, he had received his third election, and at
the hands of a nominal Democratic legislature, or
his career in the senate would have closed under it.*

* The exact conditions may be outlined for those who may not remember. We had recovered the Mississippi, and with it always bot-
tomless Louisiana. Mr. Lincoln then tried an experiment of reconstruction—his " ten per cent."—derisively called—as it took but ten
per cent. of the people to reconstruct. Congress promptly--Flanders

A word further is due the Thirty-seventh congress, of which Mr. Wade was such a conspicuous
figure, and in which his influence was so large, his
labors so great and useful. It seems to have been,
possibly, the first whose vision and grasp embraced
the continent, as well as the interests of the hum-
blest citizen. It tied the wide asunder shores of
the Pacific as with the sweep of a mighty lasso to
the Atlantic—the railroad and telegraph. It enacted the Homestead law. Perhaps the necessity
which compelled it to deal with vast sums—huge
armies, marching, fighting over a wide continent,
dealing in the huge—gave it a capacity for broad
views, while the very nature of the great contest,
quickening and inspiring the higher sentiments,
gave elevation that inspired high aims. It is

---

and Hahn were in the house—rejected his senator, and later it passed its
first act for military governors, and adjourned early in July. The President did not receive it ten days before that event, and quietly permitted
it to die. He thereupon issued his famous proclamation, setting forth
the Louisiana plan. Its tone was sarcastic toward congress, which
shared fully the estimate and spirit of the Thirty-seventh congress.
Mr. Wade and Mr. Davis rejoined in a caustic protest—they called it.
Mr. Davis was one of the ablest and most brilliant men of his time.
Mr. Lincoln long balanced Davis and Blair for his cabinet—preferred
Blair. Could Davis forget it ! Perhaps so. I don't know. He wrote
the protest—a most admirable performance, saving its tone, reviewing
the whole ground. And so the world for the first time knew how
widely asunder the President and congress were. It sided with the
President, condemned even Wade, would cut off young Garfield on
suspicion. Wade and Davis were greatly right, the President fatally
wrong, had his way prevailed. When congress re-convened it stood
by its champions and no harm came. Mr. Lincoln serenely acquiesced.
Not so much a ruler. The greatest manager of men the American
world ever saw.

not the least indication of its rare aptitude, that while it thus dealt with the highest, broadest destinies of races, as well as of the nation, it neglected no minor domestic interest, lost sight of no need or requirement of our foreign relations. The huge volume of its enactments, the most of which were of limited duration, nevertheless contributed much to the great permanent revision of 1873. The great dome, the free capital, its schools for the races, the national banks, the bureau of agriculture, are his work—a small part of it. It launched the war, made success certain—if it did criticise the President.

Its laws are found in Volume XII Statutes at Large, 1440 pages. Bulk may show diligence. Ability only by excellence and its degree. Under the conditions in which the labors of this congress were performed, they do not fall below that of any legislative body of modern history, however estimated. Its execution required quick, unerring apprehension, courage, firmness, wisdom, will, faith. The greatest of all was faith.

The philosophy of a people's history is most certainly studied in its laws, whether enacted by itself or imposed by a despot. The twelfth and thirteenth volumes of the great series of congressional statutes contain the entire legislation of the war. The Thirty-eighth but took up and completed the work of its predecessor. Amending, perfecting—not originating. Its volume is but half the size of that of the Thirty-seventh.

Incased in these two lie the skeleton of the War of the Rebellion, to be restored and clothed with life by whoever would best study that. The muscles, sinews, the intense life, the resistless energy, that endowed, animated, armed it, which went forth to work the law-makers will, departed when that will took the from of fact accomplished.

The thing—the new financial system—barely named is destined to permanency. The national banks—possibly a direct national currency in some form, the great financial convulsion inevitable of the war, will remain—an immense step forward. No good is so perfect that evils may not owe birth to it. The greenback craze was a *larve* hatched of the national currency, as its near kin the silver delusion. The enormous, growing production of silver is fast reducing it to a base metal. Experi, ment will doubtless go on till the idea is reached-and practically accepted, that money was a discovery, and not an invention of trade. Men cannot make more than a temporary representative of it—a substitute is impossible. Money—real money—is the product of the hand that imparted all intrinsic values to its products. Coining gold only declares what for the time that is. It cannot be augmented.

The Thirty-seventh, the promulgator of that joint resolution of July, '61, not only confiscated slaves, it armed them against their masters.*

---

* This thing was first brought broadly before the house in a speech the twenty-seventh of January, 1862, the first public or private utterance

The Thirty-eighth congress was elected in '62, in due time succeeding; commenced the thirteenth volume in April, 1864. Frank Blair repeated his assault of Mr. Chase, which barely escaped driving him from the cabinet, and might have led to the gravest disasters, of which, thus far, so little is known.

There, in the house, re-appeared battle-scarred and crippled Schenck,† with young Garfield, fresh from the battlefield. They to become the head and nearly the whole committee of military affairs. What a task was theirs; volunteering had ceased. The conscription law, with its twelve openings, let the whole draft through. Of three hundred thou-

---

on the subject. The house was startled. Governor Wickliffe would not believe he understood the speaker. The claim that while men of African blood were by the laws of Kentucky slaves, they were at the same time subjects of the United States, had been turned over to it, not as slaves but as persons, and owed it allegiance as such, and the Uniten States could therefore take their service spite of the master and the master' sslave law, efface for this purpose, if necessary, all semblance of servitude, seemed beyond denial. No one attempted it. After the subsidence of the first impression, many Republican along the borders dared not circulate any of the great numbers they subscribed for. Judge Thomas of Massachusetts said it would abolish slavery even in peace. Slavery was essentially abolished when the utterance was made.

†Robert C. Schenck was among the most fortunate in rendering val-uable service, the most unfortunate in fame and reward of the distinguished men of that great period. Clear, rapid, very able, of the heroic cast of men, he became a target for more unjust newspaper clamor, and an instance of the suddenness with which great men are forgotten in our time. A volume from him would tell us more of the hidden springs of power and success, than all the conflicting accounts of all the generals from Grant to Beauregard. He and the other great civilians still with us should be at work.

sand drawn, but fifty thousand were held. A new
bill was prepared and the new house of the Thirty-
eighth rejected it. Then was held that consulta-
tion in the committee room—the great President
meeting the generals and two or three others, his
sad eyes full, the solemn, inner light, by which he
seemed to see things hidden from mortals, armed,
inspired. The head and his great young second
produced their new bill—*they passed it.* A call
went out for three hundred thousand. The response from the re-aroused north—the most
pathetic and arousing lyric of the land—

> We are coming Father Abraham, three hundred thousand more
> Shouting the battle cry of Freedom.*

Where would Grant and Appomattox have been,
or Lincoln, without Schenck and Garfield?

In the dark days of December, '63, in the house,
Garfield met James Gillespie Blaine—of the same
age. Their entrance upon the public stage was of
as much significance to the republic as to themselves. Men with much of great and brilliant in
common, they yet presented great contrasts. They
became fast friends, from which flowed influences
and consequences largely shaping the affairs of
the republic; perhaps never to be understood out
of a small circle. Conkling was still in the house.
How mysteriously the fortunes of these gifted

* Frank Moore, editor of the *Rebellion Record*, has just produced
the southern popular war poems and songs.—Appleton & Company.
Some careful hand should perform this needed and interesting work for
the soldier lyrics of the north.

young men were made to mingle and inter-
depend.

The opening of '64 saw Grant on his weltering
way through the Wilderness. It saw the nomina-
tions of Mr. Lincoln and General McClellan—
George B., child of the war, an indubitable failure,
pitted against the great President, on the strength of
his *failures* mainly—and so the people were called
to pass upon them—upon the war. They declared
2,200,000 for Lincoln, to 1,800,000 for the general, who, in his days of young glory, used to
snub his chief, and who recently compared himself
with Lee—a really great captain.* Twenty-two of
the twenty-five states condemned him—under
whose eyes he performed all he ever anywhere
did.

One monument the Thirty-eighth congress
erected to itself, the thirteenth amendment of the
constitution abolishing slavery.

The year '64 lapsed to '65. The great Rebellion
came suddenly to an end.

The great President—his work done—suddenly
departed.

No creation of the tragic muse ever has or
ever will equal the dramatic effect of these closing
scenes.

Many years are left me, and Wade, the vice-
president, with a single vote between him and the
headship of the victorious, restored republic, and
the end.

---

* Written in the lifetime of General McClellan.

The war in a way fought itself. Its waste and ruin, shattered states, its political and social fragments, will not restore themselves and spontaneously take on new forms, with needed crystallizations and growths. Great care and much time will be needful for these purposes. An old civilization, old economies and industries, are to pass. There will be the old race prejudices, the greatest and hardest of all difficulties to be met. We abolished slavery. We have not yet abolished "the nigger." He is to be outgrown—evolved away by a slow process—vanished by evolution.

CHAPTER X.

THE old war horse is comparatively useless for agricultural purposes. He is alway hearing the bugle call.

Most of the men fashioned under the influence of the rising anti-slavery struggle—all middle aged men at the beginning of the Rebellion, in congress or elsewhere, in positions where they took active part in shaping, impelling, or fighting the war, whose mode and habit of thought and mind, ran in its narrow intense currents—the men in short who demolished the mushroom slave empire, destroyed the industries of its people, freed their serfs, shivered their civilization, by subverting its foundations, were not thereby, *a priori*, eminently fitted to clear the soil of the encumbering ruins, plant anew their own civilization, rebuild institutions, and reconstruct the states. This was their task without precedent in their own or any other

history, with no guide but what they knew of the
field and its occupants, whom they entirely misunderstood at the beginning of the war, and whose
good qualities and aptitudes for peaceful pursuits
they were yet to learn. Ruined, subdued, sullen,
the people still enraged, they, the conquerors in
the pride and insolence of complete and perfect
triumph, were to attempt this. Never in history
was a conquest so perfect. The war had ceased to
be civil, became national, yet no semblance of
nationality remained to the defeated, with which a
treaty could be entered into, and terms made. While
such existed the rebels had refused terms of return. The peoples were rather incongruous parts
of a whole with a once common law, a common
language, origin, history. So much to begin with.
The worst—the hardest, most persistent obstacles
were the freedmen soon to become citizens, while
the masters remained disfranchised. The first
thing to decide was the fate of the foe—the leaders
—traitors by law—eleven great statefulls. But
one state prisoner was made.

That Senator Wade would be largely and unconsciously as all were, under the full influence of
the law of human nature, the habit of mind prevailing, was very certain. The conquered were not
an enemy to be treated with, were criminals—the
great leaders—to be punished. Probably the general idea never presented itself to his mind, that
the war was the crisis of a great epoch in the history
of races, unavoidable, conducted up to in the or-

derly course of great events, and that the fallen on both sides—the losing party in the struggle of great systems, freedom and slavery—the future with the past, on the great fields of the present—were really the victims—the martyrs of that, and not the doers of otherwise punishable crimes. Few, perhaps, now give hospitality to this notion. If named to them it is rejected. For the time these leaders were great criminals, to be dealt with—some of them—as such. Mr. Davis was solemnly indicted at Richmond and incarcerated in a casemate of Fortress Monroe.*

Mr. Johnson, on accession to the Presidency, as we remember, talked savagely of inexorable punishment, would hear to nothing short. Delegations and embassies, one notable from the churches, sought in vain to soften his solemn resentment.

Mr. Wade of the God-fearing Puritans had perhaps advanced notions. He alway remembered mercy. He sought to soften the wrath of the President toward the offenders. This is the reported interview—much more was said:

President J.—Mr. Wade, what would you do, were you in my place, charged with my responsibilities?

Senator W.—I think I should either force into exile or hang ten or twelve of the worst of those fellows—perhaps for full measure, I should make it thirteen, just a baker's dozen.

President J.—But how are you going to pick out so small a number and show them to be guiltier than the rest?

Senator W.—It won't do to hang a very large number. I think if you would give me time, I could name thirteen that would stand at the

---

* He "adhered to the king's enemies." His more recent givings out throw doubt on his giving them provable "aid and comfort."

head in the work of Rebellion. We would all agree on *Jeff Davis,* *
Toombs, Benjamin, Slidell, Mason, Howell Cobb. If we did no more
than drive these half-dozen out of the country, we should accomplish
a good deal.†

The President went inexorably fuming about for
three or four weeks, in this vindictive mood.
He professed more confidence in and reliance on
Wade, at that time, than on any other man. This
was a comforting assurance to the Republicans in
congress. He was openly hostile to Mr. Lincoln's
scheme of reconstruction, and it was supposed Mr.
Seward would be exchanged for Mr. Preston King
because of that. The Republican heads who had
gathered in the capitol in dismay, doubt and great uncertainty, returned home feeling reassured. As will
be remembered, Mr. Johnson was the single repre-

---

* Mr. Davis was admitted to bail by Horace Greeley becoming
surety, and in 1868 the prosecution was dismissed. His citizenship was
never restored.

† As may be remembered, Mr. Wade was opposed to the execution
of Mrs. Surratt. He believed her innocent.

On Pennsylvania avenue, a few blocks west of the capitol, stands
the oldest bookstore in Washington. In times gone by, when book-
stores were few, this was a great resort for public men, who
dropped in to buy a periodical on their way to and from the capitol. Benton, Clay, Calhoun, Douglas and other notables were daily
visitors. Mr. Wade, who lived at No. 6 4½ street, where so many
congressmen boarded in those days, would always stop on his way to
and from the capitol and look over the latest things in books and
magazines. He seemed to take much interest in the literature of the day,
and is credited with the distinction of having bought the first copy of
Harper's Magazine ever sold in Washington. The bookseller—Joe
Shillington—who still lives, takes a good deal of pleasure in recounting
old memories, and often entertains his customers with reminiscences of
distinguished men who figured in the country's history thirty or forty
years ago. One evening lately the writer happened into the old store

sentative in either house of congress, from the eleven
seceding states, who remained loyal, and took his
seat in the senate as stated.   Mr. Lincoln later
appointed him military governor of Tennessee,
where his services were valuable, and meantime,
though elected Vice-President, he continued to
perform the duties as governor.   In this capacity
he reconstructed Tennessee in the winter of 1864–5,
and Brownlow was elected governor.   His ground
was that, mauger secession, the states were still in
the Union, which was not the unanimous opinion
of congress, which alone could settle it by admitting or rejecting congressional delegations.

The President was urged to call a session of
congress.   He declined.   He retained Mr. Lin-

---

and listened to one of his stories of the time attending the trial of the
Lincoln conspirators.   He related in this connection an episode of
Mr. Wade and Judge Advocate General Bingham, who prosecuted the
accused.   Said he :

On the morning of the execution of Mrs. Surratt, Senator Ben
Wade of Ohio, came into my store and asked if I had heard any news
in regard to the then all absorbing topic, the sentence of Mrs. Surratt.
I told him that I had heard nothing later than the newspapers gave,
except a rumor that the President had positively refused to interfere.
" Well," said Ben in his positive manner, "that woman will never
hang.   She has done nothing to justify such punishment, and it
would be a lasting slur upon our reputation for justice and honor if
Johnson allows public sentiment to murder her.   A d—— outrage,
sir, an everlasting disgrace."   After saying this, he went on toward
the capitol.   Soon Bingham (John A.) came in and wanted to know
if I had heard anything.   I told him that Senator Wade had been in,
and what he said.   " Did Wade say that?" asked Mr. Bingham in
an excited manner.   " He did," said I.   " Well," said Mr. Bingham,
emphasizing each word with a rap of his cane on the counter, "he
hasn't read the testimony, and speaks from a superficial and senti-
mental point of view."   He hurried after Wade, and I learned that he
found him in a committee room, where they had a pretty warm col-
loquy, Mr. Bingham maintaining that the evidence was conclusive
and the sentence just, and Mr. Wade holding a precisely contrary
opinion without budging an inch.—[Communicated.

coln's cabinet. Mr. Seward, it will be remembered, was then prostrate from the wound by the conspirator Payne. He speedily recovered, and came forth with a strong desire for an immediate restoration of all the states.

A man great in debate, in council, with much personal magnetism, he at once quite possessed the President, with whom he before had little in common. He charmed away his resentments toward the rebel leaders. He may have roused his personal ambitions. He certainly knew the lowly-born white, who learned his alphabet at fifteen, whose early years were spent on a tailor's board, who though a senator, a man of mind, political following, had all his life been proscribed by the slavery aristocracy, and whose highest aspiration —the dearest wish of whose heart was to be accepted in its charmed circle—and he may have suggested the magnanimous revenge of a great soul, and now become their benefactor. Through these instrumentalities Seward sought purely what to him seemed the best public good. The revolution in the President's mind and plans was undoubtedly the facile work of Mr. Seward. He held that reconstruction was properly the work of the executive. Congress could not convene till December, unless called. That, as stated, the President refused to do. All the leading Republicans whose views were well known were at their remote homes, dreaming of no ill. The time was favorable.

The President's first step was a sweeping am-
nesty and pardon, which restored citizen franchise, save to the excepted, who were arranged
in twelve or fourteen classes, and provisional
governors appointed in North Carolina, Virginia,
Tennessee, and other states—in short the President, under the counsels of his secretary of
state, placed himself fully in the arms of the
'south and of their old and alway allies, the
northern Democracy, and the Republicans who
went home returned to the capital to be confronted with the returned south, clamorous for
their old places on the old terms.

So much seems necessary to an appreciation of
Mr. Wade's position and duties, and so much of
what followed as my now limited space permits
mention of. Of course Mr. Johnson's reconstructed states, himself and policy, were promptly
rejected by congress. He and it became objects
of scorn and derision. He was belligerent, full of
courage and pluck, and struck back quick and
viciously where and when he could. Unquestionably he was advised by the ablest Democratic
lawyers to disperse the Republican congress and
reconstruct one of southern senators and representatives, with those of the northern Democracy
and such Republicans as would occupy seats belonging to them.*

---

* I was then and ever since a resident of the capital. I knew all the
leading men very well. The late Judge Jerry S. Black, in the winter
after the assembling of the Thirty-ninth congress—I believe, in my

It is thus seen that the Thirty-ninth congress met under conditions little less embarrassing than those attending the convention of the Thirty-seventh. It began with a bitter feud with the President, and when we hold as we must that it was the duty with exclusive correlative power of congress to prescribe the rule and method of dealing with the conquered states—if states they still were—it is seen that the President was not blameless. His course greatly enhanced the losses of the war, and greatly delayed a return to order and restoration. There were years of misrule, crime and blood to be charged to this unfortunate division of counsels. Nor can the northern Democracy be held less culpable through this period than during the four years of the war, and as aiding in the causes which led to that. Of course the growing gap thus opened between the great party and Mr. Seward severed all purely party relations.*

The Thirty-ninth congress met under extraordinary circumstances. Its sessions were the

---

presence and addressed to me—uttered a bitter denunciation of the President, as a weak and most cowardly man. I did not ask what instances in conduct he referred to. I had no doubt. The principal alarm at Washington was during the summer of '66, after the adjournment of congress the last of that July. We then organized a club for watchfulness. I was counsel for Mr. Stanton in various cases, and had several interviews with him on this matter. I now have no notion that Mr. Johnson ever entertained the idea of the use of force in his unfortunate contest with the Republicans in congress.

* " What a bungler Payne was," exclaimed old Thad, in one of his moments of bitter irony.

most memorable of our history. In none were
the high debating qualities of its men more
conspicuous. Many new men had entered the
Thirty-eighth, and several appeared in the Thirty-
ninth. Edmunds was in the senate, so was
Guthrie, Garrett Davis, Hendricks, and Yates.
Reverdy Johnson and Creswell were there from
Maryland ; Howard was Chandler's colleague ;
Henderson and Gratz Brown spoke for Missouri ;
Oregon sent Williams, and E. D. Morgan was
with Harris from New York. General Sprague and
Anthony represented Rhode Island. There were
other conspicuous men since we glanced at the
personnel of the Thirty-seventh. Foster of Connecticut was its president. In the house Colfax
was in his second term as speaker, ready, suave,
firm, popular. Judge Kelley, beginning in the
Thirty-sixth, had already reached a great position.
Shellebarger was back there, and was soon at
the front as one of the very ablest. Cullom
and Allison were in that house. Orth, Boutwell, Green Clay Smith, Raymond, Hale, Gris-
wold, Columbus Delano, Hayes and Spalding
were there together in that house. Randall also
reëlected—not before named—as was Stevens—
a remarkable house. Conkling, Garfield and
Blaine were still there. A very able congress.
Eminently a speaking congress, whose debates,
often with temper, were the longest, the strongest, and as ably conducted as any shown by the
annals of congress. Reconstruction was the

absorbing, all pervading subject—the condition of the south, its treatment of the freedmen, its tone, temper and attitude.

There was the great civil rights bill, the amend ment of the Freedman's bureau—both passed, vetoed, and carried over the President's head. It was on the passage of the civil rights bill that Wade made his thrilling, exciting speech—in the spirit of the old Puritans, seeing the hand of God in the prostration of its enemies, and declaring his purpose to act with the Almighty. The four-teenth amendment was wrought out at that session, largely the work of General Schenck. Some de-fections, noticeably that of Jim Lane, from his radical associates, occurred. Wade administered a rebuke to Lane, and he soon after committed suicide as did Preston King. It was supposed that remorse for his desertion was largely a cause of Lane's wretched end. It came to be midsummer ere the two houses were through with their great labors. During the following winter the citizens of Washington, on the twenty-second day of Feb-ruary, cordially supporting the President, adjourned a mass meeting to the grounds of the white house, and the President in a reckless, utterly discreditable, painful way, addressed the crowd, singling out his enemies by name, in response to voices in the throng. He did "not waste ammunition on a dead duck," (Forney). War henceforth between him and the too powerful Republicans was open, bitter past treaty or terms.

The summer following saw his famous progress through the north—" swinging round the circle." At Cleveland he got angry again.   The low-born, underbred, pugnacious, uncultured ruffian reappeared, painfully recalling the twenty-second of February, and the more humiliating scene in the senate chamber of his inaugural address, in the presence of the diplomats of western Europe. That was the summer of alleged arming of the Maryland militia, to aid the President in a supposed forcible reorganization of congress, of which no evidence has yet been produced—none exists.   That he was advised by some of the ablest of his friends to attempt such a solution, there is no doubt ; nor yet that fifty thousand of the trained veterans of the Grand Army of the Republic, under Garfield and others, were in readiness to come to the defense of the constitutional congress.   At the flash of the telegraph they would appear.   There was a very feverish state of insecurity at Washington during the absence of congress, and a small club of gentlemen, as stated, was organized to keep themselves advised of any movement that might be set on foot   Nothing occurred to warrant apprehension.   They were in frequent communication with Secretary Stanton. The alarm was never given.

The congressional elections of 1866 were most disastrous to the President and Mr. Seward.   The next house was three to one against them.   Let us hope no conditions in the future will ever produce a party powerful enough to set aside a President at will and amend the constitution at pleasure. The conditions must be full of peril. Such a party is itself a great peril. That time was the sorest test of the extraordinary qualities of the Republicans. History may convict them of mistakes—indiscretions; of a want of patriotism, firmness, large wisdom, courage, it cannot. In the ensuing session the suspended war on the President was pushed with renewed vigor. The now ten confederate states had all rejected the fourteenth amendment. They were not states. The military government act was passed, the south divided into military districts, the Freedmen were armed with the elective franchise, and the President's hands tied, by the tenure of office law—these in spite of his veto and over it.

On the second of March, 1867, Benjamin F. Wade was elected president of the senate—the congress passing out of existence with the next day.

That was a great congress. It did many things beside those named. It created the pension system, with soldier asylums. It directed a revision of the statutes; enacted the homestead law; revised and made effective the Pacific railroad charter. It passed the bankrupt act, and contributed much useful legislation of permanent value to the Republic. Its (fourteenth) volume consists of near one thousand pages.

Mr. Wade will preside over the senate of the

Fortieth congress. His election at that crisis had great significance. It marked the senatorial estimate of the times, the general estimate of the man. Many regarded it an election to the presidency of the Republic. Things had been said intimating a removal of "the executive obstacle." Mr. Johnson declared his assassination was intended, and for the first time he glorified the murdered Lincoln. Ere its final adjournment without day—save its day in history—-the Thirty-ninth congress provided by its own act, for the assembling of its successor on the day of its dissolution, March 4, 1867. That congress was to sit almost continuously. It was to see a return of nearly all the states, with their delegations in both houses, under the very doubtful plan of congress itself, against the declared will of the President, attended by the day of the "carpet bag" governments of the southern states—certainly a punishment which, if inflicted as such, the constitution forbade. It is probable that the instrument itself did not permit the preceding condition of things; but as a matter of law, it may well be doubted whether the constitution—*the law of the states alone*—can be said to exist, where and when a state as such has ceased. That is a question for legal casuists. Mr. Sumner would have divided the territory of the confederacy into new states.

The senate had received some stronger men. Simon Cameron for the third time returned to it after long absence; Morrill, fully matured; Charles

S. Drake, a strong man; Oliver P. Morton, one of the strongest, and of the Wade type. There, too, now appeared Roscoe Conkling, of full growth, presaging war. Two infinities cannot occupy the same space. Sumner was still there. Butler, Beck and others were in the house. John A. Logan reappeared there. Judd from his foreign mission. Peters from Maine.

To supplement and perfect the work of the last congress, and carry on the war with the President, was the mission of this congress. There was the now chronic thing of passing and repassing bills and thus escape "the obstacle." Meantime we saw the congressional scheme accomplished, and all the states restored at the second session. The fourteenth amendment was now ratified by states. Africa was to be represented in congress, and that body turned its attention to the vast war debt to be funded.

Already J. M. Ashley, of Ohio, as long before as January 7, '67, had risen in his place in the house, and after the imposing formula of Burke in the British commons, in his historic impeachment of Warren Hasting "of high crimes and misdemeanors," and impeached the President of the United States. It had been much talked of. The act greatly impressed the outside world. The house was not startled. The matter was sent to the judiciary committee, who reported it back the day the senate elected Wade to the presidency. On the seventh day of March, Mr. Ashley called it to the attention of the new house. The Democrats opposed. Mr. Ashley's resolution passed, and so he had launched it. Mr. Boutwell, chairman, reported a resolution ordering an impeachment. December 7, following, it was defeated, yeas fifty-seven, nays one hundred and eight. It was hoped this disposition was final.

There long had been a bitter feud between the President and the secretary of war appointed by Mr. Lincoln in spite of Montgomery Blair's strenuous opposition, and retained by Mr. Johnson over his protest. Early in August ('66) the President asked him to resign. He refused. The President suspended him and Grant took his place. Under the tenure of office act the President, on the twelfth of December, five days after the above decisive action of the house on his case, first communicated his action and reasons to the senate. He made a strong case of " incompatibility of temper." On the thirteenth of January, '68, the senate declared his grounds insufficient and "the senate does not concur." Grant never liked Stanton. He locked the war office door, and with his head pitched forward, both hands in the bottom of his pockets, took his silent, thoughtful way to headquarters. That was before he invented for himself the art of speaking. It was suggested to the President to nominate General J. D. Cox for the post—a certain graceful way out. " I take no backward step "— he had proclaimed months before. He loved a fight. He hated Stanton. Both the strongest

passions of his intense nature made him retain Stanton—or leave him where congress and his friends
found him. There was an intermediate quarrel
between Johnson and Grant meantime. The
President said the general was to hold on till the
supreme court settled the status of Stanton. The
general denied, and was lost to the President in
the war.

So the matter hung in solution till the President
removed Stanton, then in possession, and appointed
General Lorenzo Thomas secretary of war *ad in-
terim.* The general moved on the war office, made
an assault, was himself assaulted, retired, and sued
the stout secretary for $100,000.*

The house took the matter up now with decided
temper, more than that sorely tried body had
before shown. The day following the action of
the senate on the last movement of the President,
Mr. Stevens reported a new resolution of impeachment, and after each of the leaders made statements
rather than speeches—certainly not arguments—
Mr. Stevens closed pungently; the vote taken and it
passed—one hundred and twenty-six to forty-seven.
So the President soon thereafter was impeached
pro forma, at the solemn bar of the senate, March
5. Messrs. Bingham, Boutwell, Wilson, Butler,
Williams, Logan and Stevens—standing in the
order of the vote each received—Mr. Bingham the
highest, one hundred and fourteen; Thaddeus

---

* Mat Carpenter and myself were retained by the secretary—I had
defended General Terry, General Scofield and General Baker twice,
once at Trenton, and again in Washington—by his direction.

Stevens the lowest, one hundred and five—were appointed managers.

The opening of the great national court of impeachment for the trial of the President, though simple, was imposing. The great chief-justice, in his black robes of office, presided—in personnel next Washington, the grandest figure in our history. Then at his best, of all the men of his time, he stands in the field of inner vision, unapproachable and alone. By his side sat the president of the senate, sixty-eight years of age, with snow-white hair and eyebrows, his firm and fine grained face smooth shaven and florid, with his unwinking intensely black solemn eyes, in which lay the unquenchable fire under a thin veil of lashes, always ready to flash, his form a little rounded and fuller; erect, with no diminution of mental or physical force, *sui generis*, yet the peer of peers.*
There was the short, compact, fine figure of the accused, with his strongly marked iron gray face,

---

* No two men of the day presented a more striking contrast than the chief-justice and the president of the senate. An incident of the President's room, characteristic of the two, got whispered outside. During the trial this room was the robing room of the president of the court. One day, at the moment of arraying, this qualifying adjective could not be found. The attendant pages, one or two gentlemen present, the unbending chief himself took part in a search for this prefix. The case was grave. The court could not go on. At the last moment Wade, who had grimly observed the scene, saw something black under some other thing, and lunging it with his cane fished out the delinquent black samite which he irreverently held out at the cane's end with, "Here, Chase—here's your —— old gown." The pages ghastly at the speech, reverently rescued it, and the pale and silent chief-justice was befittingly robed. An added dignity sat on his regal brow all that eventful day.

dark brow, under his iron gray hair, which the iron would never leave, with his counsel, Henry Stanbery, attorney-general; William M. Evarts, Benjamin R. Curtis, William S. Groesbeck, and T. A. R. Neilson of Tennessee, on the left of the president of the senate, with the managers on the right. The senators in their seats. The accusing house ranged about in their rear. The available space of gallery, lobby, and cloak room was crowded with distinguished men and elegantly robed women, admitted by card. This on March 23, 1868.

Mr. Butler, alway an indifferent speaker, opened at great length, reading from printed slips—his nose seeming to touch the paper—to which was appended Judge Lawrence's strong brief. Then followed the accuser's evidence.

Judge Curtis opened the defense. He dissented as justice of the supreme court in the Dred Scott case, as will be remembered. One of the clearest judicial minds of his time, too judicial for the highest achievement of advocacy. His strength as a lawyer was a rare discrimination; as an advocate, in clearness of statement. Perhaps of the great array of lawyers he best met the expectation of him. Two days he held the attention of the court.

On the conclusion of the evidence, April 22, General Logan delivered a masterly summing-up for the managers. Vigor characterizes his speeches. He was followed by Boutwell in an able, perhaps

the most ambitious effort of the trial. Then came
the Tennessee lawyer, with possibly the handsomest and most rhetorical of all the performances.
Next in order was Mr. Groesbeck's speech, spoken
of as, on the whole, the most effective of the great
occasion. He replied especially to Boutwell.
Mr. Stevens, seldom happy in his studied efforts,
with not a pleasing voice or very impressive manner, worn and already feeble, gave his manuscript
to Butler—of all men—to read for him. Then
came Evarts for the defense. He never failed.
It was thought he would never end. His argument, illustration and presentation were admirable,
with some play of wit. No one could have met
the expectation of him. Those who had heard
Stanbery at his best in Ohio and wished to see
him bear the palm of this great forensic battle,
as he might once have done, were prepared for
the disappointment that strangers experienced.
Long ill-health, shattered nerves, over anxiety,
left him a splendid ruin. John A. Bingham closed
the case in an over-prepared, though able, and, in
many ways, conclusive speech. I've heard him
much more effective, notably in reply to Wads-
worth's ʼmasterly and brilliant first speech in the
house of the Thirty-seventh.

The case was submitted.

On May 11 the senate, in the midst of the
profoundest excitement, voted on the eleventh
article. The vote stood—*guilty* 35, *not guilty* 19.
Later the vote was taken on such other of the

articles as the managers desired, with the same result, the senators each gave the same vote on each issue. The President was acquitted. The impeachment court adjourned *sine die*. Those who voted *guilty* were Anthony, Cameron, Cattell, Chandler, Cole, Conkling, Conness, Corbett, Cragin, Drake, Edmunds, Ferry, Frelinghuysen, Harlan, Howard, Howe, Morgan, Morrill of Maine, Morrell of Vermont, Morton, Nye, Patterson of New Hampshire, Pomeroy, Ramsey, Sherman, Sprague, Stewart, Sumner, Thayer, Tipton, WADE, Willey, Williams, Wilson and Yates. *Not guilty*—Bayard, Buckalew, Davis, Dixon, Doolittle, Fesenden, Fowler, Grimes, Henderson, Hendricks, Johnson, McCreery, Norton, Patterson of Tennessee, Ross, Saulsbury, Trumbull, Van-Winkle and Vickers. It was thought after the first vote that Ross would vote guilty on the later tests. It is thus seen that a change of one, of several Republicans from the negative, would have convicted. It was best as it was.*

Mr. Wade was criticised in some quarters for his votes on the final question. It was said he was directly interested, and voted for himself. This is an unjust view. On the trial he was a senator. He and a majority of his state, believed the accused was proved to be guilty as charged. So believing, and appointed to the duty of passing

---

* The writer, then practicing law at the capital, was asked to be retained to prepare the evidence against the accused. He deemed it unwise to accuse, and declined. He always honored Fessenden and Trumbull for their votes.

upon the question, how could he escape the duty
and thus enable a flagrant criminal to escape punishment, remain where he was, and repeat offences
in other forms? No one for an instant supposed
he was influenced by any consideration on earth,
save his clear sense of what was due to justice and
conscience.

His public career closed with that notable Fortieth congress. He was succeeded by Allan G. Thurman.   The state evenly maintained her well established position by the exchange. Fairly estimated,
she neither gained nor lost.   Her new senator had
perhaps more culture, but not distinguished for
that.   In intellect not a whit Wade's superior.
He had a wider, larger hold of the public.   He
never attained Wade's position with his fellows on
the floor.   In down right manliness, courage, firmness and independence, he was in no way Wade's
peer.   There were but few who could claim to be.
Thurman filled a much larger space in his party,
and so in the public eye ; but, let the truth be said,
it takes a much larger man to be one of our great
Republican leaders than it did, or does, to fill that
role with the Democracy.   Wade was a singularly
unambitious man, as seeking place and preferment.
Had he been a Democrat, and covetous of leadership, he would have been a king.   Some of his
more striking qualities were at higher premium in
the Democratic party.

The mushroom negro governments were something worse than the saddest of failures.   They

seemed a necessity, originating in the blindness
and stupidity of the northern people, which, after
all, has shown itself to be something prodigious.
The adherence of the northern Democracy to the
south through the ante-war struggle, unwittingly
on its part, was a potent inducement to the south
to take the fatal initiative of attempting to dissolve
the political association. Of course, that she
would seriously attempt that, was as unforeseen by
the Democrats as the earlier Whigs and later Republicans. A party which should pursue the *ante
bellum* course of the Democracy, with no worse
purpose to gain than its continued ascendancy,
certainly is not to be convicted of sagacity over its
political enemy. It was the same stupid, blind
party after the war that it was before. It pursued
the same means to the same end. It clamored
very effectively at the north for the redemption of
the crushed south from military oppression, under
the Republican methods, devised to relieve the
Freedmen of the atrocious oppressions of the un-
regenerated masters, and, notwithstanding the experience of the northern voter with that Democracy,
he showed such an alarming tendency to again
trust it, not only with his own fortunes but with
the government of the political fragments, to which
its well-remembered misconduct had reduced the
south. The Republicans were justly alarmed.
The course pursued showed that they dared not
longer trust solely to the people of the north.
True, in a long series of years the many times

changing popular estimate of men and things settles itself into irreversible and generally just forms. The need was too great, the time too short, to trust to this slow movement in the exigency. They armed the freedmen with the elective franchise, and trusted that under the lead of Republican agents, they would stand firmly and courageously by their personal and political redeemers. Curiously enough slavery had imparted to them neither courage, wisdom nor forecast. It was supposed that an African, taught by two hundred years of personal bondage, would prove superior to the average white man under the same conditions. It needed an experiment to demonstrate the fallacy of this. Its failure was the bitterest disappointment. The great long-continued war had shattered the common basis of morals of the average man. The many agents entrusted with the construction of these anomalous political expedients, were as unfit for the task as the only material at hand for the edifices. None but the highest, rarest human qualities, never abundant, was equal to the difficult if not impossible task. Congress was armed with the power of restoring the disfranchised rebel to citizenship. It created the forms of states. It restored the disfranchised rebels, by fraud, force, guile, violence; these thrust by the cowardly, stupid, still slaves in heart, mind and spirit; and took possession of the state governments made to their hands. So the south

came back by means complementary of the blood
and revolution by which it went out.

The chief-justice, in a group of gentlemen nominally assembled for a social purpose, thus stated
the Republican position before the experiment.
The northern clamor is for restored states. It will
not cease until that is accomplished. That issue
must be passed out of the field of national politics.
The Republicans are necessary to the country.
The employment of the freedmen is a necessity to
them. The third proposition of this syllogism was
obvious. One present replied—" The condition
of the south under slave rule will appeal more
powerfully to northern sympathy than its domi-
nation under the military district law can. The
issue will not be passed out of national politics."
It was tried; what followed is history. Its example would be valuable, but conditions never can
exist when it may be useful.

With her sons in the army, Mrs. Wade who had
before been much with her husband at the capital,
took up her residence with him there, during the
later of his eighteen years of senatorial service.
They had pleasant, convenient rooms on Four and
a half street, northwest, intermediate between the
great capitol, the executive mansion and great
departments. A man of action, of silent cogita-
tion, without literary instincts, not a compiler of
reports, a composer of speeches, or a writer of
letters—(a few cramped notes, in a hand that
would have been the despair of Daniel, lie before

me)—the least social of men, unless sought in
hours when public men might be enquired for, he
was alway found at his rooms in even pleasant
good humor. Mrs. Wade, gifted with qualities
that might have made her a social leader, an orna-
ment, from the first, fully appreciating the qualities of her husband, devoted her fine powers, her
time, her life to him. They were beautiful in their
mutual self-devotion in the few eyes which saw
their secluded serene life, in the heart of the great
capital, the soul and centre of the great civil convulsion. She wrote his letters, cared for his cor-
respondence, was his thoughtful memory, a tender,
considerate part of his conscience. She read to
him, giving the charm of her voice, the grace and
help of her fine quiet elocution, to aid the delivery
of her author, to his appreciative mind. The real
unseen life of this manliest of men, and that of
one of the womanliest of women, which became
one so late in their lives, was lovely in its *oneness.*

There is a borderland, sometimes a desert, which
surrounds the public life of the capital, broad or
narrow, as the individual sharing in that life was
brief or continuing. Some never pass it successfully. Men distinguished in congress return, seek
subordinate places—haunt the capital, like souls
whose bodies are buried, but will not depart. How
many names of the first spring to mind, some of
which may be mentioned. Mr. Whittlesey lived
and died at Mrs. Hyatt's; Mr. Giddings was often
at the capital, could turn to no pursuit; Samuel

Vinton was an instance, and died in exile. Mr.
French of Maine came back, secured an auditor-
ship under Mr. Lincoln, and spent the remainder
of his life in the dingy Winder building, made
short by it. Innumerable less fortunate instances
of living men crowd the memory. The country,
the capital, are full of these restless, ruined lives.

Mr. Wade, with his noble consort, safely and
serenely made the transit of this border country.
He was never bitten of the Presidency as were Mr.
Seward, Mr. Chase, and many of our living men.
He remained steadily to the end in the bosom and
confidence of the Republican party, while, curiously enough, Mr. Seward, Mr. Chase, Mr. Sumner and Horace Greeley all died out of it—exiled
in a way by men created by the fruits of their
labors.

Something more remains to me. Not tortured
by the Presidential mania, and barely flavored with
the life at the capital—the Wades returned to their
Jefferson home. The little mud and forest-
leaguered town of his law student days had grown,
became long since a beautiful, thriving centre and
capital of one of the largest, most populous and
wealthy of the farming counties of Ohio. It now
had the appearance of an old, cultured town, conspicuous for fine residences and tastefully orna-
mented grounds. The Wade mansion was one
of the most spacious and noticeable of these.
Here, at seventy, the retired senator and his wife
renewed, rather than resumed, their former life.

Many changes had occurred. Many friends were dead or departed. A new generation were in blooming maturity. The old house was haunted with memories, cherished or sad, pleasant or depressing, seen through a softening atmosphere of time. During the black days, it was a source of light, a centre of strength, courage and hope to the hundreds of fainting men from the wide region around. How many men and incidents were recalled as the now glad survivors came to welcome them back. There was the memorable visit of the oldest brother, who pushed off first from Feeding Hills to Albany. He had grown up an all through Democrat, bitter, intense, inveterate. It was in the earlier years of the rebellion—a famous physician and surgeon, he came leisurely to visit his surviving brothers and sisters. From the opposite poles the eldest and next the youngest of Mary Upham's boys met in the Jefferson mansion and joined battle royal—the difference being mainly the merits of the respective causes each advocated, and of which he was master. From twilight deep to dewy dawn the stormy battle raged. The sun *arose* on their wrath. They did not forget their blood, heated as it became. Fiery as was Frank in matter of temper, he had the advantage of the equally stout James. Did a Wade ever yield? James was not in the least subdued nor much enlightened. Had the Democrat of that day aptitude for light?—a question, as Falstaff said, to be asked. Later, the war

did for him what it failed to accomplish for
the southern—it reconstructed his views. He
lived to rejoice in his younger brother's career. A
Wade was never heard to speak well of the
younger brothers—however glad and proud he
may have felt for the positions and distinguished
services of either.

Ohio, Ashtabula county, the Reserve, as the
whole country, had seen the course of its senator
in the Wade-Davis manifesto abundantly vindi-
cated by later light. That did not detract from
the now pathetic glory surrounding the name of
Lincoln. It did add luster to the name of Wade.
With the reticence of the Puritan, neither his old
neighbors or he ever referred to the subject, or if
they did he replied as to Clayton, "We will regard
it as settled by the statute of limitation." They—
many—must have been ashamed of many things
they had said. He did valiant service in the
Grant canvass of 1868. He was a private citizen
now, not claiming any of the privileges springing from his years, which still sat lightly on him,
and ready to meet the calls of his old constituency
and party, as a citizen might.

It was quite generally supposed at the capital
that President Grant would offer him the department of the interior. Much was buzzed about
and in his ears of it. So far as he might he
silenced the busy tongues, and seemingly entertained no thought of it. He never was in an
attitude of expectancy of any position, and had to

be sought out alway by it, as we have abundantly
seen.   He did his old work with the old effective-
ness in the unhappy Grant-Greeley campaign.
He was a chief from the San Domingo commission,
under the nominal leadership of Babcock. *   He
was of pure English descent.   Had an Englishman's instincts to dominate the earth, an American's aspiration for the advancement of large
interests by his nation.   The rejection of the treaty
was a grave mistake, due to Sumner's unworthy
hostility.   Whoever visits the islands can appreciate the meaning of geography, with any capacity
to apprehend the right uses of vast undeveloped
resources, and should, in the absence of reasonless
prejudice, see that one of the tasks of the American
people is to help the world forward by the means
to be drawn from these sources.   There is no
argument against their honorable acquisition that
would not also have barred the purchase of
Louisiana and Florida, toward which their acquisition were two inevitable steps.   "Manifest
destiny," however derided, is the law of national
advance, prematurely proclaimed, as was the
senseless cry, "On to Richmond," and as inevitable of fulfillment as that proved in the bloody
sequel.   Mr. Wade aided in the state canvass of
1875, was a delegate to the convention of 1876,
and Presidential elector.   He very promptly

---

* "Wade was the man of the commission," said General Boynton,
who attended it, on his return.

repudiated the Hayes southern policy ; as for him it was inevitable.*

Mr. Wade also was sent under the statute to inspect and report upon the construction of the Union Pacific railroad. His performance of that duty was not perfunctory. With the thoroughness with which he performed all labors, this task was executed. His report quite put an end to the uncertainty as to the actual condition of that great work. His strength and vigor remained, and these were but pleasant episodes of his later years, which were rounding and ripening an eventful life of rare symmetry and great usefulness. He was among the rarely fortunate men of his great period. The country was fortunate in his possession, fortunate in a man to do many important things beyond the reach and strength and courage of common men. She never had any cavil about his compensation or reward.

The production of these sketches was due to the cherished life-long friendship of their subject for the writer, and to the memory of one of the dearest to his affections early to fall.

It was due to our countrymen, the writers of her histories of the peoples and individuals, that some continuous record be made, and somewhere lodged, of him, to which reference may be had at least by historians.

The men of to-day are too much absorbed in the

---

* There was another side to that. The southern states were lost to the Republicans by the Grant administration. There was no use in struggling further for them.

drum and trumpet sketches of battles, the mere
mechanics of the war, to care much for the men
and their work, whose fire kept in motion the great
heart whose mighty and steady beatings, created
and sustained—made battles successful and fames
assured, to care much for the career or labors of
those who performed this task, or what may be
said of them.

Benjamin Franklin Wade died at Jefferson,
March 2, 1878.

They made his grave near the heart of his life-
long home, and set at his head a granite shaft less
enduring than the influence of his deeds for truth
justice, freedom and his country's good.

INDEX.

www.ingramcontent.com/pod-product-compliance
Lightning Source LLC
Chambersburg PA
CBHW021034030726
47496CB00006B/1529